THE COMPLETE CASES
OF BAIL-BOND DODD, VOLUME 1

NORBERT DAVIS

THE COMPLETE CASES OF

BAIL-BOND DODD™

VOLUME 1

NORBERT DAVIS

ILLUSTRATIONS BY
JOHN FLEMING GOULD

ALTUS
PRESS

BOSTON • 2015

EDITED AND DESIGNED BY

Matthew Moring

PUBLISHING HISTORY

"Murder Down Deep" originally appeared in the February, 1940 issue of *Dime Detective* magazine. Copyright 1940 by Popular Publications, Inc. Copyright renewed 1967 and assigned to Steeger Properties, LLC. All rights reserved.

"Murder in the Red" originally appeared in the April, 1940 issue of *Dime Detective* magazine. Copyright 1940 by Popular Publications, Inc. Copyright renewed 1967 and assigned to Steeger Properties, LLC. All rights reserved.

"This Will Kill You!" originally appeared in the August, 1940 issue of *Dime Detective* magazine. Copyright 1940 by Popular Publications, Inc. Copyright renewed 1967 and assigned to Steeger Properties, LLC. All rights reserved.

"Come Up and Kill Me Some Time" originally appeared in the October, 1941 issue of *Dime Detective* magazine. Copyright 1941 by Popular Publications, Inc. Copyright renewed 1968 and assigned to Steeger Properties, LLC. All rights reserved.

"The Gin Monkey" originally appeared in the January 15, 1935 issue of *Dime Detective* magazine. Copyright 1935 by Popular Publications, Inc. Copyright renewed 1962 and assigned to Steeger Properties, LLC. All rights reserved.

THANKS TO

Joel Frieman & Rick Ollerman

TABLE OF CONTENTS

MURDER DOWN DEEP

WILLIAM DODD'S BUSINESS WAS BONDS—NOT MURDER. THE MERE FACT THAT IT WAS BAIL-BONDS INSTEAD OF GILT-EDGED SECURITIES HE DEALT IN, DIDN'T GIVE HIM ANY LICENSE TO MIX INTO POLICE-WORK— BUT AN IMPOSSIBLE HOMICIDE THE COPS INSISTED ON CALLING AN ACCIDENT, AN AMAZING ARRAY OF PLEASANT DRUNKS, A BUNCH OF CARNEY FOLK AND THE PROSPECTIVE LOSS OF HIS BEST CUSTOMER ALL PROVED TOO MUSCH FOR HIS BUMP OF CURIOSITY. HE HAD TO SOLVE THE KILL—EVEN IF IT MEANT LOSING HIS SHIRT AND MAYBE HIS LIFE IN THE PROCESS.

CHAPTER ONE

THE NUDE IN THE POOL

WILLIAM DODD ran up the steps and turned down the narrow, green-walled corridor. He was a tall, shambling man, loosely built, with deceptively wide shoulders. His gray tweed suit looked expensive but it didn't fit him very well. He wore a pair of horn-rimmed glasses, patched with a piece of white adhesive tape on the bridge. Behind the lenses his eyes were wide and blue and blandly innocent.

He made the first turn in the corridor, and a little man in blue coveralls came skating down the hall toward him, flipping his ankles fancily and pushing a wide brush in front of him.

"Hi, Riganov," Dodd said. "How's the revolution?"

Riganov had a seamed, darkly drawn face and fiercely flashing brown eyes. He skidded past Dodd on the right, did a loop behind him, and came back on the left.

"*Ssst!*" he hissed dramatically. "Any day now! We are waiting for the word!"

"Tell me when you get it," Dodd requested. "I'm saving up my money for a machine gun."

"Soon," said Riganov. "Soon! *Hah!*"

DODD went on down the hall as Riganov did another of his figure-eight turns before a man sitting on a stool in front of two swinging doors with heavy, frosted-glass panels. The man was hunched forward disconsolately, looking down at the cork floor. He had a towel draped around his shoulders, and was wearing nothing else but a pair of very scanty white shorts and thick-soled bathing clops.

"Hello," Dodd greeted cheerfully. "How's for a swim?"

The man looked up and shook his head. "No," he said. He was deeply tanned and had wide, beautifully muscled shoulders.

"I mean, I want one," Dodd explained.

"No, " said the other man in a discouraged tone.

"Look," said Dodd. "My name is William Dodd. I have an office in this building, and I've paid the rent for this month, and the rent gives me the privilege of using the swimming-pool inside there whenever I want to. I hope I am making myself clear?"

"Yeah," the man admitted. "But you can't swim now." He added as an afterthought: "My name's Perkins. I'm the new life-guard and gym-attendant."

"It's a pleasure to know you," said Dodd. "But just why can't I swim now?"

Riganov had propped himself up on his brush-handle and was an interested spectator.

Perkins sighed, bringing into relief rigid, corrugated muscles across his flat stomach. "Miss Bowler is using the pool."

"She's a filthy fascist," said Riganov angrily.

"Her dad owns this building," Perkins added.

"He's a filthy fascist, too," said Riganov.

"Well now, listen here," said Dodd. "This pool and gym are supposed to be for the use of men only."

"Don't I know that?" Perkins asked plaintively. "Are you telling me, or something? Look, this gal comes in and she says, 'Scram, Tarzan, because I want to take a swim,' and I say, 'Listen, lady, this here pool is for men. There is a Y.W.C.A. right across the street where steno's and such-like can go, do they want to swim.' She says, 'I don't like their pool, and I like this one, and my old man owns this building and hires you, so scram.' So I say, 'Wait, now. I ain't supposed to let nobody swim in this pool without I'm here watchin' while they do it,' and she says, 'You ain't gonna watch me because I don't pass out free thrills, and I don't swim in a bathing-suit.'"

"So?" said Dodd, interested.

"So here I am," said Perkins. "Anyway I get fired, I can see that. If I don't swim, I get fired. If I do watch her, I get fired. If I don't watch her, I get fired for not guarding the pool while there is somebody in it, which is a very strict rule—a city ordinance or something."

"Fascists!" Riganov spat. "Comes the revolution! Then—*hah!*" He swung the brush up like a rifle. "We line them up against a wall and *bap-bap-bap!*"

"Yeah," said Dodd. "But I want to swim now. I've been looking forward to a swim all day, and I'm paying premium rent just for this swimming-pool. How long has this snooty dame been in there?"

"Half-hour, maybe," said Perkins.

"Then it's time she was getting out. Come on."

Perkins looked up, startled. "You—goin' in there?"

"Sure."

Perkins shook his head. "She's a tough little baby. She'll chew your ears right off. She said she wasn't gonna wear no bathing-suit."

"That's her worry."

"She's skinny anyway," said Riganov condescendingly.

"Come on," Dodd said.

HE PUSHED the doors open and stepped through. Perkins got up reluctantly and shuffled after him. Riganov stayed out in the hall, still leaning on his brush.

Dodd and Perkins were in a long, low room that had white-painted iron girders across its ceiling. There was a passage-way through the center with long rows of shiny green lockers on

He heaved a flower-pot at the human fly.

either side, and the air was thick and steamy and heavy with the smell of sweat and chlorine.

"Hey!" Dodd called. "Hey—you—Miss Bowler!"

His voice rang emptily, and there was no answer.

"Hey!" said Dodd again, more loudly.

"Maybe we better wait," said Perkins uneasily.

"Nuts," said Dodd.

He went striding heavily along the corridor to its end. The door to the gym was to his left, the door into the pool on the right.

Dodd stopped and called again. "Miss Bowler!"

He shrugged his shoulders then, and stepped through the right-hand door. The pool was a long, narrow oblong with the water in it flat and placid and unstirring, looking very green from the diffused reflection of the tile under it.

The low diving-board was at the end nearest Dodd, and at the other end there was a twelve-foot board braced by steel uprights that were shiny and gleaming with aluminum paint. Some benches and canvas chairs were scattered along the sides and placed helter-skelter at the ends.

There was no one in sight.

"Maybe she's takin' a sun-bath," Perkins suggested. "Out on the terrace."

The door to the terrace was at the far end of the pool, and Dodd walked in that direction, skirting the scattered chairs and benches. He could hear the clip-clop of Perkins' loose clogs coming along behind him, and then, when Dodd was almost opposite the end of the pool, the clip-clopping behind him stopped with a grinding scrape.

Perkins gave a sudden breathless grunt.

Dodd turned around. Perkins' face looked yellowish-green under its tan, and he was staring at the water under the twelve-foot board.

"What?" Dodd asked, stepping closer to the edge of the pool. "What is it?"

He could see her then, too, and there was no need for Perkins to answer. She was white and unmoving against the cool green of the tile at the bottom of the pool. She was face down with her head turned awkwardly sideways, and it was as though she were sleeping there peacefully under the soft weight of the water.

"Good God!" Dodd said in a whisper, and then to Perkins: "Get her out of there! Quick!"

Perkins kicked his clogs loose and flipped his towel aside. He dove expertly off the side of the pool, and the water closed over him with a hollow, echoing *whoom*. There was a spreading burst of white bubbles climbing up toward the surface, and waves lapped against the tiled sides of the pool.

Dodd leaned forward dangerously, and he could see Perkins swimming down with long powerful sweeps of his muscled arms. He reached the girl and tried to lift her with his hands under her armpits and she slipped out of his grasp.

He stroked hard again, getting down to her, and a sudden blob of bubbles blew from his mouth. He doubled up this time and got his feet down on the sloping tile beside her. He slid his arm under her waist, straightened up, holding her, and kicked hard against the tile bottom, shooting himself surfaceward.

He came up under the diving-board with a frothy splashing of water. He turned sideways, shifting the girl until he could get his hip under the small of her back. He slipped his right arm across her torso and stroked hard toward Dodd with his left.

He caught the edge of the pool. Dodd was crouched down now, and he leaned out to catch one of the girl's arms.

"I've got her."

He pulled her in toward the edge, caught the other arm and lifted her up out of the water. Her skin was cold and wet and smooth, slippery in his grasp. He laid her down gently on the rubber flooring beside the pool.

SHE WAS a small girl and too thin. Her hair was black, cut in a long bob, and it was plastered across her face now in stringy, wet streaks. When Dodd let go of her, her head lolled sideways into the same awkwardly crooked position it had been in when he had first seen her. Her mouth, still edged with lip-stick, was open a little. Her eyes were closed, and the lids looked bluish, almost transparent.

Perkins heaved himself up over the side of the pool with a dripping rush of water. He knelt down beside Dodd, panting.

"Telephone—in gym office. Get doctor—pulmotor."

He grasped the girl's slim hips, meaning to turn her over on her stomach.

Dodd said: "No need of that."

Perkins looked up, still breathing heavily. "Give her artificial respiration—till pulmotor gets here."

"She's dead, son," Dodd said. "She didn't drown. Her neck's broken."

Perkins let go of the limp white body, jerking his hands back. "You—you sure?"

"Yes." Dodd slid gentle, probing fingers under the back of the girl's head. "Here at the base of her skull. Snapped right off. You can feel the bones."

Perkins' face was yellowish-green again, and he shook his head once, shivering.

"She dove off that twelve-foot plank," Dodd observed. "And she went too deep. Hit her head on the bottom. I guess I better go call the doctor, though. Wait here."

Perkins was staring at the twelve-foot board, and he made a faint noise in his throat.

"What?" Dodd asked.

Perkins pointed mutely from the board to a small, streaked paint-can that was sitting back in the corner on a bench.

"What about it?" Dodd asked, his eyes narrowing suddenly.

"I—I just finished painting the brace-work," Perkins whispered, "when she came in. I told her not to use the board on account she'd get all smeared…."

Dodd looked down at the girl. There were no paint-marks anywhere on the white, nude body. He stepped quickly around the corner of the pool and examined the steel frame-work that held up the board. He touched one of the braces with the tip of his finger. The shining paint was sticky, and his finger left a dimple in it.

He examined the rungs of the ladder. The paint was smooth and unmarked. He looked further, then. There were no marks anywhere, on any of the braces.

"Well," said Dodd softly. "Well, now."

It was quiet in the room, with the disturbed water slapping slyly against the edges of the pool. Perkins was sitting back on his heels beside the white body of the girl. He kept moistening his lips.

Dodd looked at him. "You paint all of the framework?"

"Yes."

Dodd stepped back away from it and squinted calculatingly at the board. "Doesn't look to me like anyone—especially a girl as small as she is—could get up on that board without touching the framework somewhere, even if they didn't use the ladder. Can you do it?"

Perkins swallowed. "Well—yes."

"How? Show me."

PERKINS stood up stiffly. He went to the corner of the pool and backed away on a diagonal from it, giving himself room to run. He sprinted forward and then, suddenly, jumped outward over the water when he was still ten feet from the board.

He caught the board with both hands about two feet from its end. The strong wood sprang down and up again in jerking arcs. Perkins' body went up and down with it, swinging back and forth under the board at the same time.

Dodd watched, narrow-eyed. The muscles in Perkins' forearms stood out in stringy, corded cables. The board stopped jerking, and Perkins went hand-over-hand out to its end, chinned himself with a sudden bulging heave of his biceps, threw one arm up over the end of the board.

Dodd nodded. "That's enough. I can see you could do it. Drop off into the water."

Perkins let go and disappeared with another hollow *whoom*. He came up at the side of the pool, and heaved himself up over the edge and sat there. He was panting heavily.

"Any other way to do it?" Dodd asked.

Perkins shook his head silently.

"Hell," said Dodd. "She couldn't any more do that than she could fly to Mars." He thought of something suddenly and the muscles of his face stiffened, but his voice was casual. "Anybody else in here when Miss Bowler came in?"

Perkins shook his head again, watching him with a sickly smile.

Dodd's eyes grew very alert and wary, and he glanced all around him, whistling in a casual way. "Fire-escape off this terrace here?"

Perkins swallowed. "No. Don't come up to the top story."

"Any other entrance than the one you were sitting in front of when I saw you first?"

"No," said Perkins miserably.

"Sit there all the time?"

"Yes," said Perkins, more miserably.

"Stay here," said Dodd. "Right where you're sitting, and be damned sure that you do."

"Yes, sir," said Perkins.

Dodd opened the door that led to the terrace and looked out. The terrace was a bare rectangle with a shoulder-high parapet around its edges. There were several army cots and a few camp chairs on it. It contained nothing else and there was no place anything could be concealed.

Dodd closed the door again. His face looked a little strained, and he took off his patched glasses and wiped the steam from them automatically.

"Wh—what?" Perkins whispered.

Dodd was staring at the inner door at the other end of the pool, the one through which they had first come. "She was murdered, dummy. The guy must still be in here, somewhere. I'm going to look."

Perkins jumped. "I'll—I'll go with you...."

Dodd put his glasses back on. "Oh, no. I said he must still be in here. You are."

Perkins made a clutching gesture at the air. "I didn't! I—I—"

"Stay here," said Dodd. "Just stay here—that's all."

He walked around Perkins, turned the corner of the pool. He stepped over the girl's body, not looking at her. His feet were not making any noise now, and he went very quietly and quickly down the side of the pool to the inner door. He hesitated a moment beside it, muttering in an undertone to himself, and then drew a deep breath and slid through.

CHAPTER TWO

PHANTOM KILLER

DODD WALKED along the rubber carpeting, between the long row of green lockers—and as he walked he felt a little cold chill between his shoulder-blades. The outer doors were slightly ajar and he pushed them wider.

"Hi," said Riganov. "I don't hear no yelling yet."

He was standing directly across the hall, leaning against the wall with his brush for a prop.

Dodd said: "Did anyone come out of here after Perkins and I went in?"

"Nope," said Riganov.

"You're sure?"

Riganov moved his shoulders. "I was standing here all the time—continuous."

"Keep on standing there."

"You bet," said Riganov amiably.

Dodd turned around and stood with his back to the door. There were four rows of parallel lockers—the two rows that faced the middle passageway, and one more back of each of them. Dodd went down the middle passageway again, the cold chill still with him.

At the end he turned and looked back into the room that contained the pool. Perkins was sitting in exactly the same position, and his face looked like a white, rigidly strained mask. The body of the girl made a pale blur against the matting under her.

Dodd turned back the other way and went into the gym. He stepped inside the door, and the long, high-ceilinged room stretched out empty ahead of him, with the parallel bars and the rowing machines and the leather horses looking like queerly lifeless animals squatting in the shadows.

Casually Dodd reached out and picked a dumb-bell off the rack beside the door. It was a four-pound iron bell, and it gave his hand a coldly satisfying weight. He held the bell at his side, half behind his hip, and walked quickly down the length of the gym to the glassed-in office at the far end.

The little square was empty and Dodd sat down at the desk, picked up the telephone, watching through the smeared windows.

The operator's voice was cheerfully casual: "Yes, sir?"

Dodd said: "If there's a doctor in the building, tell him to come up to the men's gym quickly. If not—get one. Better call in a couple of policemen and send them up, too."

"Doctor," the girl said casually. "Police…. What? What did you say?"

Dodd hung up, still watching through the window. Carrying his dumb-bell, he walked out into the gym proper. The shower-room was at the far end. Dodd looked that way for a moment and then said to himself: "Oh, well, what the hell? You can't live forever."

He walked firmly and steadily toward the swinging green doors and pushed them open. The shower-room was empty and silent except for the cold and lonely drip of a leaking tap. Dodd went through it and looked into the washroom beyond. It, too, was empty, and when Dodd had made sure of that after looking into each one of the stalls, he felt a foolish, light-headed sort of relief.

Coming back through the gym he stopped in the outer doorway. As a precautionary measure he looked into the room that contained the swimming-pool. Perkins was still there, looking as though he hadn't moved since Dodd had first looked in, and so was the white, still body of the girl.

Perkins had found his voice now, and he said: "What—what—"

"Wait a minute," Dodd said.

He was still holding the iron dumb-bell. Now he gripped it tighter, held it up ready to strike, and went into the first locker-aisle. There was a bench down the middle, and Dodd walked along it to the end. He crossed over and walked back up the fourth locker-aisle.

He saw no one at all and stopped for a moment at the end of the aisle, near the door into the pool, drawing a long, deep breath of relief. He realized suddenly that his heart had been pounding with a beat that drummed in his temples, and that his throat was dry and tight with tension.

WHEN he went into the room that contained the pool, he looked like his normal self again, and he was grinning in a deprecatory manner.

"My mistake, I guess," he said.

Perkins was staring at the iron dumb-bell. He hitched himself along the edge of the pool, away from Dodd.

"Listen! I—I didn't—"

Self-consciously, Dodd put the dumb-bell down on a bench. "I guess I let my imagination run away with me. She probably used the same trick you showed me to get on the board."

Perkins shook his head. "Oh, no."

Dodd stared at him. "What?"

Perkins wiped his brow with a muscled forearm. "Listen. I don't want to get myself in wrong—any more than I am—but I been training for a tumbling team for five years. I tried that trick I showed you eight times before I made it. You gotta figure just the right angle."

"She couldn't do it?" Dodd asked. "You mean, I was right about that?"

"Hell," said Perkins. "Look at her. Of course, she couldn't do it. But—but she was as healthy as you are when I left her in here."

"Do you think, if she tried and missed, that short a fall would break her neck?"

Perkins looked sick. "Oh hell, no."

Dodd walked to the girl and stood over her. As far as he could see there was no slightest bruise or abrasion on her body. He stooped down, after a moment, turned her over, and then he pursed his lips and made a slight whistling sound.

"What?" Perkins demanded eagerly.

"See here," Dodd said.

There was a faint, wide, red mark across the small of the girl's back.

"Look," said Dodd. "Suppose I pad my fist up in something soft— say a shirt or a hat maybe—and I tap her a quick one on the jaw. She half falls and half slides down on her face. Then I put my knee here. See, I've got clothes on, so there'd be a little mark left by the abrasion of the cloth."

He bent his knee over the girl's prone form, and the mark—was approximately the same size as the red abrasion on her skin.

Perkins said: "But—but her neck…."

"And then, while I'm holding her with my knee, I reach down with my right hand—like this—and I catch her under the chin and give a hard jerk…."

"Oh!" said Perkins. His knees wobbled, and he held himself up against the wall.

Dodd nodded thoughtfully. "That would do it. That'd crack her neck right where it's broken. And then, not knowing about your little painting job, I'd just heave her from the side of the pool right under the diving-board, and I'd have me an unfortunate accident." He looked up at Perkins suddenly. "Wouldn't I?"

Perkins nodded stiffly. "Yes. But listen, I didn't—"

"I don't think you did. There might easily have been someone hiding in here without you spotting him, if you weren't looking particularly. But if he was in here, how in hell did he get out again, with you sitting at the only door all the time? He isn't here now. There isn't any place he could hide. I looked every place and Riganov has been outside the front door ever since we came in. I can't see…."

A UNIFORMED policeman came into the door, hesitated a moment to get his bearings, and then walked toward them, his feet plopping importantly on the rubber matting.

"Now what's all this? What—" He saw the body of the girl. "Oh!"

"She's dead," Dodd said. "Her neck's broken. I called a doctor."

The policeman came closer, looking down. "Are you— Here! You moved the body! I can see the wet marks where you moved—"

"Sure we moved it," Dodd told him. "She was in the pool when we found her. Want us to throw her back?"

The policeman had a wind-reddened face and suspicious, small, blue eyes. He moved his head back a little now, looking Dodd slowly up and down again.

"Just don't get smart, mister." He took a leather notebook and a stub of pencil from his pocket. "Now, what's your name?"

"Dodd. William Dodd."

The policeman wrote it down, working his lips laboriously. He looked up suddenly.

"There's a William Dodd that's a bondsman. Any relation?"

Dodd nodded. "Very close. I'm him."

"So," said the policeman, as though his suspicions had been verified. He wrote that down, too. "Who discovered the body of deceased?"

"Me," said Perkins, swallowing hard. "Clem Perkins. I'm the lifeguard."

"So," said the policeman. "And can you identify deceased?"

"Her name is Bowler," Dodd said.

The policeman's head jerked. "Bowler? You mean—the Bowler who owns this building?"

"Yes. He's her father."

The policeman pursed his lips. "You wait right here—both of you. I gotta telephone. Where is it?"

"In the gym office," Dodd said.

"Stay right here," said the policeman importantly. He walked down the side of the pool and out the door.

"Too big for him to monkey with," Dodd said absently. "He's calling for help. I think I'll drift along."

Perkins started to protest. "But he said—"

"I'm not hard to find," Dodd said. "See you later."

He went along the pool and out through the door. The policeman was in the glassed-in office of the gym, and he saw Dodd pass. He put the phone down quickly, and his voice came in muffled protest—"Hey! Here, you! Come back here!"

Dodd went on down the aisle toward the outer door, hurrying now.

The policeman's feet thudded on the gym floor and his voice was a commanding bellow. "Stop, you! Stop!"

Dodd slid through the outer door into the hall.

RIGANOV was still leaning against the wall, and Dodd said quickly: "There's a cop after me. Distract him for a moment."

"Sure," said Riganov casually.

Dodd went down the hall at a trot. Over his shoulder, he saw Riganov slide the handle of his brush in front of the door. Dodd turned the corner, and behind him there was a sharp breaking crack and then the sodden thud of a body falling. Riganov's voice howled in outraged protest. "Clumsy! You broke my brush handle. I'll sue you! I'll.... All right! Hit me! Go on! I dare you! I'll have the law on you! I'll protest to the governor!"

Dodd went down the stairs three at a time. At the bottom, he met a stocky man carrying a black medical bag.

"Someone up here called for a doctor...."

"Upstairs," Dodd directed. "You'll find a policeman right at the top who will direct you."

None of the offices on this floor were rented. Dodd went down another flight of stairs. There were some tenants for the offices on this floor. Dodd stopped beside a grilled elevator door and punched the button. He was whistling softly and casually to himself.

He rode down to the fifth floor, got out of the elevator and walked down the corridor to his office. The door had a small conservatively neat legend—*WILLIAM DODD—BONDS*—in the lower right-hand corner of its frosted-glass pane.

The waiting-room had no furniture at all except a big, flat desk with a swivel-chair behind it. Meekins, Dodd's runner, was sitting in the chair now, tilted far back against the wall, his feet up on the desk. He was a gaunt, faded man who might have been anywhere from thirty to sixty years old. He was bald and was sensitive about it, so he always wore his hat. He had it on now, the brim tilted down low over his sleepily colorless eyes.

He nodded at Dodd and said: "You're under arrest."

"So soon?" Dodd asked.

"Yup. Some cop with a mad on just called up and told me so."

"What did you say?"

"Ha-ha. And then, when he didn't like that, I told him to look up Paragraph Two, Page Twenty-four, of his rule book. It's illegal to make an arrest over the telephone."

Meekins could quote every rule, law, and court decision that had anything to do with the bonding business.

"Any customers this morning?" Dodd asked.

"Yeah. Small fry. Two drunk driving. Three book-making."

"Where is Bowler's office?"

"Third floor."

"Know anything about him?"

Meekins said: "He'd rather cheat you out of a dime than cut your throat—but not very much rather. He's kind of heavy at the mayor's office. They used to get drunk together before the mayor got stomach ulcers. You thinking of running up against him?"

"Yes."

Meekins shrugged wearily. "Well, it's been nice knowing you. I'll be watching the morgue for unidentified bodies."

CHAPTER THREE

THE MAN AT THE KEYHOLE

THE BOWLER BUILDING was a slim, unadorned spike, all austere white, rising proudly out of the mid-town financial district. It had been conceived and built in those dim distant days when the stock market was something that was spoken of with respect if not awe, and a stock broker was considered slightly higher in the social scale than the proprietor of a floating dice-game or the croupier at a roulette table.

It had been over-built as well as over-capitalized, of course, and its high windows came in handy for some of its lessees who decided to get to the ground the quickest way when they heard the sheriff rapping at the front door. It still staggered along under its load of debt—the two top floors empty and its directory board scantily filled with names, half of whom were dummies and the rest optimists—a monument to the fact that man can build better than he can plan.

Dodd got off the elevator at the third floor, asked directions from the operator, and went down the long, wide, marble-floored corridor. The doors were all closed along it, impressive with frosted glass and chromium and names in neat gold lettering.

Bowler's office was around a turn in the corridor at the end. Dodd wasn't walking any faster or slower than he usually did, nor was he trying to be particularly silent. He had no premonition of trouble until he turned the corner.

He could look straight ahead at the door of Bowler's office, then. The outer door of the office was slightly ajar, just enough so that Dodd could see through it and see the leg and shoulder of a man inside.

The leg was in a peculiar position and Dodd slowed up, staring curiously. The leg was bent almost double, as though its owner were in a crouch, squatting uncomfortably, on one heel. The shoulder was hunched forward rigidly, almost touching the knee.

Dodd went on his tip-toes the rest of the way and slowly pushed the outer door further open. The outer office was as small as Dodd's own, but much more completely furnished—professionally business-like with a flat stenographer's desk equipped with typewriter and dictaphone, files in a long row against the wall. There was a huge leather divan and deep cushioned chairs and a low, bronze-wood railing.

The man Dodd had seen was crouching in front of the door that led into the inner office. This door was closed, and the man had his head bent close to the keyhole, hand cupped over one ear. He was a small, pudgy man in a rumpled gray suit and a battered panama with a green ribbon band. He had a pinkly perspiring face that was twisted up now in an expression of intense concentration. He neither heard nor saw Dodd.

"Hi, pal," said Dodd casually.

"Uh!" the man said in an agonized gasp.

He whirled around, still squatting, and his head banged back against the door, knocking off the battered panama. His hair was colorless and thin, sticky with sweat. His lips opened and shut soundlessly, and he made flustered, groping motions toward his hat.

"Don't mind me," said Dodd. "Is the listening good?"

The man found his hat. "I—uh—tying shoe…."

"I could see that," said Dodd.

The pudgy man found his hat and straightened up, smiling in

agonized embarrassment, and then the door at which he had been listening opened suddenly and Bowler stepped out.

DODD had never met the man but he had seen his pictures in newspapers, and he recognized him instantly. The newspaper photographs, strangely enough, had flattered him. They had been blurred enough to take off the rough edge. Bowler was fat, but there was no softness in the fat. It was as hard as chiseled marble. It didn't hide the sharpness of his features, the greed and cruelty of his long, downturned mouth. His nose was a blob, and above it his eyes were reddish blue slits that gave his whole expression the effect of utter, uncaring callousness.

"You!" he snapped at the pudgy man. He didn't raise his voice, but the word came out as though he had bitten it off with his teeth, and the pudgy man stepped back hurriedly, half raising one arm.

"Now, Mr. Bowler, please.... If I could just have one second of your time.... If you'd just give me an inkling of your attitude.... I won't quote...."

"Get out!" Bowler said. "Get out of here!"

The pudgy man backed into the railing, stumbled, groped along until he found the gate. "Mr. Bowler, please.... It's of vital importance to my paper and its clients...."

"Get out!"

The pudgy man backed into Dodd, gave a startled squeak, and bounced off again. "I—I'll call again...."

"If you show your ugly face around this building again, I'll have you arrested! Do you understand?"

"Y-yes," said the pudgy man, ducking past Dodd and through the door. His feet pattered quickly down the hall.

"Who's he?" Dodd asked curiously.

Bowler was looking around the office, his little eyes narrowed dangerously. "Name of Green. Pip-squeak who owns a two-bit financial newspaper. Gave my secretary orders to throw him out next time he came. Where is she? Miss Mills! Miss Mills!"

There was a closed, unlettered door to Dodd's right, and now a muffled pounding sounded on it. Dodd stepped to it, snapped the patent lock. The door opened on a supply closet, and a woman half fell out of it, clutching at Dodd's arm to steady herself.

"Mr. Bowler! He—he—"

"What're you doing in there?" Bowler demanded angrily.

The woman gulped for breath. She was thin and tall and prim-looking, middle-aged, with nose-glasses that were tipped askew on her long, grayish face.

"I—I went to get some carbon paper. It's on the upper shelf, and just as I was reaching for it someone p-pushed me from behind and then shut the door on me. He—he talked to me through the door and said if I screamed he'd s-shoot...."

Bowler's long lips flattened fiercely against his teeth. "That damned meddling Green! I'll have him arrested for this! I won't be annoyed by his prying!"

Miss Mills nodded weakly. "It—it was that Green person. I—I recognized his voice."

"What does he want to know that's so important?" Dodd inquired offhandedly.

Bowler made an impatient gesture. "Some silly business about Harris bonds. Claims he has information that I'm in a pool that's trying to run them down and is trying to verify the rumor so he can print it in his paper. As if I haven't enough trouble of my own without fiddling with motor bonds.... Just who are you, sir, and what are you doing here?"

"Dodd," said Dodd. "William Dodd. One of your tenants."

BOWLER'S face seemed to tighten. "Oh. William Dodd, eh? I've been meaning to have a talk with you. You leased an office in my building giving your business as merely 'bonds.'"

Dodd nodded. "Yeah. It is."

"Bonds! *Police* bonds." Bowler spat the words.

"Sure," Dodd admitted. "Bonds, just the same."

Bowler took a deep breath. "This building, Mr. Dodd, is a respectable one. It houses respectable financial and investment firms. Its name is noted for that."

Dodd shrugged. "Well?"

"I do not desire any such tenant as you," Bowler said clearly and precisely. "I do not desire this building infested with the class of clients you cater to—criminals, drunks, vagrants, prostitutes."

"Not all of them," said Dodd.

"Enough. You took this office in my building merely to give you and your business a cloak of respectability. You don't have any staff or any organization here. All you have is one unsavory character by the name of Meekins, who contacts your clients when they are jailed. 'Runner' is, I believe, the word by which he is designated—referring no doubt to the necessary agility needed to evade the law."

Dodd straightened his shoulders. "Well, now, wait a minute, here...."

Bowler nodded coldly. "I intend to wait—just long enough for your present period of occupancy to expire. Then I'm going to have you evicted from your office—forcibly if necessary. I have no desire to have a building named for me become the gathering place of thieves and criminals and scum. I have even less desire to give space in the building to a person I consider no more than a vulture and a scavenger slavering after the spoils of law-breakers."

Dodd's nostrils looked pinched, but his eyes were as bland as ever. "That's putting it nice and plain. Thanks a lot for the boost."

"You are quite welcome," said Bowler. "Was there anything of importance you wished to see me about?"

"Yes. I've just come from the gymnasium on the top floor."

Bowler said: "You are inferring, no doubt, that you have some information about the death of my daughter."

Miss Mills gasped and clapped a claw-like hand across her lips. Dodd stared incredulously. Bowler had spoken as casually and as unexpressively as if he had made a remark about the weather. He couldn't have heard of his daughter's death more than a few short moments before, yet he showed no emotion over it.

"Well?" he inquired in a coldly even voice. "The police have already informed me of the circumstances of her death, if that was the information you had to impart."

"Oh!" said Miss Mills in a half-sob. "Oh, Mr. Bowler! That poor girl...."

Bowler was staring unblinkingly at Dodd. "I may inform you, Mr. Dodd, since you seem to be curious, that my daughter has never had the slightest respect or affection for me, and that I fully reciprocated her feelings. Her mother died when she was young, and my daughter has been viciously and willfully disobedient to my every wish since that time. She was in this office before she went up to swim—for money—the only reason she ever appears either here or at my home—and she was intoxicated then. I warned her not to swim in that condition, but she merely laughed at me in her usual insolent manner."

"I see," said Dodd slowly. "Would you be interested in information indicating her death was not—accidental?"

"Very interested," said Bowler grimly. "But not in quite the direction you evidently suppose. I'm satisfied to let the authorities handle the matter. If you interfere, I can only suppose it is because you hope to gain financially by it. I would advise you not to try that, Mr. Dodd."

"No?" said Dodd softly.

"No. Attend to your own affairs and confine your doubtless great talents to helping your criminal associates avoid the penalties for their misdeeds. Now get out of this office."

Dodd watched him silently for a moment, and then nodded once, as though he had come to a decision. "You'll be seeing me."

He went out and shut the door quietly behind him.

CHAPTER FOUR

CARNEY BACKGROUND

WHEN THE BOWLER BUILDING had been constructed a bar and clubroom—strictly private for the tenants—had been included on the second floor. This had been during prohibition, but none of the tenants considered even for a moment that the law was meant to apply to such important people as they were at the time. When repeal and the depression came along, the bar had been enlarged and opened to the public because its lessees had grown tired of putting drinks on the cuff for indigent stock brokers and bond salesmen and had decided they could do with a little cash business for a change.

Dodd came into the bar after his interview with Bowler, his wide shoulders humped forward slightly, smiling in his deceptively mild way. He ordered a straight rye and drank it, ordered another.

Setting the drink down in front of Dodd, the bartender said: "He's going to get slung in the pokey, I bet, as soon as he tries to navigate in the street, so there's a little business for you, hey?"

Dodd looked at the bartender, puzzled. "What?"

"Tipton," said the bartender, pointing. "Six double Scotch-and-sodas, he's had. He drinks 'em through a straw. Can you imagine a guy drinkin' Scotch through a straw?"

Dodd turned to look. Tipton was a short man with a cheerfully vacuous face and rumpled blonde hair. He was deeply tanned and astonishingly healthy-looking. He was at a table in the corner, half lying down in a big divan, sipping a drink through a tube of red cellophane.

Dodd knew him of old. He had bailed Tipton out on numerous occasions for disturbing the peace, drunkenness, brawling, assault and battery, and resisting arrest. Tipton's family was both rich and socially prominent and they paid up promptly every time.

Taking his drink, Dodd walked over to his table. "Hi, Tippy. How they going?"

Tipton blew through his straw into his drink, making a noise like an outboard motor. He looked up blankly at Dodd and dodged back, startled, then looked all around the room quickly.

"What's the matter?" Dodd asked.

"Am I in jail again?" Tipton asked cautiously.

"Not yet," said Dodd.

Tipton sighed with relief. "Every time I see you it reminds me of policemen and night courts and things equally unpleasant. Sit down. You must have a drink with me. I insist."

Dodd sat down. "Why?"

"This is important. Oh, very. I'm about to become a husband. Indeed, yes."

"Does your family know it?" Dodd asked.

"Yes, yes, yes, yes. That's why you must have a drink with me. They know of it and approve—my dear, dear parents. They approve most heartily."

Dodd lifted his own drink. "Here's to you."

"Thank you, thank you, thank you," said Tipton. "That's really very thoughtful of you. I am marrying a most delightful girl—oodles of money and personality, really. A trifle on the brusque side, I must admit. A little short in her conversational gambits, on occasion, yes. But a heart of gold—and not only that, but a rich father."

Dodd tilted his head, watching him. "Her name wouldn't by any chance be Bowler?"

"Right," said Tipton, amazed. "Right-o! You're a veritable mind-reader. Do you know the dear little creature?"

"I've seen her."

"Slightly on the thin and bitter side," Tipton admitted judicially.

"But my extremely sunny nature will no doubt make up for that deficiency."

Dodd rubbed his chin, not knowing just what to say.

HIGH heels made hard, angry taps coming across the floor behind him, and Dodd looked back over his shoulder as a woman stopped beside their table and stared across it at Tipton.

Tipton's mouth opened and then shut again. "Well," he said aimlessly. "Well, well, well, well. My dear Lea. My dear, dear Lea. This is an enormous pleasure."

"You rat."

"Me?" said Tipton. "A rat? Oh now, my dear, you're being unkind, I think. I do, honestly."

She was a blonde, and she looked as though she had practiced being a blonde for a long time. Her hair was brittle, glinting yellow and her eyes were narrow and coldly furious under eyebrows that went up into ridiculously high arches. She was expensively overdressed, and despite the expertly applied make-up that covered her like lacquered veneer, she must have been at least ten years older than Tipton.

She leaned over the table now and picked up Tipton's glass and threw its contents in his face.

Tipton sputtered and then said: "Really now, Lea. I've often told you I don't like to drink so fast."

"You rat," repeated Lea. "You think you're going to marry that Bowler tramp, do you? You think you can give me the brush-off, do you?"

"Why, yes," said Tipton, smiling.

Lea pointed a rigid forefinger at him. "You wait."

"Right here?" Tipton asked innocently.

"All right," said Lea vindictively. "I'll make you mighty sorry, mister. You're not through with me."

She turned around and walked quickly out of the bar.

Tipton waved a finger at the bartender. "One more, please." He nodded at Dodd. "I'm very, very popular with girls. I don't know why it is. It must be my sunny nature."

"She looked like she meant what she said," Dodd observed.

Tipton shrugged. "Kaye—Miss Bowler—will fix her in short order. Oh my, yes, Kaye has a vocabulary. You must come up sometime after we're married and hear her swear. She will singe Lea's hair. She doesn't like Lea."

Dodd was looking back at the bar. A man had come into the room and was standing at the far end.

Dodd said: "Are you going to stay here?"

"Oh, yes," said Tipton. "Indeed, I am. Kaye—Miss Bowler—brought me in and sat me down right here and told me to wait, and she gets very impatient if I don't do what she says."

Dodd got up and went over to the bar. "Hello, Spider," he said to the man standing there.

Spider was a small, very neat little man in a plum-colored suit with padded shoulders. His face was dark and narrow and hard. He looked up at Dodd—a quick, uneasy flicker of a glance.

"Hello, Dodd. Busy. See you later."

He left his drink unfinished at the bar and went out, walking with quick, balanced litheness.

Dodd raised his eyebrows, watching him go. He ordered another drink and sipped at it thoughtfully. He still couldn't decide what to do about Tipton. He didn't want to tell him about Kaye Bowler's death. He thought Tipton was too drunk to comprehend it fully, and it was none of Dodd's business anyway.

He decided to let it pass for the moment and went out of the bar and back up to his office.

MEEKINS was still there, sitting in the swivel chair in the waiting-room with his feet up on a desk-top.

"Any visitors?" Dodd asked.

"Yeah. Your pal, Lieutenant Hodges of homicide, was around passing out sour looks. He wants to see you. He's upstairs in the gym. He's mad."

Dodd nodded absently. "He always is. Know anything about young Tipton?"

"I know he's a one-man riot if you cross him when he's feeling too gay. His folks are good for it, though. Is he in jail again?"

"No. Ever hear of a girl named Lea in connection with him?"

Meekins nodded. "He's been cartin' her around a lot lately. Picked her up out of a burlesque show. She's an old-timer in spite of the stream-lined chassis, and I hear tell she's a little on the rough side."

"Yes," said Dodd, "a little. What's Spider Ladue doing now to make a living?"

"He claims he's a private detective. I suppose at that it's safer than wire-walking."

"Wire-walking?" Dodd repeated.

"Yeah. He used to be a wire-walker with street carnivals. Walked from building to building and all that—sort of a gag to pull in the rubes so the carnival boys could take 'em."

"So," said Dodd thoughtfully, rubbing his chin.

Meekins yawned. "You wanta know any more about him, go see Bish Reap. Old-time barker. Fronts for a flea-show now. You'll find him in Casey's Haven on Kester Street any time after nine o'clock at night."

Dodd nodded. "Maybe I'll go down. One more. Do you know anything about a guy named Green who publishes a paper?"

"No. Except that it's a sort of a stock tip-sheet. It ain't never right. You still pokin' your finger at Bowler?"

"Maybe."

"Don't say I didn't tell you."

LIEUTENANT HODGES, homicide, was a thick-set, ponderous man with a broad face that held a perpetual expression of sullen distaste. He was alone, sitting in a chair on the edge of the deserted swimming-pool, staring gloomily into the green water and chewing on an unlighted cigar when Dodd came in.

"Heard you wanted to see me," Dodd said blithely.

Hodges looked up sideways. "Nice of you to come so quickly. Sure you can spare the time now, or shall we put it off another month or two?"

"That's what I like about you," Dodd told him. "Always a smile and a cheering word. What did you want?"

"You've been going around making funny cracks about this business. Make some to me."

"What did you find out?"

Hodges gestured toward the diving-board. "Accident. She fell off and broke her neck."

"How'd she get up there?"

"Climbed," said Hodges.

"It's just been painted."

"It's dry now," said Hodges. "That paint dries awful fast."

"Not fast enough. It wasn't dry when we found her. Someone cracked her neck and threw her in from the side."

"Like maybe who?" Hodges asked sourly.

"I don't know."

"You're crazy," said Hodges. "Look, there wasn't anybody in here when she came in but the life-guard. He went out and left her in here. He was sitting outside the door the whole time. He's got a witness for that—a screw-ball by the name of Riganov—a janitor around here. Nobody came in or went out while the life-guard was there until you and he came in. There isn't any other way to get out of here but that door. The only person who could have done it is the life-guard—before he went out."

Dodd shook his head. "He didn't. He wouldn't have told me about the paint on the diving-board frame-work if he had, and besides he's muscle-bound above the ears."

"Right," said Hodges. "So that makes it an accident." He paused. "The mayor told the police commissioner it was an accident—positively."

"Oh," said Dodd. "I see."

"I hope you do."

Dodd said: "I want to take a look at the terrace."

He skirted the end of the swimming-pool and went out on the terrace and walked over to the parapet that bordered it. He followed the parapet along, looking carefully at the top of it.

"What're you looking for?" Hodges asked from behind him.

Dodd didn't answer. He was at a corner of the parapet now. He braced himself on his elbows and looked over. There was a ledge approximately four inches wide on the other side. The white of the building extended on down smoothly below it, down and down to the narrow gash of the street and the tiny play-figures that darted ant-like along it.

"What?" Hodges asked again.

Dodd pointed. "There's some scratches on the ledge there at the corner."

"Pigeons," said Hodges.

Dodd turned to stare in eloquent disgust. "Pigeons!"

"Tell me, then," Hodges invited.

Dodd said: "There's no buildings near this one anywhere near as high. Probably no one would notice a man if he walked along that ledge to the corner. Then, maybe, he could slide down and hang by his hands and reach the top of the window-ledge on the floor below with his feet."

"You're nuts," said Hodges, looking over the parapet and shivering at the height. "It would take a guy with a pair of wings to do that."

"Or maybe a wire-walker," said Dodd thoughtfully. "If you make a business of cavorting around on a wire above the streets, walking that ledge wouldn't be much."

"You haven't been out in the sun too much lately, have you?" Hodges inquired. "You sound goofier by the minute. I think maybe you'd better leave it be an accident like the mayor says it was. Just watch your step, Dodd."

CHAPTER FIVE

CASEY'S HAVEN

KESTER STREET was a welter of warehouses and tenements on the flats south of the bay. The dingy walled canyon was packed with the overflow from the tenements that bordered it. Children shrieked and scurried in the streets, and push-cart vendors yowled their wares discordantly.

Dodd, walking along slowly, his hands in his pockets, was two blocks from his destination when he heard Riganov. He was on a soap-box on the corner under a street-light. He still wore his blue janitor's uniform, but he was bare-headed now, and his oily black hair was down over his eyes in a ferocious tangle. He was yelling like a maniac at the ring of idlers who surrounded his box and watched him with the abstract indifference of spectators at a zoo.

Riganov had a lot of sound to compete with, and Dodd couldn't make out much of his message, but it seemed to have something to do with the near approach of a revolution which would be the death-warrant of all unbelievers and anyone who had more than ten dollars in the bank. Riganov danced and jittered on the soap-box, waving both skinny arms in the air.

As Dodd approached a policeman came around the corner beside Riganov and paused thoughtfully. Riganov went right on with his diatribe and the policeman finally edged up close, waggled his finger at Riganov. "Now, little man, come down off that box and let the revolution wait till tomorrow. You're blockin' the sidewalk."

"I won't!" Riganov yelled defiantly. "I got constitutional rights! I'm a citizen!"

The policeman reached up and lifted him down. Riganov promptly tried to kick him in the shins. The policeman slapped him with an open palm, not very hard, and said tolerantly: "Now, now. Stop it. What you need is a nice cool ride down to the station."

Dodd wriggled his way through the spectators. The policeman shifted his grip on Riganov, leaving his right hand free, and watched Dodd calculatingly.

"Officer," said Dodd, "I'm a friend of this man. My name is William Dodd. I'm a bondsman."

The policeman nodded gravely. "Heard of you. My name's Dinregan."

Dodd said: "I've bailed Riganov out a hundred times for disturbing the peace and holding meetings without a permit and what-not. I know him well. He's harmless. He only does things like this because his wife beats him."

"What?" said Dinregan, amazed.

"Fact," Dodd assured him. "His wife is twice his size. Whenever Riganov gets paid, his wife takes all his money and goes out and gets drunk and then comes home and beats him. Riganov has to show his independence some way, so he gives speeches on soap-boxes."

"Poor fella," said Dinregan sympathetically. He let Riganov go.

"Cossack!" Riganov spat at him, brushing himself off indignantly. "Filthy fascist!"

"Now, now," said Dinregan tolerantly. "Do you run along with your friend Mr. Dodd, little man, and don't be screeching on corners like a monkey on a stick. Go along, now."

"Thanks, Dinregan," Dodd said. "Come on, Riganov. I'll buy you a beer."

Riganov leered at Dinregan fiercely. "Comes the revolution!" He drew his forefinger across his scrawny throat in a meaning gesture. *"Sccrcht!* Off with their heads!"

Dodd caught his arm and dragged him down the street.

CASEY'S HAVEN was a blare of sound and winking neon on the corner. Dodd ushered Riganov, still strutting indignantly, through the door. It was a long, old-fashioned bar-room, thick with smoke and loud conversation, crowded with longshoremen from the docks. The high bar ran all the length of one wall. A mechanical piano screeched unattended and unheeded in one corner.

Dodd, hauling Riganov behind him, worked his way through to the end of the bar.

Casey, squat and round as a beer barrel, nodded gravely at Dodd. "Howdy, Mr. Dodd. Nice evening."

"A trifle noisy," Dodd said. "A couple of beers, Casey."

Casey filled two mugs and slid them along the spattered top of the bar. Dodd clicked his against Riganov's.

"Here's to the revolution. I wish you'd stop that soap-box stuff, Riganov. I wouldn't have pried you loose tonight except for that little favor you did me this morning."

Riganov was busy drinking his beer. There was a sudden lull in the uproar in the saloon.

"Oh-oh," said Casey anxiously. "Riganov!"

Riganov dropped his glass on the counter and spun around like a top. A woman was standing just inside the door. She was six feet tall and wide in proportion. She had black hair, and a face that was dark and smooth and sleek as mahogany. She was wearing a man's carpet slippers, and she shuffled forward in them like some giant beast of prey. The crowd moved back away from her warily.

Riganov gave a moan of terror. He skittered away from the bar, whirling and ducking through the crowd, darted out the side door.

The woman came on up to the bar and Casey backed away from it cautiously until his shoulders were against the shelves of glasses behind it.

"Now, Mrs. Riganov," he begged, holding up his hands in a soothing gesture. "Don't start anything. I didn't sell him that beer. I swear it. This gentleman bought it for him."

Mrs. Riganov turned darkly enigmatic eyes on Dodd, and Dodd backed up a step.

"You buy it?" asked Mrs. Riganov.

"Yes," Dodd admitted cautiously.

"Don't do it no more."

"Absolutely not," said Dodd quickly.

Mrs. Riganov nodded once, warningly, at Casey, and once at Dodd, then she turned and went shuffling silently across the room and out the side door.

"She'll catch him," said Casey, hastily pouring himself a short one. "She'll catch him and beat hell outta him. What a woman! She gives me the pixies. I'm sorry I had to poke it off on you, Mr. Dodd, but the last time I gave him a drink she busted over a hundred dollars' worth of glassware and my bouncer's right arm."

Dodd drank the rest of his beer and breathed a little more easily. "She has a certain look in her eye—indubitably. Another beer, Casey, and can you tell me if there's a man by the name of Bish Reap around here tonight?"

"In the corner over there behind the table," said Casey, bringing the beer. "If you want to talk to him, do it quick, because soon he'll be under it. Better take him a drink to wake him up a bit."

Dodd took the glass of whiskey Casey proffered and walked across to the table the bartender had pointed out. He sat down in a rickety chair and nudged the whiskey gently across the table toward the man on the other side.

"Hey, Bish," he said. "Up and at 'em. I want to talk to you."

"You see a man in the depths of a great mourning," said Bish Reap.

He had dreamy blue eyes that were open very wide now, as blank and glassy as twin marbles. His long, deeply lined face had been shaved only on one side and that sketchily. He was a tall man with a long red nose and a loose-lipped flabby mouth. He wore a frock coat that had moth-eaten velvet lapels, and his gray hair was theatrically long in back.

He picked up the drink automatically and sipped it, sighing. "In the deepest mourning, sir. Sorrow has come to me today, stealing up on sly feet. A friend is gone—gone where we all shall follow some day. Gone in the flush of her youth, and I mourn for her, because she was kind. Yes, kind to an old man clinging to the shattered remnants of greatness. I refer to myself, sir, and thank you for the drink."

"What was your friend's name?" Dodd asked.

"Bowler—Miss Kaye Bowler—a member of our financial and social aristocracy—and she graced her position with an air and dignity, I might say, that many who criticized her might do well to imitate."

"How did you happen to know her?"

"She came to me, sir, I'm flattered to say. She sought me out, and I was more than glad to give her my poor help."

"What help?"

"She sought information, and if I may say so without undue vanity, she came to the man who could give it to her and who did give it to her, unstinted."

"What information?"

"That, sir, is a secret that no force could drag from my lips."

"Did she ask you about Spider Ladue?"

The ice in Bish Reap's glass tinkled lightly. His eyes grew wider and blanker and he moistened his lips with a quick, uneasy flick of his tongue.

"Leave me, sir. Leave me to wonder at the cruel mystery of life!"

Dodd got up and went back to the bar. "Where can I find Spider Ladue, Casey?"

"In a hole on Turk Street. Four-twenty is the number. He lives upstairs in back, and I'll give you twenty percent if you can collect the bar bill he owes me, the rat."

CHAPTER SIX

DRUNK AND DISORDERLY

TURK STREET was one over from Kester, a crawling, teeming tunnel with a sinisterly quiet, shadowy life of its own.

420 was near the corner on a line with Casey's Haven. Yellow light peeped out from behind slatternly blinds. There was no light in front, and Dodd hesitated uncertainly, squinting up at the door. There was a slight movement in the darkness beside him and he saw a man leaning against the high iron railing that guarded the steep steps. A match grated and its wavering flame brought a face into view—a thin, dead-white face with a mouth like a scar. The match moved up to the mouth and touched the end of a bobbing cigarette.

"Spider in?" Dodd asked softly.

The man's palms suddenly reversed, throwing the light into Dodd's face. Dodd blinked blandly, smiling.

"Friend of his," he said.

The match winked out. "Upstairs. Third floor. Back."

"Thanks," said Dodd.

He went up the worn steps, found the door, pushed it open. There was one light far back in the hall, and the heavy air seemed to swim slowly around it, pressing it in. The stairs were shadowy to the left and Dodd climbed up them.

A baby was crying somewhere, and the voices of a man and woman cursed each other in fluent Spanish.

Dodd reached the second floor, went on up the next flight of stairs. Dirt grated under his feet and he wondered how Spider Ladue could live in this hole and keep his plum-colored suit so immaculate.

The third-floor hall was narrower than the ones on the floors below it, and the air was dead and lifeless, still holding the heat of the day. Dodd walked on down the hall, halted under its one light—a dusty unshaded globe hung by a cord from the ceiling.

There was a door directly at the back and Dodd saw when he came close to it that it was open about six inches. He slowed a little, instinctively, and then he noticed the faint, disappearing flick of a light behind it.

Dodd came up to the door in three long, silent steps and kicked it open. It flew back against the wall with a drumming thud. The light in the hall threw a grotesque, hump-shouldered shadow of Dodd across the floor inside the room. He crouched, and the light came over him from behind and showed the twisted face of Spider Ladue, shiny with sweat, the mouth gaping crookedly. He was lying on the floor on his back, and the black handle of a knife protruded from the hollow of his throat.

There was a closed door behind him, almost touching the rigid toe of one of his shiny shoes, and Dodd heard a faint, furtive scraping noise from the other side.

Dodd drew a long, gasping breath. He stepped over Spider Ladue and hit the door hard with his shoulder, reaching down to turn the knob at the same time. The door went inward, carrying him with it.

HE WAS in the black, square hole of the kitchen, and the smell of old cooking clogged his nostrils. The gray square of a window loomed to his left, and a dim figure was moving against it.

Dodd yelled and dove for the figure. His fingers rasped across rough cloth, and then a foot caught him squarely in the chest with driving force and knocked him backwards. Dodd went over a stool and crashed into a cupboard. Crockery came down around him with a jangling crash.

He fought free of it, started forward, and half fell over the stool again. By then the figure was gone through the window, and Dodd went through after it.

He barked his hand against the rough brick of the sill, dropped off twisting awkwardly and came down crouched on the slant of a roof.

It was dark here, but Dodd saw the shadowy figure ahead of him silhouetted against the moonlit sky, going over the parapet that edged the roof. Dodd ran that way, sliding clumsily against the roof slope, and brought up against the same parapet with a breathless grunt.

He started to climb over and then halted short, staring down. There was no roof on the other side of the parapet. The wall dropped off sheer, down into the black pit of an alley two stories below, and the shadowy figure was crawling down that wall, flattened against it like an enormous bug, arms and legs spraddled wide, going smoothly and easily down where there was no foothold at all.

Dodd swore, groped around in the darkness behind the parapet, blindly looking for something to throw, and his hands encountered the slick roundness of a flower pot. It was heavy with dirt and some plant in it dug spiny leaves into Dodd's fingers.

Dodd leaned over the parapet. The shadowy figure was halfway down now, almost lost in the blackness, just a vague swirl of movement there.

Dodd aimed and dropped the flower pot. He couldn't follow its swift descent, but he heard the thud of its landing, and there was a choked, agonized cry. In the blackness of the alley ash-cans suddenly rolled in a smashing clatter.

Dodd leaned far over, trying to see, and he caught just one more glimpse of the shadowy figure as it appeared against the half-lighted mouth of the alley. It was running bent over, staggering crazily.

Dodd swore again, stumbled back across the roof and in through Ladue's window. Broken crockery crackled under his feet, and Ladue was still sprawled lifelessly in the front room.

Dodd went out through the flat's front door, ran down the hall. The tenement seemed strangely quiet now, and Dodd's feet made a thunder of sound going down the stairs. He swung out the front door and down into the street. He turned to the right and headed up Turk Street, in the direction of the alley-mouth, at a dead run. When he reached it he stopped short. There was nothing in its grimy darkness and no one moving along the street close to it. Dodd went up to the corner and headed across toward Kester Street and Casey's Haven.

He was midway in the block when he saw Mr. and Mrs. Riganov outlined under a street-light, coming toward him. Mrs. Riganov had her spouse by the back of the neck, shoving him ahead of her, and every other step she would swing her free hand and catch Riganov on the side of the head with a sodden smacking sound. Riganov was yelling—one continuous protesting wail.

AS DODD watched, Tipton suddenly appeared in front of them. Tipton was so drunk his knees wobbled, and he shook a gravely disapproving finger in front of Mrs. Riganov's nose.

"Tut, tut, tut, my good woman. That is no way to treat a faithful helpmeet. Unhand him at once, at once, at once."

Mrs. Riganov hit him. She struck like a man with her closed fist. Tipton's head jerked, and he staggered sideways, waving his arms to keep his balance. He tripped over the curb and sat down.

Dinregan, the policeman, came up at a run. "So!" he said to Tipton. "I've been watching you, my smooth friend, and wondering how long before you'd start."

Tipton got up, swaying. "Hello, hello, hello," he said, smiling. "I can't hit a woman—never, never, never—but I can hit you, can't I?"

Tipton jumped for Dinregan, swinging with both arms. Dinregan dodged sideways, hauling a leather-covered billy from his hip-pocket. He flipped it up and down expertly, catching Tipton on top of the head.

Tipton sat down on the curb again. He didn't seem to be hurt much. He looked up at Dinregan, still smiling, and said, "Well, well, well, well," in a pleased voice.

Dodd ran up. "Watch him, Dinregan," he said. "He's tough as whale-bone."

"I've handled him before," said Dinregan grimly. "It's to the station for you, my boy, and no tricks, either."

Dodd said: "There's a man been murdered over on Turk, Dinregan. Spider Ladue. I just found his body."

"So," said Dinregan. "He would play cop, would he, that little rat. Wait till I phone in. A man should be twins in this district."

Dodd said: "Have you had your eye on Tipton long?"

"I saw him a half-hour ago and started after him, but he dodged me somewhere. I've been looking for him. I know what happens when he gets going. Just sit you there, my boy."

Dodd looked down at Tipton. "What are you doing in this district tonight, Tipton?"

Tipton stopped smiling. "I am looking for someone."

"Why?"

"I am going to put my fingers around his neck, very gently, you see, and then I am going to squeeze—oh, for quite some time."

"You know who killed Kaye Bowler?"

"No," said Tipton. "No, no, no. But I am going to squeeze until I find out. Yes, yes, yes."

"Who?" Dodd asked.

Tipton waggled his finger. "You would not know him, but his name is Bish Reap. I will tell you more after I have squeezed for a long time. It will be very, very good fun."

THERE was a crowd of curious onlookers ringing them around now, and Dinregan said angrily to them: "Go on. Move along now, or maybe I'll give you a ride, too."

There was the sudden racketing crash of a revolver report, partially muffled, and then a woman screamed and screamed again.

"God save us," said Dinregan. "And now what?"

The crowd of onlookers split apart, seeking cover as the swinging doors of Casey's Haven banged back with abrupt violence. Casey and a woman stumbled out and struggled across the sidewalk. The woman was holding a revolver high over her head, and Casey had a grip on her wrist, shaking it violently.

Before any of them could move, the revolver spun in a glittering arc and clunked down in the middle of the street. The woman twisted loose from Casey and ran directly toward them, with Casey right after her.

Casey was amazingly fast for such a tubby barrel of a man, and he caught the woman again ten feet away and whirled her around and threw her headlong into the astonished Dinregan's arms.

"There she is!" he panted. "Shot him, she did! Walked right in and poked a gun in his face and let him have it!"

The woman screamed again and struck at Dinregan.

"Now, now, now, now, Lea," said Tipton amiably. "The gentleman is a policeman, and as you've so often told me, it is unmannerly to strike policemen."

Lea's brassily blonde hair was down over her eyes, and her face was twisted until the veneer of make-up seemed cracked. She forgot Dinregan and tried to get at Tipton, but Dinregan had a grip on her now.

"You rat!" Lea screamed, trying to kick Tipton.

"Now, now, now, now," said Tipton reprovingly. "You're repeating yourself. And don't yell so loudly, my dear, or you'll spoil your singing voice."

"Stop it," said Dinregan, swinging her away. "Stop it, all of you. You, Casey, what is this about shooting?"

"She murdered Bish Reap," said Casey. "Right in the side door, she walked, and leaned over the table and shot him dead as a canned sardine, and I saw her with my own eyes."

"May I be of assistance?" asked Bish Reap. He was standing on the fringe of the gaping crowd, tall and somber and swaying loosely.

"Yah!" Casey yelled frantically. "Get away. You're dead!"

"Not quite, fortunately," said Bish Reap. "The lady's aim was not as deadly as her intentions. The bullet missed me by an inch or two, I think, although I didn't measure."

"You'll all go to jail," said Dinregan. "That you will—every damn one of you—and no more yelling and rioting." He pulled his revolver from his holster, still holding Lea with one hand. "March! The whole bunch of you! Right to that call-box on the corner!"

CHAPTER SEVEN

BROKEN ALIBI

THE PADDY-WAGON unloaded them in the paved court between the jail and the city hall, and their feet raised a hollow racket of echoes in the bare corridor on the way through to the booking-room. There was Tipton first, in the grip of one policeman, and then the blonde, Lea, in the grip of another. Mr. and Mrs. Riganov came next, with Mrs. Riganov hauling Riganov along by one thin wrist like a squalling child. Dodd and Bish Reap walked side by side behind them, and Casey brought up the rear, talking soothingly and persuadingly to the grim-faced Dinregan.

Some reporters saw them go past the pressroom and came in the booking-room after them. Dinregan and the booking-sergeant started yelling at each other because Dinregan had come in with his prisoners instead of staying on post, with the two other policemen trying to explain and the reporters all asking questions. The racket was deafening, and at its height Meekins drifted sleepily in from some back room and nudged Dodd.

"You caught quite a kettle of fish, but I've got a bigger one if I can land it for us."

"Who?" Dodd asked.

"Bowler."

"Bowler!" Dodd exclaimed. "They're bringing him in? What for?"

"Quiet," said Meekins, jerking his hat-brim lower. "The reporters don't know it yet. The sergeant tipped me, because I owe him some dough. It's attempted murder. You know that guy Green you asked me about? The one that runs the financial newspaper? It seems he's been after Bowler for an interview for his paper, and Bowler wouldn't give it to him, so just a little while ago Green gets up his nerve for one more try and goes out to Bowler's house. He rang the front doorbell. Bowler's butler was out, and Bowler answered the door. He had a walking stick—a heavy one—with him. He swung on Green and knocked him down the front steps. The house is old-fashioned with a high porch. There's about a dozen cement steps, and it's a damned wonder the fall didn't kill Green offhand, but it didn't, and Bowler was coming down to finish the job when some people that were walking by stopped him. It's open and shut—witnesses and all. He won't slide out this time."

Dodd was staring at the stained green walls, his eyes squinting thoughtfully behind the patched glasses.

"Maybe you were right," Meekins murmured. "Maybe the old boy had something to do with ticking his daughter off. They always did fight like hell."

Bowler came in between two radio-car men, and the racket in the room suddenly redoubled as the reporters recognized him and fought to get near him.

Bowler was white-faced and shaken. He kept making bewildered, pathetic gestures, trying to brush the reporters away, trying to conceal his face. His eyes were dazed, and the hard shell that had seemed to encase him had cracked now, and he looked sick and old and tired. He backed into a corner and stood there helplessly.

Dodd edged through the scuffling reporters and said: "Hello, Mr. Bowler. I told you we'd be meeting again, but I didn't suspect it would be in such pleasant circumstances."

BOWLER had no fight left in him. He stared at Dodd silently, and his lips were trembling. Dodd was suddenly sorry for him and angry at himself for gloating over him. Bowler was like a gaunt old wolf backed into a corner and ringed in by his enemies, knowing he is doomed, but still facing forward and not asking for any mercy.

Dodd said: "I'll help you out of this."

Bowler's voice was thin and shaking. "Thank you, Mr. Dodd. I—I have been wanting to apologize.... I loved my daughter. I was lying this afternoon. I loved her more—more than anything. But—but I could never show emotion. Neither of us could. I was hurt—more than I've ever been—because we'd quarreled over that drunken fool, Tipton, before she left.... I do apologize for attacking you...."

"Forget it," Dodd said uneasily.

Green fought his way into the room. There was an ambulance interne in a white coat behind him. Green's coat was off, and his shirt was streaked with blood. His right arm and shoulder bulked lumpily grotesque under thick bandages.

"I won't go to the hospital until he's booked!" he was yelling furiously. "I won't! He'll slip out of this if I do! I want him booked for attempted murder! I demand it!"

His pudgy face was scraped raw on one cheek, and his mouth twitched with pain.

"He's got a broken shoulder, and his arm's broken in two places," the interne said angrily to the booking-sergeant. "Maybe he's got some ribs caved in, I don't know. He's got to get to the hospital where there's an X-ray."

Dodd shouted suddenly: "Quiet! All of you! Listen to me for a moment, and we can settle all of this!"

They were all staring at him, and Dodd continued in a more normal voice, relaxed and smiling a little bit, but with his eyes coldly alert behind his glasses.

"All of us are here now. All that are alive. And I can tell what happened from the beginning, and that was when Kaye Bowler decided to marry Tipton. They had an offhanded way about it, and they were both pretty hard-boiled, but I think they loved each other more than anyone realized. Tipton had been going with this girl, Lea, and she tried to spoil things by threatening Tipton and then Kaye Bowler."

They were all listening, and for a moment the policeman who was holding Tipton forgot him. Tipton twisted away. He jumped forward and hit Lea squarely in the mouth and knocked her ten feet into a wall.

A couple of cops got hold of Tipton again, and a reporter lifted the dazed Lea to her feet. A flash-bulb popped brilliantly.

Tipton was grinning amiably. "I've been wanting to do that for some time, dear, dear Lea."

"Quiet!" Dodd shouted. "Listen to me! Kaye Bowler was the kind to fight back. She began trying to get something on Lea. Something to counteract the breach-of-promise suit or whatever it was Lea threatened, and she got it. She heard somewhere about Bish Reap—a walking encyclopedia of show history—and she went to him and asked him about Lea. What did she ask you, and what did you tell her, Bish?"

Bish Reap swayed majestically. "Her confidence, sir, is not to be profaned...."

Tipton almost broke loose from the two policemen. "You oratorical bag of bones! You'll tell or I'll...."

Bish Reap lifted one hand negligently. "Threats of violence do not frighten me, sir. I was about to say that her confidence was not to be profaned in ordinary circumstances, but due to what has happened to her and those she loved, I will say that she asked me concerning Lea, here, and I could tell her little but that Lea had once graced the platform of a carnival in the capacity of a hootch-dancer."

"A lie!" Lea shrieked furiously. "A dirty lie!"

BISH REAP went on sonorously, his blank eyes staring at the ceiling. "She wanted to know more, of course, and so I recommended the services of Spider Ladue—an old trouper turned private peep—who was an expert at the art of shadowing a suspect. She hired him through me, and he set out to follow Lea and learn more about her. I regret, sir, that I know no more about the matter."

"Never mind," said Dodd. "I can guess the rest. Lea had a pal, of course. Someone to back her up and put on the squeeze when the time came. That pal was an old-time carnival or circus man, too. When she contacted him, Ladue recognized him at once—even though he had probably changed his name—and he must have seen and recognized Ladue and traced him back to Bish Reap. But there was nothing to worry about then. Lea was entitled to have friends. Nothing to worry about until Kaye Bowler, because of what she knew about Lea, was killed—and the murderer had to be either an acrobat or wire walker or human fly to get away the way he did after he killed her—by climbing around a four-inch ledge and down the sheer side of a building fifteen stories above the street. Then Spider Ladue's knowledge that Lea's pal was one of those things became vital, and he was murdered for fear he would reveal it, and Lea tried to kill Bish to keep him from talking.

"Spider Ladue was murdered tonight—even before he had a chance to realize that he had vital information—because Kaye Bowler's death is listed officially as an accident. But his murderer knew what would happen if and when Spider did talk. He killed Spider and got away down the sheer side of a building tonight, but I dropped a flower pot on him and knocked him part way down. He fell and was hurt, but he was clever. He had already incurred the anger of Bowler—Kaye's father—under the pretense of trying to interview him. He did that in order to have some sort of an excuse in case Kaye went to her father and he interfered. The murderer would have put Bowler out of the picture very shortly had that happened. He had his alibi planted because Bowler had threatened him repeatedly before witnesses. Self-defense, he would have pleaded.

"Tonight, when I knocked him off the wall, he used the same planted alibi to cover his injuries. He went to Bowler's house and insulted Bowler. Bowler knocked him down the stairs, and there was an excuse for having the broken shoulder I gave him when I knocked him off the wall outside Spider Ladue's."

Green smashed the interne in the face with his uninjured fist and dodged for the door. Lea screamed and raked her fingernails across the face of a policeman who tried to grab him, and then Riganov, still fast in the grasp of his wife, put out one foot slyly, stretching full-length to do it, and tripped Green.

Green went down in a tangled sprawl in the doorway, and three policemen piled on top of him before he could get up again.

Dodd grinned wryly at Bowler, and then Tipton was standing beside them.

Dodd said: "Let's go have a drink, Tippy. I need one."

Tipton shook his head gravely. "No, thanks. I won't be drinking any more. Kaye, when she left me in the bar-room of the Bowler Building, asked me not to drink more than a dozen Scotch-and-sodas while I was waiting for her. I had the twelfth just before I ran into the Riganovs." He took Bowler's arm gently. "Would you like to sit down over here, sir? Mr. Dodd will arrange bond for our release shortly."

"Thank you, Tippy," Bowler said. "I am—rather tired."

Meekins was staring at Tipton unbelievingly. "Did you hear that, boss? Our best customer! Going on the wagon!" he moaned.

"Well," said Dodd, "for some reason or other I don't feel so badly about losing him."

MURDER IN THE RED

IN WHICH THAT
FABULOUS LUMINARY OF
THE CRIMINAL COURTS
AND HIS MAN, MEEKINS,
SOLVE THE RIDDLE
OF THE RED-HEADED
STREET-WALKER WHO
HANDED OUT RUBIES
TO MEN SHE ACCOSTED
ON KESTER STREET,
AND BET A BLUE CHIP
ON MURDER IN THE RED
TO WIN THANKS FROM
ONE GAMBLING MAN
AND CATCH HELL FROM
ANOTHER.

CHAPTER ONE

THE TART FROM KESTER STREET

IT WAS still raining when Dodd's taxi slid to the curb in front of the courthouse. He pulled the collar of his coat up around his throat and sloshed quickly across the sidewalk, went three at a time up the long, broad flight of granite steps. He pushed through one of the revolving doors, went into the hall, puffing a little.

Meekins, Dodd's runner, was leaning against the wall under a square gold-lettered sign that said—*Room 101, Night Court.* Meekins was small and mild and nondescript, and the only cue to his age was the fact that he was bald and sensitive about it. He always kept his hat on whenever it was possible, and he had it on now, pulled down low over his weary eyes.

"You ain't any too soon," he said. He's up now, and he's soundin' off again."

"What judge?" Dodd asked.

"Crane. He's new."

"Oh, hell," said Dodd.

"I don't know why you think you got to front for that screw-ball, anyway," Meekins said. "It ain't as if there was any dough—"

"Later, later," said Dodd, opening the door to 101.

IT WAS a long, high-ceilinged room, brightly lighted with the spectators' seats in long, curving rows in front of the railing that separated them from the court proper. There were a few bedraggled people, sitting in the seats, and sure enough Riganov was up and sounding off again.

Dodd was a big man, tall and loose-jointed, with deceptively wide shoulders, and his feet made thudding echoes as he hurried down the aisle. He wore a pair of horn-rimmed glasses patched over the nosepiece with a strip of white adhesive tape, and his eyes were blue and blandly good-humored behind their rain-misted lenses. He had to fumble with the catch on the gate in the railing.

Riganov went right on talking, loudly. "I got a right! I got a right in the Constitution! It says so. It says free speech in the Constitution, and I'm a citizen and I got a right!"

Judge Crane was a thin little man, looking shrunken and pale in his black robes, and he was regarding Riganov with an air of mildly absentminded interest.

"Quite so," he said. "Quite so, Mr.—ah—Riganov. I flatter myself that I am as familiar with your constitutional rights as you are. However, the state—in this case, the municipality—has a right, also. It is known, generally, as its police power. Under that right, it has the power to forbid acts that endanger the safety of its citizens. No one objects to your holding meetings, but you can't do it on street corners where you block traffic and menace the safety of passers-by."

"It's a plot!" Riganov yelled. "You're just a fascist tool of the special interests—"

Dodd got through the gate and reached him. He caught one of Riganov's bent, thin shoulders, whirled him around, and slammed him down in a chair.

"Shut up!" he whispered fiercely. He straightened up then, smiling,

It was just at that point that Mrs. Riganov went to work with her flat-iron.

apologetically, and said: "Your honor, I'm sorry to interrupt the court in this abrupt manner, but may I be allowed to speak for the defendant?"

"Who are you?" Crane asked mildly.

"My name is William Dodd, sir."

"Are you an attorney, Mr. Dodd?"

"No, sir. I'm a bondsman—the defendant's bondsman."

"That's interesting," said Crane, "but hardly relevant at this stage of the proceedings. You may well be the defendant's bondsman, but that doesn't give you any status in this court."

Dodd nodded. "I know that. I'm not acting in my professional capacity, your honor. I've furnished bond for the defendant several times, but I've never received any money for it. He's just a friend of mine."

"A philanthropic bondsman!" Crane said. "That's astonishing, Mr. Dodd. In fact, almost unbelievable. You've succeeded in arousing my curiosity. Go ahead."

Riganov popped out of his chair. "It's a plot! It's a filthy fascist plot to silence—"

Riganov had a shock of bushy black hair, and Dodd put his hand on top of it and pushed hard. Riganov sat down.

"Your honor," said Dodd in his most persuasive manner, "this man is the janitor in the building where I have my offices. He's slightly cracked on the subject of fascist plots, but other than that he's perfectly harmless."

"He's charged with holding an unauthorized meeting on a street corner, blocking traffic and disturbing the peace. I understand he has been arrested repeatedly for the same or similar offenses."

"That's correct," Dodd agreed. "But he's still perfectly harmless. He only does things like that because his wife beats him."

"Ah?" said Crane in amazement.

Dodd nodded earnestly. "She beats him. He has to express his defiance and independence and general manhood in some way, so he gets on a soap-box and yells at people."

Riganov didn't get up this time. Instead he wriggled forward in his chair and twisted his thin, brown face into a horrible grimace. "Any day, now," he said, "we blow up all courthouses!"

"All of them, Mr. Riganov?" Crane inquired, interested.

"Yes!" Riganov snarled dramatically. "All! This one here, I attend to myself personally. I put ten tons of dynamite in the cellar and then *whoom!* Nothing but a hole in the ground!"

Crane looked at Dodd. "That's a rather dangerous program for him to advocate."

"It doesn't mean a thing," Dodd insisted, glowering at Riganov. "He'd run like a rabbit if he saw a stick of dynamite."

"And jails!" said Riganov. "We let everybody out of jail and arrest all policemen and judges and put them in!"

"Your honor," Dodd said desperately. "I've known Riganov for a long time, and he never does anything but talk. He has a good job, and if he's put in jail he'll lose it."

"He doesn't sound very safe to me," said Crane.

Dodd said: "He's trying to get you to put him in jail, your honor."

"He has a good chance of succeeding," said Crane. "But just why does he want me to put him in jail?"

"His wife is here waiting for him."

Crane looked up at the audience. "If Mrs. Riganov is in the court, will she stand up, please?"

A woman sitting in the front row of spectators' seats stood up slowly. She was six feet tall, but she was so enormously broad she looked much shorter. She had a round, impassively smooth olive-skinned face and dark, narrowed eyes that had dangerous greenish flecks of light in them. She was hatless, and she wore an old man's overcoat fastened with a safety pin in front.

"Yes," said Crane thoughtfully. "I can understand that Mr. Riganov might have reason to be apprehensive if his wife disapproved of his actions."

"She outweighs him by a hundred pounds," Dodd said. "And she gets mad when he talks on street corners."

Crane stroked his chin. "Well, I'll tell you, Mr. Dodd. I appreciate your motives, and after seeing Mrs. Riganov, I'll discount a lot Mr. Riganov has said, because I can understand that he'd probably prefer the safety and quiet of a jail to having an interview with his wife in the privacy of their home. But nevertheless, in view of the defendant's record, I can't just simply dismiss his case. I'll put him under a hundred-dollar peace bond, Mr. Dodd."

"A hundred dollars?" Dodd said, swallowing.

"Yes. You may furnish it if you wish. Arrange it with the clerk."

"Thank you, sir," Dodd said glumly.

HE ARRANGED for the bond with the clerk. Riganov was still sitting in his chair with a look of dazed despair on his face, and Dodd hauled him up with a grip on one thin arm and steered him through the gate in the railing and on up the aisle. Mrs. Riganov padded quietly and sinisterly along behind them.

Safely out in the hall, Dodd let go of Riganov and said: "Now, listen, you. I—"

Riganov suddenly thrust against him, pushing him back into Mrs. Riganov, and darted frantically for the front door. Mrs. Riganov got Dodd out of her way by the simple method of cuffing him one alongside the head and knocking him into the wall. She went after Riganov in a deadly swift, ponderous rush and caught him just at the door.

Riganov squealed once. His wife took a good grip on the back of his collar and dragged him back to Dodd. Dodd was feeling gingerly of the ear that had stopped her slap.

"What?" Mrs. Riganov asked gutturally. "What happens in there?"

"He's loose—for the time being," Dodd explained. "I put up a peace bond for him."

"Peace bond? What is that? Money?"

Dodd nodded sadly. "And how. A hundred dollars. If he gets arrested again, I lose it."

"He makes speeches—you lose money?"

"That's it."

"He don't make speeches," said Mrs. Riganov. "He—don't—make—speeches." She emphasized her words by hitting Riganov four times—twice on one side of the head and twice on the other. Riganov's head bobbed like a punching bag.

Meekins came down the hall, making a cautious detour around Mrs. Riganov, and spoke to Dodd. "There's some more comin' in now. Women. We ain't got any in this batch, so can I go out and have me a beer?"

"I guess so," said Dodd.

The prisoners came in through the passageway that led across to the jail. There were six of them in charge of two matrons who looked enough alike to be twins, and were almost as big as Mrs. Riganov. The prisoners filed along toward the rear door of the night court with an air of dispirited defiance—bedraggled drabs seined up out of the city's slums—all except the last one.

Dodd stared at her unbelievingly.

SHE WAS swaggering along with her head up in the air and her hands in the pockets of a fur jacket that had cost plenty of money. She was slim and very young, and she had bronze-red hair and a pert, tip-tilted nose. She looked like she knew just what she was doing and was very proud of herself for doing it.

"That last one?" Dodd asked Meekins, watching her disappear through the door.

"I thought so, too," said Meekins. "The coat is worth six months of what you laughingly call my salary, but she wouldn't put it up for security, and she hasn't got a dime cash on her, and besides she told me to scram."

"What's her name?"

"Tessie Smaltz—she says."

"What's the charge?"

"Soliciting. She must be dumber than hell. She talked back to a plainclothesman down on Kester Street, so of course he run her in."

Riganov coughed. "She stops me too."

Mrs. Riganov shook him viciously. "What? What?"

"Wait," Dodd said. "Wait, now. What's this, Riganov? That girl—Tessie Smaltz—stopped you?"

"Yes. I am hurrying to make my speech, and she stops me and says, 'Wait a minute,' and I say, 'I got no time, please,' and start to walk away fast, and she stops me again and puts her fingers in my pocket to hold me, like this…."

Riganov poked two fingers in the breast pocket of his coat to illustrate, and his voice trailed off into a mumble. He opened his mouth and shut it again, carefully.

Mrs. Riganov grabbed his wrist and hauled his hand out of his pocket. Expertly she opened his clenched fingers. A flat red stone gleamed with incredible fiery brilliance against the grime on his palm.

"*Whooie!*" Meekins said in a reverent whisper.

Mrs. Riganov slapped her husband and then slapped him again, harder. "So! Taking jewelry from no-goods!"

"No!" Riganov wailed. "No, no! I didn't! I didn't know it was even there!"

"Let me see it," said Dodd.

"Give," said Mrs. Riganov.

Riganov handed the stone over. "But I didn't know! She puts it there when I don't know! I didn't—"

"Liar," said Mrs. Riganov, slapping him.

"Wait, now," said Dodd quickly. "What happened after she put her hand in your pocket?"

"I knock it away," said Riganov plaintively. "I am in a big hurry to make my speech. I don't say nothing else to her at all, and I don't even see her again until now. Honest!"

"Is it real?" Meekins asked in the same reverent whisper.

Dodd nodded. "Yeah. Get in there and pay her fine. Quick."

Meekins darted through the front door of the courtroom.

Mrs. Riganov pointed a finger. "You keep."

"Keep—this?" Dodd asked, holding up the stone.

"Is no good. Is no good to take jewelry from bum girls."

"Mama!" Riganov protested. "Mama, but—"

She slapped him. "Shut up. You come home. I fix you."

She dragged him down the hall. Riganov tried to hold back, wailing tearfully, but to no avail. Mrs. Riganov hauled him through the door and out into the night.

CHAPTER TWO

VANISHING REDHEAD

MEEKINS CAME out of the courtroom so fast his hat-brim was blowing up in front. He stopped beside Dodd, skidding his heels on the damp tile.

"Listen, boss! Sam Rudolph is in there. He got the clerk to call her case first, plead her guilty, and paid her fine without batting an eye. They're coming now."

"Rudolph," Dodd repeated thoughtfully. "What's he doing in a night police court?"

Meekins had no time to answer because Sam Rudolph and the girl with the bronze hair came out of the night-court entrance and started down the hall.

"Hi, Sam," said Dodd getting in their way.

Sam Rudolph was a thin little man with a pouter-pigeon chest. He wore specially built-up shoes, but even they weren't enough to bring the crown of his carefully creased hat higher than the top button on Dodd's vest. He had a dark, sharply sallow face and a voice so gratingly unpleasant that it was rumored judges gave him his many successful decisions just to keep from having to listen to him any longer. He was a crack criminal attorney, with all that implied. The Bar Association had been following him around for years, but had never been able to catch up with him.

He tilted his head back and scowled up at Dodd. "Uh? Oh, hello, Dodd. Busy, now. Some other day."

"Wait a minute," said Dodd easily. "You've got enough time for me to say a word or two to Tessie, here, haven't you?"

"No!" said Rudolph, trying to get around him.

But the girl with the bronze hair pulled back on his arm, anchoring him. She looked even better at close range. She had a clear tanned skin and nice blue eyes that she had opened very wide now in a burlesque imitation of a baby stare.

"Oh, let's talk to the nice man. You are a nice man, aren't you?"

"Positively," said Dodd.

"Are you a reporter, too?"

"No!" said Rudolph sharply. "He's a bail bondsman. Come along."

The girl still dragged back. "But I want to see a reporter! I thought there were always reporters in courtrooms to take your pictures and things."

"This is night court, Tessie," Dodd said. "But you can talk to me. I talk to easily, even if I don't carry a camera."

Rudolph put his hand against Dodd's chest and shoved. "Now, listen here, Dodd! You stop annoying my client! I'm in a hurry—"

Outside, in the street, there was a sharp, cracking report that multiplied itself in fluttering echoes. Instantly after it there was another.

"Shots," Meekins exclaimed.

He darted for the front door with Dodd pounding heavily right behind him. They stopped for a second on the wet granite steps, staring both ways through the mist.

"There!" Meekins said, pointing to the left.

A tavern occupied the corner a half-block away, light showing orange and dim through its painted windows. Its front door was open now, swung wide, and a man lay flat on the sidewalk in the column of light that splashed through it.

"Hey!" said Meekins. "That—that looks like—"

"It's Riganov!" Dodd said.

He went down the steps in long, awkward leaps, skidded dangerously on the smeared sidewalk, and then hunched his broad shoulders forward and ran for the corner. Several of the saloon's customers had their heads poked cautiously out the door now, looking at the sprawled body on the sidewalk with stupid curiosity.

Riganov lay half twisted on his side, as though he had started to turn and got his legs tangled in the process. One arm was out limp beside him and the other was across his eyes, hiding his face.

Dodd knelt down beside him, swearing in a whisper. Gently he moved the arm that covered Riganov's face. All the animation seemed to have fled from it, and it was stiff as wax. There was a deep, slashed cut over the eyes, and the nose was flattened and slewed sideways. Blood mixed with rain ran messily down both Riganov's sallow cheeks.

MRS. RIGANOV appeared silently and ponderously out of the wet darkness. She shoved at the tavern customers that had ventured outside to form a ring around Dodd and Riganov, knocking several of them aside.

"Get out! You get out!" She knelt beside Dodd and put one square, muscle-padded hand softly on her husband's shoulder. "He is dead?"

"No," said Dodd. "He's been knocked around plenty, but I can't find where any shots—"

"They don't shoot at him, they shoot at me."

Around the corner a siren sounded in a long dismal wail. Dodd stared at Mrs. Riganov. Her smooth face was as impassive as ever, but her eyes were all green now, as round and luminous as a cat's.

"You?" said Dodd.

"Yes. I leave him here while I go inside to get a beer. He cannot have a beer because he makes speeches after I tell him no. Two men come and hit him on the head and knock him down. I run out and chase them. They shoot at me." She touched a long rip in her overcoat, waist-high on the left side, and shrugged indifferently.

"They don't shoot so good, but they run good."

The ambulance on call at the police station whipped around the corner, skittering wildly on the wet asphalt, and bore down on them with the siren still wide open.

Meekins was standing on the running-board, holding on to the door-post with one hand and the brim of his hat with the other. He hopped off when the ambulance pulled in to the curb.

"Is the little screw-ball dead?" he asked anxiously.

"No," said Dodd. "A couple of birds hammered him around with brass knucks. Got a concussion, I think."

The ambulance attendants were handling Riganov's limp body with expert precision. They lifted him quickly and gently on a rolling stretcher.

Mrs. Riganov stood silent and impassive, watching them.

Dodd pulled at her sleeve. "Did you recognize the birds that hit him?"

"No. I not see good. I find, though."

"What?" said Dodd.

"I find," said Mrs. Riganov. "Nobody hits my husband but me. Nobody. I find." She nodded her head once at Dodd and climbed into the back of the ambulance with her husband.

Dodd leaned in and called to the attendant. "Doc! Give him a private room and the trimmings. It's on me."

"O.K., Dodd. Roll her, Casey."

The back doors slammed shut, and the ambulance bored away into the night with another rising howl from the siren.

Dodd suddenly remembered Sam Rudolph and the girl with the bronze-red hair. He turned hurriedly to go back to the courthouse and nearly fell over Meekins.

"They beat it," Meekins said, divining the cause of Dodd's sudden move. "Rudolph had that green locomotive of his parked in front of the courthouse. She got in it with him, and they went off in a cloud of smoke."

Dodd squinted thoughtfully through the moisture that smeared the lenses of his patched glasses.

"You think them two birds were after that red rock Riganov had?" Meekins murmured.

"Maybe," Dodd said.

"You sure it's real? I didn't get a good squint at it."

"It's real. I can't tell whether it's flawed or not, without a glass, but it's a swell job of cutting."

"Ruby?"

"Yeah."

"Boy, oh, boy!" said Meekins. "Oh, boy! Do you suppose the dame really slipped it to Riganov like he said?"

Dodd nodded. "Yes. He wouldn't have tried to sell his wife such a goofy story if it hadn't been true. Anyway, you could tell from his face that he didn't know it was in his pocket until he reached in there."

"Do you suppose," said Meekins, "that the dame has any more like that? Do you suppose she'd maybe hand us over a half-dozen or so if we asked her pretty?"

"I'd like to know," said Dodd.

"And me," said Meekins. "And how! Hey, look. When I ducked through the station on the way to get that ambulance, I spotted a dame that might give us some business. Want to see her?"

"Yes. I'd like to find Rudolph and Tessie Smaltz, but there isn't much chance of that if he wants to keep her under cover. He's got too many hide-outs."

THEY walked across the street and diagonally across the small park south of the courthouse. Behind them, a radio car rolled up in front of the tavern.

"Remind me I got to make a report on that as an eye-witness," Meekins said. "I told the boys I would when I flagged the ambulance through. You better, too. I didn't want Riganov lyin' there on the sidewalk until them dopey cops got through with their pinochle game and got around to answerin' the call."

"All right," said Dodd absently.

Meekins jerked at his soaked hat-brim. "Gee, you finally did cash in on that little screw-ball, didn't you? I couldn't figure why you was always fronting for him for no dough."

"I wasn't trying to cash in on him," Dodd said shortly. "I like him. He's a harmless little devil, goodhearted as the day is long, even if he does have nitwitted ideas. I didn't want to see him get thrown in jail and lose his job."

"All right, all right," Meekins said soothingly. "But I'd sure hate to be the birds that pasted him. I wouldn't want that wife of his on my tail. Them eyes of hers give me the assorted shivers."

They went around the back of the courthouse and along a dimly lighted alley and across the paved court toward the green light that marked the side entrance of the police station.

"In here," said Meekins.

Dodd preceded him through the door and down the grimy, stale-smelling hall past the deserted pressroom. The sergeant in charge was the only officer present in the booking-room. He had his elbows on his desk and was looking wearily at the girl who stood on the other side of the wooden railing in front of it.

"Well, really," she was saying in a clear, arrogant voice, "it doesn't seem to me that you can be very intelligent."

"Oh, I'm hellishly intelligent," the sergeant said. "All us cops are."

The girl was slim and tall and young. She wore a close-fitting blue tailored coat with a high fur collar. Her hair was blue-black, cut in a long page-boy bob, glistening sleekly with moisture now, and her eye lashes were long and langorous, over sleepily dark eyes. She was staring at the sergeant as though he were some form of lower animal life.

"It's a plain question," she said. "Surely you can answer it if you want to try."

The sergeant shook his head sadly. "Look, lady. I sit here eight hours a day, doin' nothin' but bookin' people in. How can I remember what one particular dame looks like?"

"You could remember this one. She looks very refined, and she has red hair."

"Red hair," the sergeant said slowly. "Refined. Sorry, lady. It don't mean a thing. Hello, Dodd."

Dodd nodded to the girl and said: "Perhaps I can help you. You were looking for a girl with red hair?"

She tilted her head back to stare up at him. "And just who are you, may I ask?"

"I forgot," said the sergeant. "Pardon me. She don't speak to strange men without a proper introduction. If you'll allow me, lady, I'll present you to Mr. William Dodd."

"Are you a reporter?" she asked Dodd flatly.

"No, lady," the sergeant answered for him. "He's a bail bondsman. That's a brand of vermin that infests police stations. We can't get rid of 'em. We tried fly spray and rat poison and what-not, but they're a hardy breed."

Dodd smiled at her. "You were looking for a girl with red hair? Was she wearing a short mink jacket?"

She was suddenly eager. "Did you see her?"

Dodd shrugged. "Maybe. What's her name?"

"That's none of your business!"

"Oh," said Dodd. "Well, I guess I haven't seen her, then."

"You have! You're lying!"

"You're probably right, lady," said the sergeant. "Do you want to bet on it, Meekins?"

"The hell with you," said Meekins. "You've won enough of my dough."

The sergeant rubbed his hands. "That reminds me, Meekins, my friend. There was a little matter of two dollars on that fight last night."

"Collect from Dodd," Meekins said glumly. "He owes me last week's salary."

The dark-haired girl stamped one small, high-heeled pump. "You! All of you! Answer my questions!"

"Well, now," said Dodd blandly, "if you'd only tell me your friend's name, perhaps I could tell you if I'd seen her."

"I won't! It's none—"

Running feet thumped along the hall, and a man came through the door and jerked to a breathless halt when he saw the girl.

"Donna!" he exclaimed, staring in bewilderment from Dodd to the sergeant to Meekins. "I got here as soon as I could. What—what is it?"

He was a young man with a finely drawn, pale face. He was wearing a long blue overcoat with velvet lapels over a dinner jacket. He took off his black felt hat now and brushed absently at the moisture on the brim, watching with worried eyes.

The girl took him by the arm, pulled him into the far corner of the room and whispered urgently in his ear. Dodd and Meekins and the sergeant watched curiously.

The young man had white, thinly nervous hands, and he kept jerking them in subdued gestures of protest as the girl whispered to him. Finally she finished and gave him a little push in the direction of the railing.

"But, Donna!" he protested. "I can't—"

The girl nodded her sleek, dark head determinedly. "You do it."

He shrugged and came up to the railing and spoke to the sergeant. "I'd like to inquire whether or not a girl has been booked here tonight?"

"Name?" the sergeant asked, interested now.

The man made a helpless gesture. "I don't know her name. I can give you a description—"

"If it's the same one she gave me," the sergeant said, jerking his head to indicate the dark-haired girl, "I already told her at least a hundred times I don't know who you mean."

THE YOUNG man drew in his breath.

"I'm an attorney, Sergeant, and the girl in question is my client. I have a right to know whether or not she's being held here and the charge."

"Attorney?" said the sergeant. "What's your name?"

"Howard Linden."

Dodd looked at Meekins and nodded. Meekins went quietly back along the hall to the pressroom, and Dodd could hear him dialing on one of the telephones there.

"Look, Mr. Linden," said the sergeant. "I'm not trying to put anything over on anybody. I don't remember anybody like the lady describes, but that don't mean she ain't been here. If you give me her name, I could look it up, but if you don't, I can't. There's been about a hundred prisoners in here tonight. Some of 'em are still here and some of 'em went through night court already and some are goin' through now. If you wanta, you can inquire over there."

Linden nodded. "Thanks." He turned to the girl. "That's the best thing to do, Donna. It's no good staying here."

The girl pointed at Dodd. "He knows."

"Do you?" Linden asked.

Dodd shrugged and smiled blandly.

"Offer him money, you fool," the girl said.

Dodd smiled more broadly. "No. You tell me the girl's name, and I'll tell you whether I've seen her or not."

Linden turned to the dark-haired girl. "Donna, can't I—"

"No!"

"Then, no sale," said Dodd.

Linden looked around helplessly and then said: "Come on, Donna. Perhaps at the night court...."

She let him lead her out, turning for one last arrogantly angry stare at Dodd.

Meekins came in and said to Dodd: "Linden is connected with McKay, Dunlop and Riley, and they're hot-shot legal guys that handle corporate and financial stuff only. No court work. Linden ain't a partner or anything. Just sort of a glorified office boy."

"Nothing much there," said Dodd. "He and the brunette are evidently friends of the redhead. See if you can find out the brunette's last name. The first is Donna."

"I'll find out," said Meekins. Dodd knew he would, too. Meekins had weird and wonderful sources of information.

"What's all the gagging?" the sergeant asked.

"We're trying to find out," Dodd answered. "Look up Tessie Smaltz and see what address she gave when she was booked."

"Oh, is that who they were after?" the sergeant said, pawing through an index. "Why the hell didn't you tell 'em?"

"I didn't want to," Dodd said. "I've got a reason."

"Here," said the sergeant. "She gave her address as Thirty-seven-sixteen West Forty-fifth."

"Dummy," said Meekins. "There ain't no such number. Forty-fifth ends in the thirty-four-hundred block."

"Oh, hell!" the sergeant exclaimed. "That's right."

Dodd shrugged. "Well, that's that. Let's go over to night court, Meekins. They might dig something out of the clerk over there, and maybe we can tag along."

Meekins nodded at the sergeant. "Tell the boys in car twelve I'll make out an eye-witness statement before I leave tonight."

"You'd damned well better, smarty," the sergeant told him, "or you won't leave for very long. And don't forget that two dollars."

CHAPTER THREE

GUS GILLEN—GAMBLER

MEEKINS AND Dodd came in through the back door of the courthouse and walked around the turn in the corridor in time to see Howard Linden and the girl called Donna coming out of the entrance of the night court. She was talking to him with a sort of angry disgust, and her voice carried plainly.

"Well, you did it, and you should have had better sense. The idea of telling a person a thing like that!"

"But, Donna!" Linden protested. "I didn't know. I didn't think. I supposed of course she knew."

"You're a fool, Howard," Donna said shortly. "Now who is this man Rudolph the clerk told you about?"

"He's a criminal attorney. He has a very shady reputation."

"How would he know her? Why should he pay her fine?"

"Donna, I don't know! I haven't the faintest idea!"

"Then we'll have to find him and ask. Come on."

Without even looking in the direction of Dodd and Meekins, they went along the hall and out through the front entrance. They met a man at the wide doors, and he stepped aside quietly to let them pass. They didn't notice him.

Meekins nudged Dodd. "They're going to have one hell of a time finding Rudolph if he don't want them to. Rudolph is—" He let his voice trail off, staring.

"What?" Dodd asked.

Meekins moistened his lips. "That guy, there. That's Gus Gillen!"

The man Donna and Linden had passed in the doorway was coming down the hall now. He was short and pudgy, and he had a round face that was pink as a baby's. He wore a shiny blue suit that didn't fit him very well and was spotted on the shoulders with rain drops. He wore thick, rimless spectacles, and he had an amiable, shy smile.

"Who?" Dodd asked out of the corner of his mouth.

"Gus Gillen," Meekins whispered. "Big shot from the West. Hangs out in Reno."

Gillen came right on toward Dodd and Meekins and stopped in front of them. He lowered his head a little to peer over the tops of the thick glasses.

"You recognized me?" he asked in an embarrassed tone.

"Yes," Dodd admitted. "If you're Gus Gillen."

"That is my name. And yours?"

"Dodd. I'm a bail bondsman. This is Meekins. He works for me."

"Dodd," Gillen repeated gently. "Dodd. I'll remember. I came in tonight on a hurry-up trip. It is private business, purely. I would rather it were not known I was here."

"Oh," said Dodd noncommittally.

"You were watching the young couple who just went out. You are interested in them?"

"After a fashion," said Dodd.

"A bail bondsman wouldn't be interested in them."

"No?" said Dodd.

"Maybe I should say a bail bondsman *shouldn't* be interested in them," Gillen said, correcting himself. He was still smiling.

"We ain't interested in them," Meekins said quickly. "Not any more, Mr. Gillen. Not a bit!"

Dodd looked at him indignantly and was about to say something to Gillen, when a man came around the curve in the corridor behind them and said: "Hi, Dodd. Hi, Meekins. Say listen, either of you two know anything ripe about a gal with red hair and some rubies?"

HIS WORDS echoed a little in the emptiness of the corridor, and after that the silence seemed to grow so heavy it was like a thick weight pressing down. Gillen was wearing yellow shoes with upturned toes, and he rocked forward and back on them, making them squeak gently.

"Well," said the other man. "Do you?"

He was taller even than Dodd, and much thinner, and he had a harassed air, as though he had a lot of things to do and not enough time to do them. He was wearing a ragged raincoat hung around his shoulders like a cape, and he held a blackened, stubby pipe in one corner of his mouth.

"Is it a riddle?" Dodd asked smoothly.

"Huh? No. Somebody called up and rooted me out of my evening's siesta and told me to come down to the court-house if I wanted something hot. I said I'd heard that one before, and they said to look for the redheaded girl with the rubies. I thought it was a rib at first, and then I got to thinking about it, so I trailed down here."

"It must have been a rib," said Dodd.

"Undoubtedly," said Meekins.

The tall man was looking at Gus Gillen with a calculating squint in his eye. "Seems like I've seen you before somewhere, mister. Not in person, but your picture."

"Perhaps you have," said Gus Gillen gently.

"This is Mr. McCray," Dodd said to the tall man, indicating Gillen with a wave of his hand. "Mr. McCray is a—a real-estate broker

from—out of town. Mr. McCray, this is Donald Craig. He's a reporter on the *Times.*"

"It's a pleasure to meet you," Gillen said politely.

"McCray," said Craig. "Real estate. That doesn't sound familiar.
Must be you look like someone else. Dodd, are you sure you haven't
seen any redheaded gals or rubies around here?"

"Oh, no," said Dodd.

"Absolutely not," Meekins seconded.

"Was it a man or woman who called you?" Dodd asked.

"Woman," Craig answered. "Sounded young, if that means anything.
That's why I thought it was a gag. Thought it was some chorus biddie
looking for publicity."

"Is that all she said?" Dodd inquired.

"Yeah. But somebody called right afterwards and said, 'Who's this?'
and I said, 'It's the *Times,* if it's all the same to you,' and they hung
up on me without another peep. The funny thing was though, that
on both calls there was music playing in the background, and it was
the same piece. Damn funny music, too. It sounded like somebody
playing swing on a fire-siren."

Meekins made a strangling noise in his throat and Dodd said
hastily: "It certainly is wonderful the things people will do for a gag
these days."

"Yeah," Craig said sourly. "Very wonderful, indeed. If I catch
pneumonia, I'll laugh myself to death. Well, I'll dodge into night court
and see what gives. So long."

He went through the back door of the night court and left Dodd
and Meekins looking at Gillen.

"Thank you very much, Mr. Dodd," Gillen said shyly, "for not re-
vealing my identity. If you'll excuse me now, I will go into the court,
too. I find night sessions very instructive and stimulating."

"Oh, very," Dodd agreed vaguely.

HE WATCHED Gillen until he had disappeared through the front
entrance of the court and then turned on Meekins.

"Well—why the funny noises?"

Meekins looked like he had been holding his breath. "What Craig
said—that the music sounded like swing played on a fire-siren! A
couple of weeks ago we pulled a guy named Windy Moore out of the
pokey when he was in for getting on a marihuana jag. This Moore's

an entertainer. He plays pieces by blowing up an inner tube and letting the air come out through a rubber squee-jee on the valve. I heard him. It sounds like a fire-siren. He's playin' now at Shine Brevani's clip-joint on Clark just off Kester."

"Well," said Dodd thoughtfully. "On Clark off Kester, huh? And the redheaded doll was picked up on Kester."

"Listen, boss," said Meekins earnestly, "I think we better take that red rock and get ourselves under cover somewhere. Real far under cover."

"How so?" Dodd asked, annoyed.

"Look," said Meekins. "Riganov got batted around with brass knucks on account of that ruby, and that's all right. I'll fight with them knucks for a purse like that any day. But I don't want any part of Gillen or Shine Brevani."

"I'm curious," Dodd told him. "Here's a nice-looking girl hanging out on Kester Street giving strange guys rubies and getting hauled up for soliciting and getting Sam Rudolph to front for her. I want to know why."

"I don't," said Meekins. "Don't let that mild air of Gillen's fool you. He's big-time in the gambling racket in Nevada, and he's got his fist in lots of other things, I hear tell. And not only that but he knows a hundred guys who'd just as leave rub you out as spit. And Shine Brevani is just naturally bad from way back. I positively don't want to get in between him and Gillen."

"I think I'll look around," Dodd decided, ignoring him.

"Where?"

"On Kester Street. What plainclothesman picked the redhead up?"

"Harris. You can catch him in the back room of Casey's Haven. He ducks in for a drink every hour or so. But listen, boss, if I were you—"

"You aren't, so don't let it worry you. You get to work and find out what Donna's last name is and anything else you can pick up in a hurry. Call me at Casey's Haven."

"I'll call you," Meekins agreed gloomily, "but I don't know as you'll hear me."

CHAPTER FOUR

OLD SMOKE

DODD CAME in through the swinging green doors of Casey's Haven and breasted a solid wave of noise that beat up unavailingly against the low ceiling. The longshoremen and dock-workers—heavily muscled men with big voices and bigger thirsts—were crowded three deep along the bar, and clouds of rank tobacco smoke swooped and swirled crazily over their heads. Dodd stepped over a redfaced man who was squatting on the floor pounding on the bottom of a brass spittoon with an empty beer bottle and howling some queerly rhythmic dirge. He worked his way through the press to the hinged gate at the end of the bar.

Casey, himself, was there, sitting on a spindle-legged stool and looking wearily philosophical about it all.

"How's it going, Casey?" Dodd asked.

"You can look around this mad-house and ask that?" Casey said.

"How many fights tonight?"

"Six—not counting a political argument."

"I'm looking for Harris. Have you seen him?"

Casey stared up at the cracked dial of the clock over the back-bar. "He'll be here any minute. Your man, Meekins, wants you to call him at the police station."

"Thanks. Fix me a rye highball."

Dodd pushed through to the phone booth in the corner, got the police operator, the booking-sergeant, and finally Meekins.

"Well, what?" he asked.

"Hot stuff," Meekins said. "Sam Rudolph had an argument about the right-of-way with a lamp post over on Center Street. They had to scrape his car off the pavement."

"How about the redhead?" Dodd demanded.

"She wasn't with him. Sam's got two cracked ribs and a couple of black eyes, and he isn't talking very much. He said he skidded, but that's hard to figure because it happened in the middle of a block, and there wasn't any traffic. I think the dame decided not to go any further with him and just gave the wheel a jerk and steered him into the lamp post and then beat it."

"Probably," Dodd agreed. "Anything else?"

"I always save the best for the last. Donna's last name is Barstow, and her old man is E.P. Barstow, and he's a heavy market-operator in mining stock. I found that out from Craig. So then I called up the Barstow joint and gave somebody a little song-and-dance about being a society reporter, and this somebody tells me that Miss Donna Barstow is home on vacation from Miss Wiggenbottom's Seminary for Girls and get this…. She has as her guest, during the vacation, another student from the same school, her room-mate, by the name of Patricia Gilwyne! And this Patricia Gilwyne has very beautiful auburn hair!"

"Ah!" said Dodd triumphantly. "Good work!"

"I always deliver," Meekins said modestly.

"Call me back if you get anything more."

DODD went back to the end of the bar. Casey had set out two drinks. He pointed to one and said: "This is yours. Harris is in the back room now. You can take the other one to him."

Dodd paid for the two drinks and took them with him through the rear door of the saloon and down a narrow, dark hall to another door that was marked *Private—No Admittance—This Means You* in large red letters. He opened the door, maneuvered himself and the drinks through, and kicked it shut behind him.

"Hello, Harris," he said. "Have a drink with me?"

"That I will," said Harris heartily.

He was a tall, enormously broad man with a red, square face and blue eyes that had little white laughter creases at the corners. He took the drink from Dodd, threw it down with one big gulp, and waited for it to hit bottom.

"Ah!" he said in a satisfied tone, when it did. "There's nothing like good Irish whiskey. Damn all water, I say, and especially when it's rain. How are you, Dodd?"

"Good enough," said Dodd. "And expecting to be better shortly, I hope. I want to ask you a question. Do you remember a redheaded girl who gave her name as Tessie Smaltz? You picked her up tonight earlier."

"Ha!" Harris grunted. "Do I remember her! Ha! Are you going to use that drink of yours, or are you just going to sit and hold it?"

"Take it," Dodd invited. "It's rye."

"Better than nothing," Harris said, pouring it after the first one. "Tessie Smaltz, eh? Sure I remember her. I spotted her over near Clark, and I thought she'd be one to watch on account of the coat she was wearing. You see, I used to work on the Loft Squad, and I know mink when I see it, and there's others around here who do, too, but not for the same reason. So I thought she'd wind up in an alley with a sore head and no coat to cover her if I didn't keep an eye open. And then what do I find but that the little tart is going along hitting guys up on Kester."

"And then?" Dodd urged.

"So I stop her, and I say, 'Listen, cutie, run yourself home to your mama before I sick the truant officer on you.' Ha! And what did she say? She said, 'Listen, ape-face, I'll do what I damn please and walk where I damn please.' So I say, 'No, you won't, my dear. You'll ride to the station.' I was just bluffing, hoping it would scare her, but she laughed in my face, so I had to send her along. She was a crazy one, but then the young ones are all crazy now. She had no eye for prospects, I'll say that. She hit up two of the worst you could find if you sifted this town like sand."

"Only two?" Dodd asked casually.

"Yup. One was Riganov, that screeching little crack-pot who has a wife that would cut his ears off if he looked at another woman, and the other was Old Smoke."

"Old Smoke?" Dodd repeated.

Harris laughed. "That old stew-bum! He'd rather look into a glass of whiskey than into the eyes of any woman that ever lived!"

"Where could I find him?" Dodd asked.

"Old Smoke? He lives in a shack on Butcher Flats, on a little spit that sticks out just south of Crane's Packing House. He'll be drunk by this time—stiffer than a log."

Dodd stood up. "I'll take a look."

Harris pointed a thick forefinger. "Watch your step, my boy, down that way. It's one of our most exclusive neighborhoods. Exclusively bad."

THE TAXI bounced over a culvert with a sideways twist that made the springs groan protestingly and pulled up to a stop under the feeble yellow glow of a streetlight.

"We're at the end of the line, doc," the driver said. "This here is a taxi, not an ocean liner."

Dodd got out and paid him. "I won't be long. Will you wait for me?"

"Doc," the driver told him, "in this neighborhood at this time of night, I wouldn't wait five minutes for the King of England. There's guys around here that would cut your throat for a dime, and I mean ten cents."

"All right," Dodd said.

He started down the slanting, slick cobblestones. Behind him the taxi's motor made a fluttering blast as it backed and turned hurriedly. It banged back over the culvert, and then the sound of its motor faded smoothly into the distance.

It had stopped raining, but there was a yellow, moving mist in the air that felt slickly smooth against Dodd's face. There were warehouses all around him, great blocks of them hunched in squat darkness. Somewhere close ahead water slapped monotonously against a piling, and the sour salt smell of the bay floated heavily in the mist.

Dodd came to a corner, under the feeble yellow eye of another streetlight. He turned around very quickly there and ducked down a little, staring up the slant of the street. He caught the dim sway of a figure outlined for a second against the first streetlight. It was gone instantly, and it didn't appear again. Dodd swore to himself in a whisper.

The sound of the slapping water was closer, and he walked in front of a warehouse on planks that were ground to rough splinters by the constant wear of the iron wheels of hand-trucks. A red light on a buoy dipped and swayed tipsily making ruddy, gleaming streaks on the greasy surface of the bay.

Dodd went on past the warehouse and ducked into a velvet-black niche between it and the next one. He stood flat against the wall there, waiting. A boat whistle sounded low and dull, off somewhere in the night.

Footsteps touched the splintered planks and came along in a quick, stealthy shuffle. Dodd could hear the man breathing before he saw him, and then he was just a dark, bent outline. Waiting until he was even with the niche, Dodd stepped out behind and slid his right arm across in front of the man's throat.

"Hah!" the man said in a sudden shrill gasp that ended when Dodd tightened his arm and bent slightly sideways, pulling the man against him and bending him backward across Dodd's out-thrust hip. The man fought, clutching desperately with both hands, trying to kick back at Dodd's shins.

"Quit it," Dodd said, "or I'll crack your neck."

The man relaxed instantly, with a choked gurgling noise. Dodd relaxed his strangle-hold slightly, and the man sucked in air with a wheezy sob.

"Let go! Let go me! I didn't—I wasn't—"

"Oh, hell!" said Dodd in a disgusted tone. He released the man and gave him a shove. "So it's you, is it?" He found a match in his pocket, snapped it on his thumbnail, and held it in front of his own face.

"Hah! Dodd!"

"Yeah. I didn't think I'd see you again, Maxie, since you owe me ten bucks. Haven't got it on you, have you?"

The man's voice dropped into an accustomed whine. "I'm just dead broke, Dodd. Honest. I ain't got enough to eat, even."

"That certainly isn't food I smell on your breath," Dodd agreed. "So you've taken to rolling lushes now, have you, Maxie? Better watch your step. One more trip-up and they throw the book at you."

"I got to have something to eat—"

"Ever think of working?"

"I can't get no job, Dodd. Them cops keep after me all the time—persecutin' me and houndin' me. I ain't got a place I can turn, and I ain't got a friend—"

"Too bad, too bad," said Dodd unfeelingly. "You should write a letter to the governor about it, only don't forget to tell him you had three jobs since you got paroled the last time, and lost them all because you couldn't keep your mitts out of the cash register. But never mind that. Where does Old Smoke live from here?"

"Down the next block and through that alley toward the bay. What's everybody want that old stew-bum for?"

"What do you mean—everybody?"

"There was a guy after him earlier."

"How do you know? Try to stick him up?"

"No! I never did! I just asked him for a match, and he stuck a gun right in me. He was a reporter, he says. Name of Craig. And he wanted to interview Old Smoke. I say it's a hell of a fine note for a reporter to stick guns in people!"

"If it was Craig, it was probably just a pipe."

"A pipe! No, it wasn't no pipe! I know a gun when I see it, and that's what this was he stuck in me. He ain't got no right to stick a gun in a person just because a person asks him polite for a match."

"You don't seem to be having very good luck tonight. Don't follow me around any longer, because I might get mad."

"Sure not, Dodd. Say, could you maybe spare four bits for an old pal that ain't had a bite to eat for three days? Just four bits, huh, Dodd? I'll pay you back next week."

Dodd gave him a coin. "All right, all right. But when you get picked up drunk tonight, don't holler for me to go your bail, because I'm not going to."

"Thanks. Thanks, pal. I ain't drinkin' no more. No, sir. I turned over a new leaf, Dodd. Thanks."

"Scram."

"Sure, Dodd. Sure. Thanks. I'll pay you back next week. Honest. So long."

DODD stood and watched the bent shuffling figure until it went under the yellow circle of the streetlight and turned up the block.

He shrugged then and turned around and went past the next warehouse and across another of the narrow, cobble-stoned alleyways. The shoreline turned a little here, and there were warehouses on both sides of Dodd again. He went along in between them accompanied by the hollow, empty sound of his footsteps, until he saw a blackened notch in the solid walls.

Dodd turned into it, slowing up. The ground softened, and his feet crunched on soggy refuse. He went on, feeling his way with one hand against the rough stone of a wall, and suddenly the alley opened out and he almost fell into a pond of scummed, stagnant water.

He stopped, squinting ahead through the mist, and made out the shadowy blur of a shack straight ahead. Ten feet to his right there was a long board stretched across the pond. Dodd tested the board with his foot, gingerly, and then walked quickly across it, balancing himself with his arms extended wide. The board slapped the water under him, groaning with his weight.

He jumped the last five feet and landed in mud that sucked hungrily when he pulled his feet free. The shack was directly ahead of him, a sagging patternless pile of battered odds and ends of lumber that had been salvaged from the bay. One window in the wall on Dodd's side stared like a bleary blinded eye.

"Smoke!" Dodd called. "Old Smoke!"

His voice bounced off the warehouse walls and echoed flat and empty across the water. There was no answer.

Dodd walked around the shack, his feet slopping wetly in the mud, and found what served as a door. He pounded on it and shouted again.

"Hey, Smoke!"

There was no stir and Dodd muttered disgustedly to himself: "Must be drunker than an owl." He put his weight against the door and pushed. The hinges groaned dolorously, and the bottom scraped against rough board.

Putting his head inside, Dodd breathed in stale air loaded with the odors of sweat and burned grease and alcohol.

Dodd struck a match on the wall, and the flame sputtered up yellow and wavering and showed a blurred, impressionistic picture of the cave-like interior of the shack.

It was like a medieval horror painting, with the wasted form of Old Smoke lying on the soiled mattress in the corner, spread-eagled there with his arms flung wide and his eyes staring glassily at the ceiling. There was a round black hole punched in the skinny muscle of his neck, just under the angle of his stubbled jaw, and the blood had seeped down and soaked into the blanket that was twisted under him.

Dodd stood there, frozen, until the match burned his fingers. He dropped it then, and lighted another, breathing heavily. The blood had turned the blanket into a purple, clotted mass. Dodd stepped closer, forcing himself to hold the match steady, and saw that every one of Old Smoke's pockets had been turned inside out.

The match went out and he dropped it and found another, fumbling in his haste. He held this one high over his head, staring around the shack. The place was filthy as a pig-sty, but it gave no evidence of having been searched.

"He found it," Dodd said in a whisper.

He felt the cold moisture of perspiration on his face, and it was hard for him to breathe.

DODD stepped outside the shack, slamming the door shut behind him. He wiped the back of his hand across his forehead, staring blankly at the greasy water of the bay.

"Craig," he said slowly. "Craig, hell!"

He jerked himself into motion then, and dodged around the corner of the shack and trotted back to the board that bridged the stagnant pool. He wasn't so careful this time. He went across the board, taking long, hurried steps, and when he was in the middle of it, it cracked gently under him, slipped side-ways and then turned.

Dodd went up in the air and came down again, churning his arms and legs frantically. He hit the water with a hollow, dull splash and turned it into dirty froth.

It was only knee deep, but there was a foot of soft mud under it. Dodd staggered to his feet, cursing and spluttering. He fought his way through the mud to the edge of the pond.

He was soaked through, and the mud was thick and slimy on his face and hands. He fumbled with stiff fingers, still cursing monotonously, until he found his handkerchief. He made a damp, wadded ball out of it and swabbed the mud out of his eyes. His patched glasses were floating placidly on the roiled water, and he leaned over and groped until he got hold of them.

He began to trot back through the alley, his trousers slapping wetly and uncomfortably against his legs. He turned out into the narrow street and back past the warehouse where he had tackled Maxie. He turned again under the street-light and labored up the slant of the street to the intersection where he had left the taxi.

His breath was beginning to burn in his throat now, and his heart made pounding thunder. He kept at it, trotting steadily along with the water squishing in his shoes, heading back toward the blurred color-smear of lights that marked the downtown section of the city.

It was fifteen minutes later, and he was staggering on numb sticks of legs that had no feeling and no give at the knees when he came out on a wider street and saw the red and green lights of a cruising taxi a half-block away. Dodd had just enough breath left to whistle. He put his fingers in his mouth and did the best he could.

The taxi kept on going, floating tantalizingly away from him, and

Dodd collapsed on the curb. He was all through. He didn't even have energy enough to swear, but he began to think dizzily of the things he was going to say when he did.

Then the taxi slid up and stopped beside him, and the driver said, without much hope: "Taxi, mister?"

Dodd got up and grabbed the door handle before he could get away again. "Aragon Apartments," he managed to gasp.

"Hey, listen!" the driver protested. "You're all fulla mud. You're gonna get my cushions all smeared—"

"All right, all right," Dodd panted. "I'll sit on the floor and pay double the meter. Just get going. I want a bath and I want one right now!"

CHAPTER FIVE

RUBIES AND A REDHEAD

THE ARAGON APARTMENTS had a small, austerely correct lobby, but there was no desk in it, and it was late enough now so that all the tenants had retired to their respective apartments, if not to bed.

Dodd was glad enough to have no audience. He went across the lobby in a hurry, still trailing dribbles of muddy water behind him, and took the self-operated elevator to the third floor. He went down the long hall, still hurrying, fumbling with wet, muddy fingers for his key ring.

He fitted the key in the lock of the door of his own apartment, but it wouldn't turn. His fingers slipped off it once and then again. He swore in an undertone and wiped his hand on his coat, smearing his fingers more than before. He tackled the key again, and this time the door opened of its own accord, and left him standing there, staring incredulously.

Craig, the reporter, was sitting in the big chair under the crook-necked bridge lamp. He was sitting there very still, looking awkward and gaunt and uncomfortable, and he was watching Dodd with eyes that were wide open and that didn't blink.

Dodd said: "Well—" and then didn't finish the sentence.

Craig's stubby pipe had fallen from his mouth. It was lying in his lap, and the ashes in it had spilled a gray streak across one trouser-leg.

There was a hole like an oversize black period in the center of Craig's forehead. Not very much blood had come out of it.

Dodd released his breath in a long sigh. He stepped into the apartment and closed the door quietly and firmly behind him. He stood there for a moment, still staring incredulously, and then stepped closer.

"Yeah," a voice told him. "He's still here."

Dodd spun on his heel. There was a man standing in the open doorway of the bedroom. He was a small man with a face as pale and shiny as old parchment and his eyes were flat and deadly close on either side of the swollen, formless bulge of his nose. He was wearing a pearl-gray derby, the crown spattered with rain drops, and a greenish pin-stripe suit. He was holding a .45 automatic that looked grotesquely huge and deadly clasped in his thin hand.

He nodded gravely and said: "Hi, Dodd."

Dodd moistened his lips. "Hello, Luke. I didn't know you were back. I thought this town was too hot for you."

"Not any more," said Luke. "Shine Brevani is taking care of me now. He wants to see you."

"Does he?" Dodd asked absently.

The front door of the apartment opened, and another man slipped inside. He was squat and bow-legged, with long muscular arms out of all proportion to the rest of him. His eyes were shifting, colorless little pin-points under glove-scarred brows, and his left ear was bent over and thickened.

"Well," said Dodd. "Shine sent a regular greeting committee, didn't he? Hello, Mushy."

Mushy lifted his rubbery, thickened upper lip in a leering half-smile. "Yah," he said in a whispering croak.

"Go over him," Luke ordered.

Mushy slid around behind Dodd and slapped his pockets with quick deft hands. "No gun, Luke."

"That's why he went out," Luke said. "He was ditching it, but what I want to know is where? Where, Dodd?"

"Where, what?" Dodd asked.

"The gun. Where'd you put it?"

"What gun?"

Luke jerked his head toward Craig.

Dodd grinned wryly. "Hell, you're not trying to talk me into thinking I killed Craig, are you? That's the kind of stuff you go in for, Luke. I had you tagged for the job."

"I was afraid maybe you had," Luke said softly. "Take another look at his pockets, Mushy. Careful this time."

Mushy went through Dodd's clothes with the expert precision of a pickpocket and found the ruby in Dodd's lower vest pocket.

"Yah!" he said triumphantly, showing it to Luke.

Luke watched Dodd silently for a moment and then said: "We'll go see Brevani. We got a car downstairs. You want to walk to it, or do you want to be carried?"

"You'll frighten me if you don't watch out," Dodd answered, "but I'll walk. I'm hardly wearing the proper dress, though, to appear in such a tony dive as Shine runs these days."

"You might look worse—later," Luke told him.

IT WAS a small, black sedan, a new one and indistinguishable from thousands of others that had come off the assembly line before and after it. Mushy was driving, and Dodd was sitting in the back seat with Luke. Luke wasn't holding the .45 on Dodd. He had it deposited casually in his lap, and apparently he wasn't even looking at Dodd, but Dodd knew that he was watching out of the corners of his eyes, waiting for Dodd to make a move. Luke was an old hand at this, and Dodd sat carefully still.

Mushy turned the sedan off Clark into a narrow alley and coasted along it slowly until he came to a board fence that barred the end. He stopped there, and Luke picked up the automatic and said: "Out, Dodd. And don't try to be funny."

"I'm fresh out of jokes," Dodd said.

He opened the door and stepped down on the rough paving. Luke slid out behind him. Mushy used a key to open a padlock on a gate in the board fence. He preceded Dodd and Luke through the gate, closed it behind them, and then led the way around the corner of a building and across a small back yard to a door in the rear of another building.

"Servants' entrance?" Dodd asked.

Luke said: "Just keep the trap shut."

Mushy opened the door, and the three of them went into a long, dimly lighted hall. When Mushy closed the door, Dodd could hear the faint clatter of plates and tinkle of silverware. At the back of the hall, a narrow carpeted stairway led up to the second story, and Dodd climbed the steps with Mushy ahead of him and Luke close behind.

There was another closed door at the top of the stairs, and Mushy scraped lightly on its panel with his thumb-nail and then turned the knob.

"In," said Luke, pushing Dodd with the automatic.

Dodd stepped into Shine Brevani's private office. It was a small, square room, its one window masked with heavy black drapes. The big, flat desk in the center filled up most of the floor space, and Shine Brevani was sitting on a corner of it, casually swinging one leg back and forth.

Shine Brevani took his name from his hair. It was so black it looked purple in streaks along the top where the light caught it, and it was so heavy with grease that it didn't look like hair at all, but a flat, viscous mat curved sleekly over the bony outline of his skull. He had a long, sallow face and a mouth that was a pursed, colorless line. He was dressed very dapperly in a navy blue tuxedo, and he wore patent-leather shoes and gray spats.

He looked at Dodd and waved one hand languidly.

"Over there."

Mushy put his hand in the center of Dodd's chest and shoved him hard. Dodd stumbled backwards, and his knees hit the edge of a chair. He sat down in it with a thump.

Shine Brevani turned his head back again and continued to stare thoughtfully at the girl with the red-bronze hair. She was sitting in a chair beside the desk, and she didn't look proud or confident any more. She looked scared, but still defiant, and she was holding her hands clasped tightly together in her lap.

Luke still had the big .45 clasped casually in his right hand, and he stepped into the center of the room where he could watch Dodd without turning his head.

"Where'd you get her?" he asked Brevani.

"She just walked in," Brevani explained. "Right after you left. So I brought her up here to have a chat. So far we haven't been getting on too well. All right, cutie. Once again. What's the big idea?"

The girl's lips were pressed into a determined line, and she shook her head stubbornly.

Brevani leaned forward and slapped her in the face, hard. Her head jerked sideways with the impact, and her blue eyes widened with a sort of unbelieving terror.

"Speak up, cutie," Brevani said.

"Slap her again, and you'll have a one-man riot around here," Dodd said flatly.

Mushy was standing beside his chair. He brought his fist out of the sagging pocket of his coat now. He was wearing a set of brass knuckles, and he slashed downward at Dodd's face with them. Dodd jerked his head aside, and the brass knuckles struck his shoulder with a force that numbed his whole side.

Luke raised the .45 automatic and leveled the heavy barrel at Dodd's chest.

"Never hit a man with glasses on, Mushy," Brevani advised gently. "You know that's against the law."

Mushy grinned and flicked out the stiffened fingers of his left hand, knocking Dodd's patched glasses on the floor. He raised his right fist in a glinting arc, aiming more carefully this time.

"Oh, don't!" the girl gasped in a sickened whisper.

Dodd stared at Brevani, blinking a little. "What I said still goes. I can take it. I hope you can when it gets around to your turn."

"He means it," Luke said. "He don't scare very easy, or maybe he's only nuts."

"Cut it, Mushy," Brevani said. "So you think we're going to get a turn, hey, Dodd?"

"You'll want bail some time."

Brevani laughed contemptuously. "You think we'd ask a two-bit operator like you for it?"

"No matter who you ask you won't get it if I put the finger on you. Bail bondsmen stick together."

Brevani's face grew tight and still. "Maybe you won't put the finger on anybody but a couple of fish at the bottom of the bay. Let's hear you do some talking. Ever see this before?"

BREVANI picked up a round blue circle from the desk and flipped it at Dodd. Dodd batted at it nearsightedly, knocked it to the floor by his glasses. He leaned over and picked it up, his glasses too. It was a poker chip, and he turned it over in his fingers and saw the name *Brevani* printed in small golden letters on its back. He looked up.

"You still running games here?"

"Two roulette tables and craps and a black-jack layout," Brevani said. "But I asked you a question, Dodd."

"No. I've never seen this chip before—nor any other one like it. I didn't even know you were running tables here now."

"He had one of the red rocks on him," Luke said. "Give it to Shine, Mushy."

Mushy handed Brevani the ruby he had taken from Dodd. Brevani turned it over in his fingers absently and then showed it to the girl.

"Yours, cutie?"

She nodded her head once, still holding her lips pressed tightly together.

"Where'd you get it?" Brevani asked Dodd.

"From Riganov. She gave it to him. He gave it to me before Mushy clipped him. You might as well break down and tell me what this is all about, Shine."

"That's what I want to know," said Brevani. "This doll comes in early this evening. She wants to see me, and when I let her, she asks me what I know about Gus Gillen. I know plenty about that baby-faced, double-crossing rat, and I told her some of it. So she just sits and takes it without a peep, and then says 'Thanks' and goes over and sits by herself in a corner of the bar. I noticed when she talked to me that she's wearing this ruby and another one like it in a big dinner ring. I tell Mushy to keep an eye on her. So she borrows an ice-pick from the bartender and starts taking these two rocks out of their setting."

"It's my ring," said the girl. "It's my business what I did with it."

"Shut up," Brevani ordered. "So Mushy can't figure that one out, and he's too dumb to come and tell me. So the doll makes a phone call. Mushy does spot the number and calls it back and finds out she talked to the *Times*. She beats it then, and Mushy comes and tells me, so I send him and Luke out to see what she's up to. She stops that little screw-ball, Riganov, and Old Smoke, and then she runs up against Harris who pinches her."

"I knew that," Dodd said.

"Never mind what you knew. So Luke sees Old Smoke lean over to pick up a snipe, and one of these rubies pops out of his pocket. Old Smoke grabs it and rushes into a bar. Luke and Mushy can't get at him in there, so they come back. I called up Sam Rudolph and told him to get the doll out and find out what the hell eats her, and send

Luke and Mushy down to back his play. They see Riganov and figure he's got the other rock and make a play for him and botch it. The doll gets loose from Sam. So Mushy and Luke went down to Old Smoke's joint, and they find the old stew-bum with a bullet in his gizzard, and they find that blue chip from my joint lyin' on the floor beside him."

"So?" said Dodd.

"So, I'm in the middle here, and I don't like it. Suppose the cops find Old Smoke croaked and that chip on the floor with my name on it? They come right back here, and they find out about this red-headed doll and her rubies startin' out from here. Then where do we go?"

"For a ride in the paddy wagon," said Dodd. He looked speculatively at Luke. "So maybe you didn't knock Craig over?"

"What?" Brevani demanded sharply.

"Craig," said Luke. "Reporter from the *Times*. We found him in Dodd's apartment—deader than a kippered herring."

"Yeah," said Dodd. "And Craig was writing a series of articles on vice and gambling in the city, wasn't he?"

Brevani came up off the desk as though something had stung him. He stood rigid for a second, staring hard at Dodd, and then sat down slowly again. He swore in a low, bitter monotone.

"That Gus Gillen. That damned back-stabbing Gus Gillen." He glared at the redheaded girl. "Listen, cutie, I got no more time to stall around with you. What's your name?"

"Patricia Gilwyne," Dodd said.

THE GIRL jerked her head around to look at him. Surprise wiped away the lines of sullen defiance in her face, and it looked round and soft and childish.

"You—!" Dodd blurted in amazement. "Gilwyne—Gillen! You're some relation to Gus Gillen! You look like him!"

She drew a long, tremulous breath. "I'm his daughter."

There was a dead, tense silence and then Brevani said very softly: "So? Gus Gillen's daughter. His daughter, hey?" He slid off the desk. "Then we'll just forget about the rubies. Yeah. They don't matter much. I've been lookin' for a chance like this. I owe Gus Gillen a thing or two." He stepped slowly closer to the girl, and he was grinning with a sort of savage vindictive glee.

"Here!" said Dodd sharply. "What—"

Brevani didn't even turn his head. "Take him, Mushy."

"Yah!" said Mushy thickly. He raised his brass-knuckled fist.

Dodd ducked sideways, swinging both stiffened legs sideways, and knocked Mushy's feet out from under him, and in that same instant the door-latch made a soft click and one of the hinges creaked a little.

Dodd lunged forward, ignoring the menace of Luke's gun, and landed with both knees in the middle of Mushy's stomach. Mushy grunted in agony. He heaved up in an arc and threw Dodd off him, and as Dodd rolled away from him, he caught a hazily blurred picture of the rest of the room.

Mrs. Riganov was standing in the doorway.

"I find," said Mrs. Riganov.

Luke was spinning around, and as he turned he fired with the big automatic. The blasting roar of the report filled the room, and Dodd saw the .45 buck up in Luke's hand and saw the bullet rake a long, splintered gash in the door-post.

Mrs. Riganov didn't seem to move fast. She raise, her right hand. She was holding a flat-iron in it. It was not an electric iron. It was an old-fashioned flat-iron—an, ugly wedge-shaped piece of solid metal—and Mrs. Riganov threw it at Luke.

Luke tried to dodge but he was too close. The flat-iron hit him in the face with a sound like a board slapping water and carried him clear across the room and smashed him into the wall. He dropped to the floor and didn't move.

Mushy was up on his knees. He struck viciously at Dodd now with his brass knuckles. Dodd ducked the blow by falling flat on his face, and then Mrs. Riganov leaned over and clipped Mushy neatly across the back of the neck with the hard edge of her palm. Mushy's head jerked, and he seemed to come all unstrung. He flopped limply over on top of Dodd.

Brevani had lunged clear over his desk and was frantically jerking at a drawer on the other side, trying to get it open. Mrs. Riganov got her hands around his thin neck, picked him up off the desk and slammed him head-first into the wall. Brevani screamed shrilly. Mrs. Riganov drew him back and slammed his head into the wall again, harder.

Dodd was trying frantically to scramble out from under Mushy. "Wait!" he yelled. "Don't!"

Brevani screamed, and Mrs. Riganov slammed him into the wall again with methodical precision.

Brevani quit screaming with horrible abruptness.

Dodd kicked Mushy off him and got to his feet. He grabbed Mrs. Riganov by one massive arm. "Wait! You'll kill him!"

"Sure," said Mrs. Riganov.

"Wait," Dodd groped for an inspiration. "Listen! If you kill him I'll lose that money I put up for a peace bond for your husband!"

"Oh," said Mrs. Riganov. "All right. I don't kill him—now." She dropped Brevani in a limp sprawl on the floor and eyed Patricia, who was still sitting stiffly terrorized in her chair. "She's the one that starts this?"

"No, no," said Dodd quickly. "Oh, no! She didn't have anything to do with these others. She's a friend of mine."

"Ummm," said Mrs. Riganov doubtfully.

"Positively," Dodd hastened to assure her. "How did you find these boys, anyway?"

"I ask. I ask every woman on this street. One sees them following this girl and knows they are Brevani men. I guess they don't beat my husband up no more."

"I'll bet they don't either," Dodd agreed emphatically.

CHAPTER SIX

THE BLUE CHIP

THE TAXI made a U-turn in the middle of the wide, tree-lined street and rolled to a stop in front of an apartment house that was a massive, dark peak of granite with high, needled spires on its four corners. Dodd got out and held the door open for Patricia Gilwyne. She was still remembering the scene in Shine Brevani's office, and her face had a drawn frightened look.

"Would—would you come up with me?" she asked. "I'd like awfully to explain—"

"Sure," said Dodd. The mud on his clothes had dried and stiffened now, and he crackled every time he moved. His shoulder ached, and his glasses were twisted at the patch so that one lens sat high and the other low, but he was feeling very pleased with himself in spite of all that.

He paid the driver, and he and Patricia were going up the steps of the apartment building, when there was a long, high squeal of skidding tires behind them, and Donna Barstow's voice called: "Pat! Patricia!"

She was driving a long maroon roadster, and Howard Linden was riding with her. They both got out of the car and hurried across the walk.

"Patricia!" Donna said. "We've been looking everywhere for you! I got the note you left for me saying you were going out to get yourself arrested, and I simply couldn't understand—" She recognized Dodd under the mud and said, instantly arrogant: "And just what are you doing here?"

Patricia held out her hand pleadingly. "Donna, please. He's my friend. He—he's been so decent and so kind—"

Donna accepted Dodd on that recommendation without the slightest hesitation.

"Oh, I didn't know. I'm sorry. Now, Patricia, what in the world does all this mean?"

Patricia nodded toward Linden, who was fidgeting uneasily in the background. "Didn't he tell you about—about my father?"

"He did," said Donna. "And I told him what I thought about him for telling you."

Linden protested: "But I didn't realize you didn't know, Pat. I'm sorry. I—"

"You're a fool," said Donna. "Really, Howard, you are, and I'm getting very annoyed with you. Now what's all this got to do with your father, Pat?"

"He's a crook and a gambler and a m-murderer. He's so crooked that even other crooks don't trust him!"

"*Pooh!*" said Donna, dismissing it with a wave of her hand. "That doesn't matter a bit!"

"It does, Donna! He never told me anything about his business— just that he was a banker. And—and I was so proud of him! And I've been going to Miss Wiggenbottom's school and being entertained at all the best homes—like yours—and all the time my father is a notorious criminal!"

"Oh, *pooh!*" said Donna. "That's not your fault. What do I care what your father is? Now you come up to the apartment and forget all this foolishness."

"But your father— He's so-well-bred."

"Bah! Come along. And you, too, Mr. What's-Your-Name. And I guess you can come, Howard, although I'm pretty well disgusted with you for telling Patricia about her father."

Linden appealed to Dodd. "It wasn't my fault. I was looking over some old newspapers, looking up publication on a divorce hearing, and I saw Gus Gillen's picture. I thought he looked like Patricia, and the name was similar, and so I just saved it and showed it to her as a joke. I never thought of it being her father. I had never seen—"

"Oh, be quiet," said Donna. "Come on."

THEY went through the severely modernistic lobby and up to the tenth floor in a self-operated elevator. The Barstows' apartment evidently took up the entire floor. There was only one door off the small entry-hall. Donna opened that with her key, and they went through into a long, low living-room.

A spindle-legged ornamental desk that evidently belonged discreetly in one corner of the room had been hauled out in the middle of the floor, and a man who could have been no one but E.P. Barstow was sitting on a chair in front of it. He was a short, bald-headed man with a fiery red face. There were papers scattered on the desk and in a loose circle on the rug around it. Barstow was chewing on the end of a pencil and staring in grim determination at the papers. As they came in, he spat out part of the pencil's eraser, picked up a bottle of beer from under the table and took a big swallow.

"Dad!" said Patricia in a choked voice.

Gus Gillen was sitting quietly on the couch in the corner. He smiled and nodded shyly.

"Uh?" said E.P. Barstow. "Oh, hello, Donna. This is Gus Gillen, Patricia's father. You've never met him, have you? Gus, this is Donna, and that one is Howard Linden. I don't know your other friend, Donna."

"The name is Dodd," Dodd told him.

"I have met Mr. Dodd," Gus Gillen said, smiling.

"All right," Barstow said, beginning to chew the pencil again. "If you want to make noise, go somewhere else. I've made a mistake here and I can't find it."

"Dad!" said Patricia in an agony of embarrassment. "What—what are you doing here?"

E.P. Barstow looked up. "What? What do you mean, what is he

doing here? Can't I even entertain my partner in my own house any more?"

Patricia stared. "You said—partner?"

"Yes, yes!" E.P. Barstow barked. "Partner! He furnishes the money and the brains, and I do the work."

Donna said: "Dad, you never told me—"

E.P. Barstow glared. "Do I have to tell all my business to everyone? Gus is my silent partner. Now, go away, all of you. I'm trying to add these figures."

"No," said Patricia. "No, wait. I want to know—to understand—" She was looking at Gus Gillen. "I saw—an old paper today. There was a picture of you in it. It said that you were a notorious g-gambler and had been arrested in connection with a murder."

"Murder!" E.P. Barstow exploded with laughter. "Gus? What a joke!"

Gus Gillen blinked apologetically. "My dear, that was just the work of a young district attorney who was making publicity for himself. I had met the murdered man only once. He was killed in New York, and I was in San Francisco at the time and easily proved it. I wasn't even held for questioning."

"But Shine Brevani said you—you—"

Gus Gillen sighed. "I own stock in three race tracks, Patricia. Brevani tried to fix a race at one of them, and I caught him and had him ruled off every track in the country for life. He's tried to get even with me several times since."

"But you told me you were a banker!"

"Well, I own a bank."

"Three," E.P. Barstow corrected. "And not one worth a damn if you ask me. Gus bought them up to keep them from going under during the depression."

Patricia still looked dazed. "The paper said—gambling—"

"Sure," said E.P. Barstow. "Gus owns three clubs that run gambling in Reno and Las Vegas. That's his end of our partnership, along with the race tracks."

Dodd cleared his throat. "It's legal to gamble in Nevada, Patricia."

"Well, sure it is," said E.P. Barstow. "What do you think we are—crooks or something?"

Patricia seemed to crumple a little. "Dad! Why didn't you *tell* me?"

GUS GILLEN looked worried in a bewildered way. "Well, dear, you see your mother used to worry terribly about these speculative businesses of mine. She was afraid I'd lose all my money—and I did, too, several times—and I didn't want you to worry at all. I wanted you to feel secure and—and happy—"

Patricia straightened up. "Oh, I've been a fool!" She stared at the others blindly. "You see, when Howard showed me that old paper with Dad's picture in it, I—I just couldn't believe, couldn't think straight. I thought I had been going under false pretenses and that my father was a c-crook. I'd heard Shine Brevani was a gambler, and I went to ask him, and he told me those lies about Dad. So—so I decided that no matter what my Dad was, he was my Dad, and I was proud of him. I decided I wouldn't pretend any more to be what I wasn't. I was going to get arrested and get my picture in the paper.

"I gave those rubies to those funny men because I wanted to make a good story out of it. I was going to say I was d-drunk, and everyone would be trying to find the rubies, and the story would go all over the country, and all my friends would see it, and that would show them I didn't care what my father was, and that I was just as bad as he was, and that if they didn't like him, they didn't have to like me any more, either. Oh, I've been such a fool!"

"You don't seem to have very good sense," E.P. Barstow agreed. "But then maybe you'll grow up after awhile. Now, will you please kindly get out of here so I can add these figures?"

"Wait a minute," said Dodd. "Speaking of those rubies. There's a couple of things I don't understand, Linden. Mud and your shoes."

"Mud?" Linden said blankly. "My shoes? There's no mud on my shoes."

"No," said Dodd. "That's what I can't understand."

Donna said: "Well, Howard, you know very well your shoes were covered with filthy mud, and that I took you home to change them—"

"Yes," said Dodd. "I thought so. I used to have a customer by the name of Grouchy Smith. He was an expert pick-pocket. He taught me some of his tricks. Look." He held out his right hand and opened his fingers. A flat ruby glowed red on his palm. "I got this out of your pocket on the way up in the elevator, Linden."

Linden slapped his hand against his lower vest pocket. "You lie! You couldn't possibly—" He stopped short, his thin face suddenly sickly white.

"Yes," Dodd agreed amiably. "I lie. The twin of this ruby—the one you took from Old Smoke when you shot him—is still safe in your pocket."

"You—you're crazy," Linden whispered.

"No. You showed that picture to Patricia on purpose. You were sure it was her father, and that she didn't know he was a gambler. You told her about Shine Brevani and followed her to his place because you knew Brevani hated Gus Gillen. He's always popping off about it, and you gamble there a good deal. You figured Patricia would be sick with the shock, and that then you could move in and offer her the sanctity and purity of your honored name, and that she'd jump at it like a shot rather than be known as the daughter of such a notorious character as the newspaper and Shine Brevani painted Gus Gillen as being, and that you would then be in line to get some of Gus Gillen's dough. You weren't making any progress in your attempt to marry Donna for her money, so you thought you'd try someone else."

Linden backed against the wall. "That's a lie!"

"I don't think so. You were desperate for money, and when you saw Patricia give those rubies away, you went after them. You tackled Old Smoke first. He was drunk on the credit he got on the strength of the ruby, but not drunk enough not to know that it was worth a lot more cash than you were offering. He wouldn't deal with you, and you shot him. You thought probably you had been seen and noticed in that district, so you tried to poke the thing off on Craig.

"You knew Craig and knew he was a newspaperman because it was from the *Times* you had gotten the old newspaper you showed to Patricia, and the interview gag was the best reason you could think of at the moment for anyone prowling around and looking for Old Smoke in the middle of the night. But, unfortunately for him, Craig also knew you. My man, Meekins, questioned Craig about Donna and you, and Craig began to connect things up. He didn't know about Old Smoke but he knew about you and the old newspapers, and he found out from the court clerk about Patricia and Sam Rudolph, and he must have remembered who Gus Gillen was. He had seen Gus Gillen at the night court. Why were you there, Mr. Gillen?"

GILLEN shrugged, still looking anxiously worried. "I always go to night court when I can. I was just passing the time away, waiting for Ed."

Barstow was staring grimly at Linden. "Gus pays fines for bums in night courts. That's his private charity."

Dodd said: "Craig went to my place to wait for me. He wanted some more information. He was an expert at picking locks, and he let himself into my place and made himself comfortable. While he was waiting, he called you up, and he said too much. You knew he could and would connect you with Old Smoke's murder as soon as he got the lowdown on Patricia and the rubies. You went to my apartment and shot him."

Donna said in a sick voice: "Howard, that was—was the phone call you got at your apartment when you were changing you shoes, and that—that was where I drove you afterwards—"

Dodd went on in the same casual tone: "Also you dropped a poker chip in Old Smoke's shack. That tripped you up badly, because Shine Brevani thought someone was trying to frame him."

Linden stood stiff and white and still against the wall. "You couldn't prove it," he whispered. "You couldn't—" He made a stiffly awkward gesture with his right arm, and then he was holding a small nickel-plated automatic. "Stand still! All of you, stand—"

All in one motion, E.P. Barstow leaned over and picked up the beer bottle and threw it with an expert backward flip of his wrist. The heavy end of the bottle took Linden squarely between the eyes. His head banged into the wall back of him, and then he dropped loosely to his knees and slid forward on his face.

"Hah!" said E.P. Barstow. "See that, Gus? And I haven't heaved a beer bottle since I used to tend bar."

"Dad!" Donna shrieked. "*You*—a bartender?"

"Sure," said E.P. Barstow. "That's how I met Gus. I was tending bar at the *Golden Lady* at Frying Pan Creek when Gus was running the faro game there. I was a damn good bartender, too, I'll have you know, young lady. I'll prove it. Dodd, you sit down here, and I'll fix you a drink. We might as well be comfortable while we wait for the police, and I want to talk to you about writing some fidelity bonds for some of my employees, and then, damn it, I want you all to get out of here, while I add these figures. Gus is going to think I'm holding out on him if I don't get the right answer soon."

THIS WILL KILL YOU!

IN WHICH THAT
EXTRAORDINARY
LUMINARY OF THE
CRIMINAL COURTS
INVOLVES HIMSELF
IN THE COMPLICATED
AFFAIRS OF MR. BANNER-
PENNANT-OR FLAG AS HE
WAS SOMETIMES CALLED.
AND MAMA MANDALAY,
THAT RIBALD AND
SAGACIOUS EX-DOXIE
DE LUXE RALLIES ROUND
WHEN MURDER REARS ITS
HYDRA HEAD TO HELP
DODD CLEAN UP THE
KILL-PUZZLE.

CHAPTER ONE

THE SOUSE WHO DIDN'T DRINK

DODD WAS having one of those horribly realistic nightmares. He was dreaming that he was in his coffin and was smothering and that someone was nailing the lid down with dull smacks of a hammer. He heaved himself up frantically, waving his arms like a swimmer in heavy surf, and the pillow fell off his face.

He was wide awake instantly, then, and he remembered that he had put the pillow over his head himself to drown out the howl of an overloud radio from the apartment below. He sighed with heartfelt relief, but the hammering on his coffin was still unaccounted for, and he finally traced that down to the front door of his apartment. Someone was knocking on it loudly.

"All right," Dodd said. "Coming."

He turned on the night lamp and saw that the jagged hands of his stream-lined electric alarm clock were just getting together chummily at the hour of midnight. Dodd found his patched glasses and set them on his nose, kicked his feet into worn slippers.

The knocking on the front door went on persistently.

"All *right!*" Dodd called. "I said I'm coming!"

He shuffled out of the bedroom, turned on the lights in the living-room and opened the front door.

"Well, what?" he demanded. "Oh, hello, Mr. Grillman. What's the trouble?"

Mr. Grillman was the manager of the apartment building. He was a bald, ineffective, worried-looking little man. He was wearing an old-fashioned flannel night-shirt and a suit-coat with the collar turned up tight around his scrawny throat. His wrinkled face was screwed up as though he were ready to cry, and there were actually tears in his eyes.

"Hah!" said Mama Mandalay.
"Made him jump!"

"Oh, Mr. Dodd!" he said breathlessly. "I'm so sorry to wake you up, but they've arrested him! What will I do?"

"Who arrested whom?" Dodd asked.

"They arrested Mr. Brown."

"Brown," said Dodd thoughtfully. "Brown. Oh, yes. You mean your pal. What for?"

"I don't know," Grillman wailed. "They called up and asked if he lived here and said he was in jail. I asked them what he was in for, and they just said, 'Plenty!' Mr. Dodd, what will I do? That jail is a horrible place, and Mr. Brown is a gentleman and refined. You know about these things, Mr. Dodd. Please tell me what I can do to help him."

Dodd blinked through his glasses reflectively. He didn't know Brown, except to say hello to casually. As he recalled, Brown was a tall, austerely correct, elderly man. He had lived in the apartment house long before Dodd had moved in. He was retired, living on some sort of annuity. He and Mr. Grillman were great cronies. They sat in the lobby for hours every day, playing chess, while Mr. Grillman kept an eye on the desk.

"He's *such* a gentleman!" Grillman repeated plaintively. "What can I do to help him?"

"Come on in," Dodd said. "I'll see." He went to the telephone and dialed the number of police headquarters. When a voice answered, he said: "Hennessey." He waited for a second and then said: "Hennessey? This is Dodd. Is Meekins around there somewhere?"

"Sure," said Hennessey. "That bum haunts the joint. Now listen, Dodd, I want to ask you something. Don't you ever pay him anything? He owes me ten dollars, and he told me you hadn't paid him any salary for two months. Now that's not right, Dodd. How can he support himself and pay his debts, if you never give him his salary?"

"I'll pay him tomorrow," Dodd said sourly. "Get him on the telephone. I want to talk to him."

"Hi, boss," Meekins greeted cheerfully.

"You louse," said Dodd. "What's the idea of going around saying I don't pay you?"

"That's just my sales talk. It keeps my creditors happy. Did you want something?"

"Yes. What about a bird named Brown?"

"Hah!" Meekins chortled. "Drunk driving—homicide. We couldn't bail him out with less than a first mortgage on the mint."

"Tell me some more, Meekins," Dodd invited.

"He drove right up over the sidewalk and smacked a girl at Tenth Avenue and San Pedro. He smashed her like a bug. He was still in the car when the cops got there, passed out, reeking like a distillery. There weren't any witnesses, but the setup is plain as a neon sign."

"Wait," Dodd requested. He put his hand over the mouthpiece and turned to Grillman. "This is my man, Meekins, on the telephone. He says that Brown killed a girl driving while he was drunk."

"Oh!" Grillman gasped, horrified. "No! That can't be true, Mr. Dodd! Mr. Brown never drinks! Never, never drinks! Not even a drop!"

Dodd looked skeptical. "You sure about that?"

"Oh, I am! I am, truly! You see Mr. Brown has a very, very acute heart condition. He can't drink anything at all, ever. I *know* that, Mr. Dodd. I've visited his doctor with him several times. He couldn't possibly drink anything. It would kill him. The doctor assured me of that. There must be some horrible mistake! There *must* be!"

DODD spoke into the telephone. "Meekins, one of Brown's best pals is here with me, and he says that Brown never drinks anything at all. He can't. He's got a very bad heart."

"Well, if he ain't drunk as a skunk," said Meekins, "he's sure giving a good imitation of it. He's still passed out."

Grillman intervened. "Mr. Brown can't even smoke, Mr. Dodd. He has to be awfully careful all the time."

Dodd nodded absently. "Meekins, get the doctor to look Brown over carefully. Get a blood test."

"You mean—now?" Meekins protested. "This late?"

"Yes, I mean now. Get going. I'll be down soon."

Dodd put the telephone back in its cradle and squinted thoughtfully at Grillman. "I'll go down and see what I can do about this, Mr. Grillman. Frankly, it looks pretty serious. I'm taking your word for it that Brown can't drink. If that isn't true, it's going to make me look pretty silly."

"It is true! Oh, it is! Mr. Brown told me all about himself. He was in bed for two years with his heart—couldn't even get up. And now he can't smoke or drink or even walk fast. He has to be very careful all the time."

Dodd started to pull his pajama-top over his head. "O.K., Mr. Grillman. We'll see what's what."

"Thank you, Mr. Dodd," Grillman said. "I'm so grateful. I just didn't know which way to turn. I've never had any experience…. Mr. Dodd, I have a little insurance, and I could borrow on it if—if…."

Dodd got out of the pajamas and settled his glasses back on his nose again. He grinned at Grillman, and the grin fanned little wrinkles at the corners of his eyes and belied his ordinary cynically hard-boiled expression. He was a big, rangy man with wide shoulders, slightly stooped, and a flat-muscled stomach.

"We'll talk about that later, Mr. Grillman. Don't worry about it now. By the way, what would your pal Brown be doing at this hour down near Tenth Avenue and San Pedro? That's a crummy district. Nothing there but a lot of old warehouses."

"Oh, he was helping Mr. Sellers. He does that every Tuesday and Thursday night."

Dodd put on his shorts and began to hunt around under the chairs for his shoes and socks.

"Who is Sellers?"

"He's a nice old gentleman. I've met him several times. He is night watchman at a warehouse owned by the Milton Medicine Company on San Pedro Street."

Dodd found his shoes under the couch and retrieved them. "Is he a friend of Brown's?"

"Oh, yes. They both used to work for the Milton Medicine Company. Mr. Brown was with them for thirty-five years. Mr. Sellers worked for them for almost that long. He lost his money in a bank failure, and the company gave him this night-watchman job to keep him going. Mr. Brown goes down twice a week and stays with him to keep him company. He does it just as a favor to Mr. Sellers, because Mr. Sellers gets so lonesome there all by himself every night. He has no family."

Dodd was pulling on his pants. "I see."

"It's all a terrible mistake," Grillman said, worried. "I know it is. And I'm so grateful to you, Mr. Dodd. If I can ever do anything…."

"You might tell that bird below me to play his radio a little more softly," Dodd said.

"Mr. Pennant," Grillman said sadly. "I know, I know. I've told him again and again. I've had any number of complaints. But he doesn't pay any attention. I guess I'll have to ask him to move out, but I hate to do that… Well, I'll go back to my apartment and wait, Mr. Dodd. Please call me as soon as you find out about this, and I do want to thank you again…."

"Forget it," Dodd advised. "I'll telephone you from the police station a little later."

CHAPTER TWO

A FRAME—AND A CUTE ONE

DODD CAME in the side door of the police station and went down a long dingy hall lined on both sides with tall green police lockers. He stopped at the squadroom and peered through the door.

Two detectives he knew, Limes and Lillicott, were playing a game of two-handed rummy at the center table. They played with a sort of weary disgust, as though they didn't care much for the game or each other, and as a matter of fact they didn't. They worked as a team, but not from choice. They were beefy, heavy-set men, looking enough alike to be brothers, and they both had the same dour, coldly suspicious manner.

Neither one looked up at Dodd now, but Limes said: "I smell something."

"There's one thing that makes a bigger stink than a bail bondsman," Lillicott observed, "and that's a bail bondsman who thinks he's a detective."

"My kindest regards," Dodd said. "And both of you can go to hell."

Meekins came down the hall from the other direction. He was small and shabby and nondescript, and he always managed to wear an air of sleepy nonchalance. He was wearing it now, even though his colorless eyes glinted triumphantly. "Thought you'd be coming along soon," he said.

Dodd jerked his head to indicate the squadroom. "What's the idea of the sour off-stage voices?"

"You mean those two dopes?" Meekins asked, loudly enough so Limes and Lillicott could hear him. "They're assigned to this Brown case. So they bring him in and turn in a manslaughter-drunk-driving report and sit around on their fat cans to wait for Brown to come to so they can question him."

"And then?" said Dodd.

Meekins chortled. "So, like you tell me, I beef at the doc until I get an examination and a blood test for Brown. So what does the doc find? Brown ain't drunk. He ain't had even a drop. He's been banged on the head—plenty hard. He's got a concussion. Not a bad one, but enough."

"That's a relief!"

"But wait," said Meekins. "When the doc examines Brown's bean, he finds out whatever gave him the concussion cut him a little bit on the back of the head. So I wonder how he got a bump and a cut there. So I go and examine the car. Not a window broken in it. No loose glass. But in the back seat I find a big monkey wrench with some blood and hair on it. Get it?"

"I'm beginning to," Dodd admitted.

Meekins nodded excitely. "It's a frame, and a cute one. Somebody laid for Brown and bopped him on the bean and put him in the car and poured whiskey all over him. After I got that, I looked over the front of the car. It's all smeared up and dented, but it ain't dented in the right places. Somebody hammered it with the same wrench they cracked Brown with. That car never ran over the dame. No car did. Somebody just naturally knocked her brains in and fixed up this Brown deal to cover it."

"Yes," Dodd said slowly.

"And those two chumps," Meekins said. "They fell for it. Now they got to eat their report." He leaned in the doorway of the squadroom. "Detectives! Yah!"

"Yah!" said Limes.

"Yah!" echoed Lillicott. "Wait until you try to borrow some money, cutie-pie."

"Yah!" said Meekins. "Wait until I pay you what I already owe you."

"Quit it," Dodd ordered. He walked slowly down the hall with Meekins tagging along. "What about the girl who was killed?"

"No identification," said Meekins. "No purse, no papers, no labels in her clothes. Just another orphan lost in the storm."

"I'll take a look," Dodd decided.

Meekins stopped short. "Whoa!"

"Well?" Dodd queried.

"You ain't seen that doll, pal, and I have. She ain't pretty at all."

"I can probably live through it."

"That ain't all," said Meekins. "Look, Dodd. You wanted to shake Brown loose, and we did. He's free and clear on the deal, after this. But the guy who really knocked this dame off just naturally hammered her face clear in. What I mean, he's not the kind of a guy you'd want to invite over for dinner. You don't want any part of him."

"Come on," said Dodd, starting down the hall again.

"Oh, hell," Meekins said resignedly.

They went around a turn in the hall and down a short flight of worn stairs.

"Who tipped the police off?" Dodd asked.

"Phone call—anonymous. It was probably the guy that killed the girl. He wanted the cops there before Brown came to. I don't want to meet that boy, Dodd. Every time I think of what he did to that girl it gives me the shakes."

"Come on," said Dodd impatiently.

THE TEMPORARY police receiving-morgue was in the basement of the station, and Meekins and Dodd went down a long cement corridor with their footsteps echoing hollowly ahead of them and pushed through the brown, slickly varnished door at the end.

The morgue office was no bigger than a hall closet. Green filing-cases towered against its four walls, and a flat desk filled the space in between them. A solemn, spectacled young man was sitting behind the desk, peering owlishly at a thick medical text-book.

"Hello, Dodd," he said absently, marking his place in the text with a forefinger. "Hello, Meekins. What do you want?"

"Let's have a look at the dame that just came in," Dodd requested. "The phony drunk-driving case."

"Sure. Come on in."

Dodd and Meekins squeezed around the desk and followed the young man through a door at the back of the office. They were in a low-ceilinged room with greenish walls and floor. The heavy door wheezed shut behind them, and the air felt dead and cold and stagnant.

There were three long waist-high tables in the center of the room with droplights hanging low over each one.

"Here," said the young man, turning on one of the lights.

The table held a rigidly still form covered completely with a coarse linen sheet.

The young man took hold of the upper end of the sheet. "Better take a deep breath," he advised Dodd. "She's not in very good shape."

Dodd nodded. "Go ahead."

The young man pulled the sheet back. Dodd winced and turned his head aside involuntarily, shivering.

"I told you," said Meekins.

Dodd forced himself to look again. The blood had been sponged away, and the effect was all the more horrible because it had. The girl's face was a raw, blue-black mass with bits of bone and teeth glistening right through it.

"Going to have trouble getting an identification here," the young man observed casually. "No chance to make a mask. Bones and everything shattered."

Dodd swallowed and found his voice. "Any identifying marks on her?"

"Nope. Look." The young man pulled the sheet the rest of the way down. "She was knocked around some here." He pointed to blue-black lacerations on the smooth white torso. "Not as bad as the face, though."

"About twenty to twenty-five years old," Dodd murmured, half to himself. "Black hair. Light brown eyes. Five feet three or four. Hundred to a hundred and ten pounds."

"Close enough," the young man agreed. "Look here." He prodded the white, flaccid concavity of the stomach with his finger. "Plenty of muscular development. A lot for a girl. And here on the thighs and calves. Her feet are short but broadened out across the toes. No excess fat at all. She took very good care of herself."

"Dancer?" Dodd hazarded, glancing at Meekins.

Meekins nodded. "Probably. So what? Dancers are a dime a dozen in this burg."

"Cover her up," Dodd said to the young man. He sighed with relief when the sheet once more concealed the still, mutilated body. "How about the clothes?"

"Nothing there," said the young man. "You can look if you want, but they're just ordinary good stuff. The labels had been cut out of them."

"I know," Dodd said. He looked at Meekins. "Where is Brown now? I want to talk to him."

"Over in the jail surgery."

"All right. Let's go."

"Now why?" Meekins demanded plaintively. "Ain't this enough for you for one night? You're going to snoot around until you get yourself parked on a table right beside this poor dame. I don't think—"

"No," Dodd agreed. "You don't. Go on. Shove off."

THE JAIL surgery was all glistening, antiseptic white with chromed surgical instruments glittering in graduated rows in glass-doored cases. Brown was sitting in one corner under a powerful observation-lamp. He was wearing a neat, turban-like bandage on his head and under it his face, tanned from sun-baths on the apartment house roof, was the color of smoothly dark ivory. His eyes were bloodshot, and his lips trembled uncontrollably.

The jail surgeon, Doctor Murray, was sitting in another chair facing him. He was a heavy-set gray-haired man with a cheerfully impersonal smile. He had one finger on the pulse of Brown's right wrist, and he looked up and nodded when Dodd and Meekins came in.

"Hello, Dodd. Your friend, here, has really got a bad ticker. I gave him a stimulant, and it seems to be taking hold all right. You feeling better now, Brown?"

"Yes, thank you," Brown whispered.

"You being treated for this heart?"

"Yes. By Doctor Stietzer."

Murray nodded. "He's the best around these parts. You'd better go mighty easy for a while."

"A fine thing," said Meekins contemptuously. "A fine thing, when a guy who claims to be a doctor can't tell whether a guy is drunk or has a bad heart. What do you do when you operate on anybody stupid enough to let you—just cut 'em open and prowl around inside until you find something to take out?"

"So you're in again," said Murray. "Sometime I'm going to mistake you for a microbe and pour some carbolic on you. Listen, Dodd. Those two dopes, Limes and Lillicott, brought Brown in and swore he was drunk. He looked drunk and he smelled drunk, so I didn't even examine him until this screw-loose runner of yours started yelling. How was I to know this particular case had a bad heart? We get over a hundred drunks every night."

"It's O.K. Not your fault."

"O.K., he says," Meekins put in. "But I don't say so. I'm a tax-payer and—"

"Ha!" Murray snorted. "A tax-payer! What tax did you ever pay—except on liquor?"

"Shut up," Dodd said to Meekins. "Mr. Brown, you remember me, don't you? I live in the same apartment building that you do."

"Yes," said Brown in his shaky whisper. "Doctor Murray has told me that you are responsible for extricating me from this—this horrible affair. I'm deeply grateful. I don't understand...."

"Mr. Grillman asked me to help you," Dodd told him. "And I was glad to do it. I'd like to ask you a few questions if you feel strong enough to answer them."

"Of course, Mr. Dodd," Brown said.

"Not too many," said Murray.

"The expert," Meekins said sarcastically. "The voice of authority speaks. Did you ever think of taking up horse-doctoring, Murray?"

"Be quiet," Dodd snapped. "Mr. Brown, can you remember anything that happened this evening?"

Brown swallowed painfully. "I left the warehouse—you knew about that?—at a little before eleven. There's a narrow alley that leads to the street—very dark. I was walking along it, going slowly, when—when something hit me from behind. I saw no one—I had no slightest warning. Just the blow. It felt like the whole world had smashed in front of my face. I don't remember anything else until Doctor Murray brought me around."

Murray nodded. "That's right. He wouldn't be doing any brain work after a sock like that. If you want me to, I'll be glad to prove it by demonstrating on Meekins."

"I'll tell you what we know, Mr. Brown," Dodd said. "Whoever struck you put you in your car, drove it up on the sidewalk, and arranged things to look like you had struck down and killed an unidentified girl. It was a clumsy and hurried job, done in desperation on the spur of the moment, I think. Have you any idea who could have done that? Have you any enemies?"

"No," said Brown, bewildered. "Why, no. As you probably know,

I'm retired. I have a small income from an annuity. It ceases when I die. I'm not in business. I go out very little socially on account of my health. No one would have any reason to be my enemy, Mr. Dodd."

"No," Dodd admitted. "Well, take this girl you were supposed to be accused of running down. Twenty to twenty-five, five feet three or four, dark, slim, probably pretty, probably a dancer or entertainer. Know anyone like that?"

Brown shook his bandaged head slowly and carefully. "No, Mr. Dodd. I really know no young people at all. I don't have any oppor- tunity to meet them. I—I can't understand any of this. It's ghastly that I should be involved, and if it hadn't been for your help...."

"Would you mind just taking a look at the girl?"

"Not if I'm responsible," said Murray firmly. "He's had enough for one night."

"I—don't feel very well yet," Brown said. "If—I could just go home and rest...."

"Sure," said Dodd. "You're still under technical custody, but there won't be any objection to giving you bail. Meekins will fix it up."

Murray adjusted his stethoscope. "Wait a second until I listen to his heart again."

Dodd took off his glasses and rubbed his eyes. "That girl—the whole nasty mess—it makes no sense. If I could only figure out why—*why*...."

"Why is O.K. with me," said Meekins, "just so you don't start on who. I still don't care to meet the gent who did that little piece of work we just looked at downstairs."

"Listen to me," Dodd ordered. "You take care of Brown, here, and then I want you to get to work and find out who that girl is."

Meekins growled reluctant assent.

"I'm going down to look over the scene of this alleged accident. If you want me, call me at Milton's warehouse. They'll have a phone there. It's required. Brown can tell you the number. Now get busy. This is important. I think we stepped into something that's liable to backfire right in our faces if we don't do some scrambling around."

CHAPTER THREE

THE WATCHMAN
WHO LIKED HIS NAP

THE TAXI rocked and swayed and bounced over the cobbles. At the corner under the wan yellow glow of the street-light, it skittered sideways in a half-circle and ended up against the curb with a neck-cracking jar.

"This is the place," the driver said. "Such as it is."

Dodd got out and paid him.

"I should charge you double, that's what," the driver informed him, hunting for change half-heartedly. "I bet the last six blocks took six thousand miles out of my springs. I can't change a dollar, Colonel."

"Keep it," Dodd said absently.

"If you insist."

The driver slammed the door hastily and swung the cab around. It banged off noisily down the street, its red tail-lights doing a jitter-dance behind it.

Dodd stood where he was for a moment, staring around him thoughtfully. As far as he could tell there was no living thing other than himself in this neighborhood of gloomy warehouses. And after the rattle of the taxi had died away, there was no sound.

He snapped a match on his thumbnail and applied it to the limp cigarette he was holding between his lips. The flame made a flat yellow glow against the lenses of his glasses. He walked along the curbing until he found a pool of blood on the sidewalk about ten feet above the intersection on San Pedro.

The blood had coagulated and hardened into a slick black smear. There was not very much of it. Dodd began to whistle thoughtfully. He stepped off the sidewalk, struck another match and cupped it in his hands, looking for skidmarks on the cobblestones. There were none.

"Well," he said to himself, puzzled.

He hunched his shoulders suddenly, giving it up, and began to walk down San Pedro Street.

He found the Milton Medicine Company's warehouse and the

alley Brown had described on the other side of it. The alley was narrow and dark with only a faint trickle of light coming through a smeared window to mark the far end of it. Dodd went into it, feeling his way along carefully with one hand trailing against a rough brick wall.

Coming closer, he saw that there was a door beside the lighted window, and he knocked on it loudly. There was no answer and he rapped again and again, while the echoes chased themselves back and forth in the narrow confines of the alley.

Finally the light from the window dimmed a little more, and Dodd could see the flat, strained blur of a face pressed close against the dirty panes, hands making twin semi-circles on either side of it as its owner attempted to peer out.

"All right," Dodd said. "Open it up."

The face jerked away from the window and a quavering voice sounded close on the other side of the door.

"Who—who's out there?"

"Open up," said Dodd. "I'm from the police station."

"Oh! Oh, all right."

A key ground in the lock, and a latch chain rattled metallically. The door inched itself open.

Dodd pushed it back the rest of the way and stepped into a close, hot little room with stained plasterboard walls. There was an army cot with a rumpled blanket on it in one corner and a chair made out of an old auto cushion in another. An oil stove burned smokily in the middle of the floor.

"Sellers?" Dodd asked.

"Yes, sir. That's my name."

HE WAS an old man, much older-looking than Brown, and painfully emaciated. He looked scared and sick and shaky. There were yellow smears under his watery eyes, and his back was bent into a permanent crook. He wore a blue suit that was shiny and frayed with age and what appeared to be a conductor's cap. He was holding his right hand behind him and he backed away from Dodd, nodding and smiling uncertainly.

"You can put it away now," Dodd said, indicating the hidden hand.

"Yes, sir," said Sellers. He brought his right hand into sight, holding a cheap nickel-plated revolver. "It—it isn't loaded, anyway."

"That helps," Dodd commented.

Sellers sat down gingerly on the cot. "Won't—won't you sit down in that chair, sir?"

"No, thanks," said Dodd. "Do you know your friend Brown was arrested a while ago for running over and killing a girl while he was tight?"

Sellers gulped. "Yes, sir. Another policeman—a uniformed man—came and told me. It—it's a terrible mistake, sir. Mr. Brown never drinks at all. He can't, even if he wanted to. There's something wrong with his heart. I told the policeman that, but he just laughed at me."

Dodd nodded. "I see. The accident happened not far from here. Did you hear it happen?"

"No, sir. I told the other policeman that."

"Hear anything else about then or just before then? Any shouts or screams—anything at all?"

"No, sir. Nothing. It's very quiet around here."

"So I notice," Dodd agreed. "I understand that Brown comes here twice a week regularly. What does he do while he's here?"

"Just—just sits in that chair, sir."

"Just sits," Dodd repeated. "Is that all he does? Doesn't he talk to you?"

"No, sir."

"What? Why not?"

"Because—because I'm asleep, sir."

Dodd stared at him. "Asleep!"

Sellers nodded agonizedly. "Yes, sir. You see, I'm an old man and it's hard to change habits, and it's very noisy in the rooming-house where I stay. I have a very hard time sleeping in the day-time. At night, I can hardly keep awake, sir. Mr. Brown found that out, and he was kind enough to come down here and sit and watch while I get a little nap. It's just from the kindness of his heart that he does it, and—and now he's gotten into this terrible trouble because of it…."

"I wouldn't worry about that," Dodd said in a more kindly tone. "I don't think Brown—"

Footsteps made a sudden clatter in the alleyway outside and a loudly important voice called: "Sellers! Oh there, Sellers!"

"It's Mr. Milton!" Sellers said excitedly. "The man who owns this warehouse. I called him…." He got up off the cot. "Yes, Mr. Milton. Yes, sir. Coming!"

Milton stamped inside the room, blowing his breath out in a sudden puff of relief. "Dark as the inside of your hat in that alley. Have to get a light…. Eh? Who's that? Who's that fellow, Sellers? What's he doing in here?"

"He said—from the police…" Sellers quavered.

MILTON looked Dodd up and down and snorted once as though he didn't approve of what he saw. Milton was chubby and round-faced, with an air of bouncing, inexhaustible energy. He looked very dapper and prosperous in a long gray tailored topcoat and a gray bowler hat. He opened the topcoat now, as though he meant to get right down to business, hooked his plump thumbs in the arm-holes of his neat gray suit.

"Police! Police, eh? You don't look like a policeman to me, sir. Not a bit. Show your authority. At once, I demand it."

"I'm not a policeman," Dodd said amiably. "I said I came from the police station."

"An imposter!" said Milton. "What do you mean by coming in here, eh? This is private property. Explain yourself at once and no evasion, sir."

Dodd said: "I'm a bondsman and I'd like—"

"Bondsman," Milton repeated blankly, and then suddenly understanding, "A bail bondsman! One of those vultures! Are you trying to extort money from poor Sellers on some subterfuge? Are you, eh? Answer me!"

"No, no," Sellers said. "No, sir. He just—"

"Quiet," said Milton. "I'll handle this fellow. I've dealt with his type before. Sharp customers, Sellers, every one of them. Now, you. What's your game, eh? I suppose you've heard about poor Brown and are trying to turn some profit out of that unfortunate affair. Let me inform you that Brown is a very old and respected employee of mine, just as Sellers is, and that if either one of them needs any aid of any kind, I will furnish it myself without any help from any denizens of the underworld who masquerade—"

"You'll run yourself all out of breath in a minute," Dodd said solicitously.

"Eh?" said Milton, startled.

"If you'll turn off the faucet long enough to give me time I'll explain that I furnished bail for Brown—"

"Eh?" said Milton. "You did! Then I'll pay you for it. I consider it my duty to an old employee. How much, sir? Quick, now. No haggling. Name your fee and be done with it."

"I don't know as yet," Dodd said patiently, "because I don't know the amount of the bail. If you're so anxious to pay for it—"

"Anxious and able, sir. Remember that. Able. If you don't know your fee now, bill me when you do. Any reasonable amount. Now, sir, I consider our conversation at a close. Please leave. Leave this property at once. I do not care for you nor your business nor your meddling in affairs that don't concern you. It has been the policy of the Milton Medicine Company for sixty years to safe-guard the interests of its own employees."

"Former employees, too?" Dodd asked.

"Exactly, sir. In the case of Brown, most certainly. He was our star salesman for a matter of thirty years. Had it not been for that infernal heart of his, he would be a vice-president right now. Vice-president at the very least, sir. But that is none of your concern. That, sir, is the door. See that you use it. Good-night!"

Dodd shrugged and smiled. "Be seeing you."

He went out into the alley and the door slammed emphatically behind him. The sudden change from the light inside made the darkness seem like a soft jet-black bandage clapped over Dodd's eyes. He went stumbling along, fumbling against the wall to guide himself, and he had no slightest warning that there was anyone else in the passage with him until he heard a sudden grunting exhalation of breath directly in front of him.

Dodd stopped and drew his head back instinctively. Because he did, the blow didn't land quite squarely. It clipped him above the right ear, and it was like being hit with a ball bat. He fell back and sideways into the wall, and the second blow struck him on the forehead above his glasses and knocked him flat on his back.

He wasn't unconscious, and he had sense enough to roll toward and not away from the man who had hit him. He rolled into moving legs, wound both arms around them, and heaved. His attacker went over him with a strangled shout. Dodd got up to his knees, and then someone else close behind him said: "You dope."

THE OWNER of that voice hit him in the back of the neck. Dodd went down on his face and felt his cheek rub grindingly against rough brick. He was numb from the neck down. He couldn't move his arms or legs, couldn't even breathe.

The man he had thrown was up again, stumbling around, and one of his heels ground on Dodd's hand.

"Give it to him, you clown," said the owner of the voice.

One or both of them were kicking him. They were trying to kick him in the head, and Dodd felt the kicks without any pain, like light, dull pops against his consciousness. The darkness swam in a greenish, spangled swirl of flame.

And then the door of the warehouse opened.

"Here!" Milton shouted angrily. "What? What?"

"Beat it," said the voice.

Feet clattered in the passageway, running.

"Stop!" Milton yelled. "Stop! Sellers, give me that gun. Give it to me, man!"

Dodd heard the repeated *click-click-click* of the revolver hammer on empty chambers.

"What!" Milton said. "What's the matter—"

"It—it isn't loaded, sir."

"Great Scott!" The revolver made a sudden ringing *spang* as Milton hurled it over Dodd's head and down the passageway. One of the running men yelped, and then they were out of the passageway, and the clatter of their feet died in the street.

Dodd was on his hands and knees now, his head hanging. Every breath was like living, burning flame in his throat.

Milton caught him under one arm and heaved him up to his feet. "Great Scott, man! What happened? Who were those thugs? What did they want?"

"Glasses," said Dodd.

"Eh? What's that? What are you saying?"

"His glasses, sir," Sellers said. "Here they are. They aren't broken, just twisted a little."

Dodd put them on, fumbling clumsily. "Let go."

"Eh? Here! Where are you going?"

"After 'em."

Milton grabbed him more firmly. "No! You can't, man! You're hurt. Come back in the office. Sellers, take his other arm. Smartly now!"

"Go—after 'em," said Dodd stubbornly.

"No!" said Milton. "They're thugs, man! Thieves, footpads! You're in no shape to chase them. You're hurt! Come back in the office. Sellers, help me!"

Dodd allowed himself to be led back to the office. His feet felt loose and strange and detached under him. Sellers and Milton deposited him in the auto-cushion chair. The room swam around crazily in front of him and Milton's face, staring down at him anxiously, was distorted out of all proportion.

Water ran gurgling—somewhere, and then Sellers said: "Here's a wet towel, sir. It's clean...."

"Let me," Milton said impatiently. "Let me."

The cloth felt cool and soft and soothing against Dodd's face. The pain was beginning to come now—in short, electric waves that seemed to go back from his eyes.

"Great Scott!" said Milton. "His eye and his cheek, here, and his mouth...."

"His neck," said Sellers. "In back."

"Yes, yes. Here, wet this towel again."

Dodd finally got his eyes to focus properly, and he said thickly: "Thanks."

"Thanks!" Milton blurted. "Thanks, nothing! I apologize, sir! I apologize from the depths of my heart! Without a doubt those thugs had trailed me in here and were lurking there waiting for me to come out. Instead, you came out—and because I sent you! I feel responsible, sir! You've been beaten terribly by those ruffians, and it was my fault! Sellers, what ever possessed you to keep that gun unloaded? I would have picked them both off. I won a trophy only last month at the Hunt Club. Sellers, give me that towel, and call the police and report this piece of infernal villainy."

"No," said Dodd. "No police. I'll take care of it."

Milton stared. "Just as you say, sir. But imagine the insolence of it, if you please! Lying in wait for me on my own property! Beating up people in front of my very door! Did they have a chance to rob you, sir?"

"No," said Dodd.

"You're going to have a black eye," said Milton. "A beautiful black eye, and your lips are swelling already, and that place on the back of your head must hurt like the very dickens! You need medical attention, sir. I insist!"

"Never mind," Dodd said. The pain was steadier now, rolling over him in black, lengthening waves.

The old-fashioned wall telephone jingled suddenly and unexpectedly. Sellers shuffled across the floor and took down the receiver. "Hello, hello! What? What's that? Who did you say? No, you have the wrong number. There's nobody by the name of Dodd around—"

"Me," said Dodd.

He got up and staggered to the phone. He held the receiver against his ear and propped himself up against the wall by one bruised shoulder.

"What, Meekins?"

Meekins said: "I got Brown all fixed up, like you said, and shipped him home in a taxi. And I got some more dope for you by the exercise of the ingenuity and originality for which I am noted far and wide."

"Spill it."

"What's the matter with you? You talk like you had mush in your mouth. You drunk?"

"No. Get on with it."

"O.K. Well, the only place to start on that dead doll was the clothes. So I thought of Lisping Lester, who runs the dress shop over on Fifth. He should know about clothes for gals if anybody does, and we've done him a favor or two. So I routed him out and made him come down here and look at them. No luck with the dress and coat and shoes and stockings. Just ordinary stuff, Lisping Lester says. Could get them at any big department store. But the girdle, that's different. You know what a girdle is, Dodd?"

"Yes. Keep talking."

"You sure sound drunk. I hope you're not so pie-eyed you can't understand me. Lisping Lester says this girdle is a fancy custom-built model. Worn by singers and dancers and dolls that want to put lots of emphasis on the stream lines under a spotlight. Only one joint in town sells this kind. Lisping Lester knows the doll who runs the joint, so he calls her up and describes the corpse—he's still sick from looking at it, moaning around here like a lost calf—and the dress-shop doll remembers the sale because the girdle was one of a new lot. Are you listening to me, or have you passed out?"

"I'm listening."

"O.K. So the dress-shop doll can't tell me the name of the girl who bought the girdle, because she didn't give any name, but she did have it sent out, and it was sent to 619 Pearl Street. And here's the kick—guess who's place is at 619 Pearl Street?"

"I don't want to guess!" Dodd said savagely.

"All right, all right. But you'll be surprised. 619 Pearl Street is Mama Mandalay's place."

"What!" Dodd exclaimed.

"See?" Meekins chortled. "Jolted you, didn't it?"

"I didn't know Mama Mandalay was running a joint now."

"She ain't. Not the kind of joint you mean. I asked all around here, and everybody tells me that Mama Mandalay is going straight now. She's running a boarding-and-rooming house and running it on the up-and-up. That last trip up the river didn't do her health any good, so now she has retired."

"O.K.," Dodd said. "Good work, Meekins. I'll come in a little later, if I get around to it. I've got an important appointment with a couple of guys, as soon as I find out who they are."

HE HUNG up the receiver and turned back to Milton. The pain was localizing in his head now, thundering between his temples like a giant drum.

"I didn't have a chance to ask before. What do you store in this warehouse?"

Milton said anxiously: "I wish you'd at least sit down here and rest a while, sir. I feel very guilty.... This warehouse? It's full of white elephants. I mean, figuratively speaking, of course. The Milton Medicine Company has been making patent remedies of various kinds for over sixty years, and in that time we've made a lot of mistakes of one kind and another. A good many of them are stored here."

"Are any of them valuable?"

Milton snorted. "Valuable! I only wish they were! No! This place is full of cough syrup that curdled and laxatives that turned green and dandruff eradicator that made people's hair fall out."

"What are you keeping them for?"

"Why not? We've got a ninety-nine year lease on this warehouse and nothing else to put in it. Besides, I've been meaning to salvage some of the bottles sometime if it was feasible. But it would be a lot of work to empty them all. There are thousands and thousands stored here."

Dodd nodded. "Another question. The girl that Brown was accused of running over. She's small, dark, slim. Probably was pretty. Wore her hair in a long bob. Probably was a singer or a dancer or both. I don't know her name. She lives at Mama Mandalay's place on Pearl Street. Know her?"

Milton clapped his hand over his mouth. "Did—did you say Mama Mandalay?"

"Yes."

Milton cleared his throat. "There was a Mama Mandalay who ran a—a place on Fulton Street...."

"That was ten years ago, or more."

"Yes," said Milton uncomfortably. "Yes. I—ah—visited the place several times.... There might have been a small dark-haired girl...."

"Not this one. You haven't seen Mama Mandalay since that time?"

"No. I understood she was sent to prison."

"She was. She's out now. Can you describe either one of those gents that jumped me?"

"No. I'm sorry, but the light was in back of me. They were just dim outlines. If that gun was only loaded.... Can you describe them, Sellers?"

"No, sir. They just looked medium-like."

"O.K.," Dodd said. "Well, I'll be going now."

"Your hat, sir," Sellers said, brushing at it. "I picked it up...."

"Thanks."

Milton said: "My dear sir—Dodd, isn't it?—you should really lie down and let me call a doctor. I feel a grave responsibility for this regrettable affair, and you may be more seriously injured than you think...."

"I couldn't be," said Dodd. "Thanks, though. I'll be seeing you again."

"At least," said Milton, "take my taxi, Mr. Dodd. I told the driver to wait for me under the street-light a block up the street. Perhaps he saw those two miscreants who attacked you and can describe them."

The taxi-driver hadn't and couldn't for the very good reason that he had been sound asleep with a newspaper over his face ever since Milton had left him. He awoke, complaining bitterly, and drove Dodd over to Pearl Street.

Dodd got out at Fourth and walked down to Sixth.

CHAPTER FOUR

MAMA MANDALAY

THE HOUSE at 619 was old and gaunt and bleak with the top-heavy fretwork of its second story making a bulged, frowning brow over the narrow slits of windows on the first floor. There was an old-fashioned iron picket fence in front, enclosing two precise oblongs of faded lawn separated by a narrow cement walk.

The gate was open and Dodd went through it and on up the high, shadowed stairs to the front porch. The front door had a long frosted-glass panel and light showed very faintly through it.

Dodd grinned a little to himself, feeling the skin stretch taut across his swollen lips, and punched the door-bell in a patterned series of rings—two long ones, two short ones, and then another long. The street was quiet, and he could hear the trilling of the bell plainly.

The light behind the glass panel grew brighter, and then the door opened and clinked against a chain that held it. A dry, thin voice said: "You don't get in here without a warrant."

Dodd said: "Hi, Mama."

"Dodd!"

The chain clinked again, and the door swung wide. Dodd stepped into a narrow, high-ceilinged hall.

"Still getting tough with cops, Mama?"

"I can afford to now, Dodd," Mama Mandalay said. She was a thin, incredibly wrinkled little woman. She was dressed in a black silk wrapper, and she was wearing carpet slippers. Her hair was pulled up into a tight, small knot on the top of her head. Her eyes, almost hidden in folds of wrinkled, parchment-like skin, were black and beady and incredibly wise.

"Been fighting, Dodd?" she asked, and then without waiting for an answer: "Come on in here."

She snapped a switch and led the way into a living-room that opened off the hall. The furniture was as old-fashioned as the house, with gnarled heavy legs and plum colored plush upholstery.

Mama Mandalay went to a cupboard and took out a bottle of whiskey and a water glass and put them on the table beside Dodd's chair. Dodd poured the water glass half-full and drank the whiskey in two swift gulps. It burned like quick flame in his throat, expanded into a slow glowing ball in his stomach. The ache in his head lessened slightly.

Mama Mandalay was sitting on the couch, watching him unblinkingly. "They gave you quite a working over, Dodd, but no more than you deserved, probably. You always were nosy."

High heels tapped on the stairs, and a girl stopped in the doorway in dramatic startlement. "Oh, I'm sorry! I didn't know you had company!"

She was a very tall, very blonde girl, wearing very sheer silk pajamas, and she stayed in the doorway with the light from the hall behind her, making it obvious that she had a nicely proportioned figure.

Mama Mandalay said thinly: "I told you before that this is a decent place. You want to wander around the halls, you put on more clothes. Beat it."

The girl shrugged her shoulders haughtily and her heels tap-tapped up the stairs again.

"She's no good," said Mama Mandalay. "And I should know what I'm talking about. I'm going to throw her out one of these days. What do you want with me, Dodd?"

"A girl's name. Not that one's, though. This one is small and dark and slim. Has black hair and wears it in a long bob with bangs in front. Dancer or entertainer of some kind."

"Nobody like that around here."

"Now, Mama," said Dodd. "If you've had her around here, it's important. She's lying down in the police morgue now. Murdered."

Mama Mandalay didn't move, didn't even blink. After a long minute, she said, "Ah!" with a soft exhalation of breath. She got up and got another glass out of the cupboard. She poured whiskey from the bottle in it, put some more in Dodd's glass. She drank it as he did, with a quick up-fling of her head that showed wrinkle-lines stretched white across her scrawny throat.

"Maybe it isn't the same girl," Dodd said. "I identified her by a special dance-girdle. It was sent to this address."

Mama Mandalay nodded stiffly. "Yes. She was wearing it tonight while she pressed her dress—before she went out. Her name was Lulu Trent."

Dodd nodded once to himself, triumphantly, and watched her silently.

MAMA MANDALAY said: "She was decent, Dodd. Only trouble with her was that she thought she knew too many of the answers. She didn't."

"Where did she work?" Dodd asked.

"Harry Trill's place."

"So," said Dodd slowly. "Harry Trill, hey?"

"Did a song-and-dance solo."

"Harry Trill," said Dodd. "Well, well. Harry used to manage a string of fighters before he got that place of his. Still got a couple of them around, hasn't he?"

"Yeah. Dutchy and Lug—a couple of punk welters. They fight each other in preliminaries once in a while and take turns winning. They're bums."

"Dutchy and Lug," said Dodd. "Yes, yes. Yes, indeed. Have you got a pair of brass knuckles, Mama?"

"Sure."

She went out of the room, and Dodd heard her open and shut a drawer. She came back with the brass knuckles and gave them to Dodd. He put his fingers through the metal loops and doubled his fist experimentally.

"O.K.," he said and went into the hall.

Mama Mandalay took her right hand out of her wrapper pocket. She was holding a revolver—a .38 Colt Police Special. "Take this along, too, Dodd."

Dodd put the gun in his hip pocket. "Thanks. Be seeing you, Mama."

He opened the door and stepped out on the porch. There was a flat, smashing report from across the street. The bullet hit the glass panel of the door beside him at an angle and instead of boring a hole through it, blew out a piece of glass the size of a man's outspread hand.

The broken glass jangled on the floor. Dodd dropped on his hands and knees and scuttled back into the hall.

"Turn off that light!"

Even as he said the words, Mama Mandalay clicked the switch. Dodd pulled the .38 out of his pocket and knelt against the door-post. He could hear Mama Mandalay's harsh, even breathing over his shoulder.

"Where?" she asked.

"In the alley over there."

There was a quick streak of flame from the alley-mouth. The bullet chunked into the wooden part of the door inches from Dodd's face, went through, and hit something that jangled musically at the back of the hall. Dodd fired back instantly. The echoes roared in the hall, and the smell of powder smoke was thinly acrid.

"Hit him?" Mama Mandalay asked.

"No. The gun pulled over when I shot."

Upstairs a girl started to scream hysterically.

"Stop that, you damned canary!" Mama Mandalay shouted.

The gun across the street banged again, and the bullet knocked another piece of glass out of the panel. Dodd moved the door back and gathered his feet under him.

"No." Mama Mandalay's fingers dug into Dodd's shoulder. "Don't try to rush him, Dodd. He'd have you against the light. Smoke him out of there."

Dodd rested the short barrel of the revolver against the door-post and fired twice, aiming carefully. Something in the alley tipped over with a jangling crash.

"Hah!" said Mama Mandalay. "Made him jump!"

Dodd waited, staring with squinted eyes at the black pocket of the alley-mouth. A siren began to wail, faint and eery in the distance.

"Those damned radio cars," Mama Mandalay said. "You beat it out the back way, Dodd. I don't want you around here when the cops come. Wait until I get you some more cartridges."

Her slippers shuffled away. Dodd stayed where he was, staring intently at the alley mouth. The siren was much closer now, coming fast.

Mama Mandalay came back and said: "Here. Out the back way now. Quick. Be careful where you leave that gun. It's registered in my name."

"I'll bring it back."

"Mail it back. Don't come around here again. You always bring trouble with you. Careful. Here's the door. Over that fence and over the next one and then across a yard and through a hedge and you'll be in Garnet Street. Keep going."

"Thanks, Mama," Dodd said in a whisper.

The siren welled up to a driving, deafening wail. Dodd ran through the black shadows of the yard toward the high board fence.

CHAPTER FIVE

WITH A PAIR OF BRASS KNUCKS

HARRY TRILL'S place—*Trill's Grill*—was closed now. The green neon blinker on the roof had been turned off, and the graveled parking-lot was empty of cars, but dim light showed through the shutters that masked the front door.

Dodd took the gun out of his hip pocket and put it in the left-hand pocket of his coat. He slipped the brass knuckles on his right hand and tapped with them on the glass of the door. The sound was a metallic clatter in the quiet emptiness of the street. He had to tap again and then a third time before the shutters moved and a face appeared behind the glass.

The face had a flat nose and thickened lips, and the eyes, under scarred lumpy brows, were narrowed angrily. The face jerked sideways in an unmistakable command for Dodd to go away.

Dodd pulled his hat brim low to cover his own features and tapped again, harder, with the brass knuckles.

The lock clicked, and the door opened six inches.

"Beat it," the man inside ordered gruffly. "Beat it, dope. This joint has been closed for two hours. It's after four in the morning, or can't you tell time?"

Dodd thrust his shoulder hard against the door, forcing it open, and stepped into a narrow entry-hall with white walls and a livid green carpet on the floor.

"Hey!" said the other man. "What—"

Dodd hit him with an overhand right, putting all he had into the blow. The brass knuckles took the man squarely on his half-open mouth. He spun around once and dropped on his hands and knees.

Teeth came out of his mouth and made white, glistening dots on the green rug, and then blood came out after them in a welling gush.

Dodd took one step forward and deliberately kicked him in the temple. The force of the kick turned the man over in mid-air, and he flopped on his back and stayed there, unmoving. The blood still welled out of his broken mouth.

Dodd watched him for a moment in a thoughtfully calculating way, and then he hooked his toe under one of the man's arm-pits and flipped him over on his stomach so he wouldn't choke to death on his own blood.

A voice from another room said: "Lug! What the hell are you doing in there—wrecking the joint?"

Footsteps sounded approaching along a hall, and Dodd was waiting in front of the rear door of the foyer when the second man came through it. The man stopped, but not soon enough.

Dodd hit him with the same overhand right. The man went backwards into the wall, and Dodd caught him with a short right hook when he rebounded. There was the crack of breaking bone on the second blow, and the man spilled down against the wall like a loosely filled sack.

Dodd watched the two of them for a second and then said softly: "How do you like it, boys?"

He took the .38 out of his pocket and, holding it in his left hand, went through the door and quietly down the hall through which the second man had approached the foyer. The door to the bar-room and dance floor was at his left, and at his right there was another narrower door masked with green drapes.

Dodd pushed the drapes aside and went softly up a narrow, dark flight of stairs. The door at the top was open, and Dodd slid quietly through it and into Harry Trill's office.

It was a nice office. There was a divan covered with dark, richly brocaded cloth in one corner and an overstuffed chair that matched it in the opposite one. There was a stream-lined water cooler and, in the center of the room, a flat modernistic desk.

Harry Trill was sitting behind the desk, mumbling to himself as he added a column of figures in the big leather-bound ledger he had open in front of him. He was an enormously fat man, and his face was a formless quivering blob under the smooth greasy dome of his bald head. Little rolls of glistening flesh crowded out over the top of his stiff collar.

"Get out," he said absently, not looking up. "I told you I was busy—" He sensed something wrong then and jerked his head up and stared at Dodd.

Dodd didn't say anything, and there was no sound in the room until the thick fountain pen dropped out of Harry Trill's fingers and made a little clatter rolling across the desk.

"Dodd," said Harry Trill, and cleared his throat with a sudden gasping cough. "What—what— I mean, you startled me, coming in so quietly...."

Dodd cocked the .38. "Keep your hands on top of the desk."

Harry Trill got another breath. "Dodd, what's the matter with you? I mean, what's the idea?"

Dodd said: "You fat rat, do you think you can pull your snide tricks on me and get away with it?"

"Wait, now," said Harry Trill quickly. "Wait, Dodd. I mean, I don't know what you're talking about. You—you look like somebody beat you up...."

"Surprise, surprise," said Dodd.

There were sudden beads of sweat on Harry Trill's face. "Lug and Dutchy! They beat *you* up!"

"How'd you ever guess it?" Dodd asked.

"Wait!" said Harry Trill frantically. "Wait, now! I mean, this is all a mistake!"

"A bad one," Dodd agreed. "For you."

"Wait, Dodd! Listen, now! I can explain—"

"Stand up."

"Ah?" said Trill in a choking gasp.

Dodd moved the revolver. "Stand up, unless you want to take it sitting down."

Harry Trill half rose, holding onto the desk. "No, no! Dodd, you can't—"

Dodd took a long step closer and struck with his right hand. It was a slashing circular blow that hit Trill on the bridge of his nose. It knocked him clear over his chair, and he slammed down, half lying, on the divan. The springs made a sudden groaning *whang* under his weight.

He lay there, his head propped up awkwardly against one of the cushions. He had both hands over the lower part of his face. Blood from his shattered nose squeezed out between his fingers and rolled down sluggishly and stained the white starched cuffs of his dress shirt. His eyes glistened with fascinated terror. He tried to speak and choked wetly.

DODD sat down on the corner of the desk. He kept the gun in his left hand pointed casually at Trill. There was a cut-glass decanter sitting on a tray beside the ledger, and Dodd pulled the stopper out—his fingers clumsy and stiff in the loops of the brass knuckles—and took a swig of the liquor it contained.

"Not bad," he said. "Start talking, Harry."

"Dodd, listen! It's all a mistake! I mean, I didn't know anything—"

Dodd pointed the .38 at Trill's battered face and pulled the trigger. He had his thumb on the hammer, and he didn't let it fall on the cartridge in the chamber. He pulled the hammer back to full cock again.

"Don't!" Harry Trill screamed. "Don't do that! Your thumb will slip...."

"It certainly will," Dodd agreed, "the next time. Tell me all about it, Harry. All about Lulu Trent and Lug and Dutchy beating me up and taking pot shots at me."

"Pot shots!" Harry Trill gasped. "No! They never did that, Dodd! I swear—"

"Don't swear. Just talk. Now!"

"Wait. Give me a chance, Dodd! Look, there was a guy coming in the place all the time and sort of hinting around. I mean, he had a proposition, and after he sounded me out for a while he came across with it. He had some M, see? He didn't know what to do with it. He wanted a market."

"M," Dodd repeated. "Morphine, you mean?"

"Yes. So I said—said I could maybe handle it. He started bringin' it around. It was liquid, not powder—pure stuff. Like they use in a hospital. This guy brought it in every week."

"Keep talking."

"So—so I thought maybe I'd like to get a bigger supply of the stuff. I didn't know this guy—I didn't know where he was getting it. So I had Dutchy and then Lug and then both of 'em try to follow him. He slipped 'em every time. He was too smart. I tried it myself, and he slipped me."

"Get around to Lulu Trent."

"Yes, yes. Listen. She was working here, see, and she's kind of halfway smart. So I put it up to her. I'll give her a couple hundred if she can spot the guy for me. I thought he wouldn't be suspicious of a girl trailing him, and I was right. She got closer than we did. She trailed him to that old warehouse district, but it's dark down there and there's nobody on the streets, and she missed him somewhere. She's been hanging around down there trying to spot him again, and then tonight...."

"Yeah," said Dodd. "Tonight."

"I heard—there was a skirt biffed down there...."

"That accident set-up didn't fool you, did it? You knew the guy Lulu Trent was trying to follow had caught her at it and knocked her brains in."

"No! No, I didn't—"

Dodd clicked the revolver hammer again.

"Don't *do* that!" Harry Trill screamed frantically. "It'll slip.... Yes. Yes! I figured that, and I sent Lug and Dutchy down to look for that bird, and they mistook you for him!"

"I'll bet they'll be more careful next time," Dodd observed. "Now, what about the bird with the morphine? Don't hold out on me, Harry. My thumb's getting tired."

"Listen, I never saw him before he come in here. I mean, I don't know who he is. He said his name was Banner. He's a tall guy—tall as you—but skinnier. He wears glasses, and he keeps his hair slicked down with a lot of grease, and he's got a black mole right at the corner of his mouth. He drinks like a fish, but he ain't on the dope."

"How old?"

"About as old as you are—maybe not so old. Listen, Dodd. I mean, you got to listen to me. This was all a mistake that Dutchy and Lug made —"

Dodd got up off the desk. He picked Harry Trill up by the front of his coat and hit him with a right upper-cut. Harry Trill hit the back of the divan and went clear over it. He landed in the corner with a sodden crash. His feet stayed in sight, sticking straight and motionless up over the back of the divan.

Dodd watched the feet for a moment and then went back to the desk and picked up the telephone. He dialed the number of police headquarters, requested Hennessey, and when he got him, said: "This is Dodd, Hennessey. Is Meekins there?"

"Sure. Listen, Dodd, you remember you promised to pay him tomorrow? On account of you said you would, I lent him another two bucks, and he promised—"

"Yes, yes," Dodd said impatiently. "Put him on the wire, will you?"

"Hi, boss," Meekins said. "Any luck?"

"Yes. I identified the girl. Her name is Lulu Trent, but keep it under your hat. Now I want you to find a guy for me. His name, he says, is Banner. He's tall, wears glasses, keeps his hair slicked down. Has a black mole at the corner of his mouth. He's a great guy to kick around night clubs, and he absorbs alcohol like blotting paper. Find me that guy. I want him in a hurry."

"Listen, Dodd. Is he the bird who did the job—"

"Never mind that. You find him. Get busy."

"Well… O.K. You better not play around—"

"I'm going home. Call me there when you spot him, and if I don't answer, keep right on calling until I do."

CHAPTER SIX

THIS WILL KILL YOU!

IT WAS dawn now, and a thin, misty grayness overlay everything. It changed the street in front of Dodd's apartment building until, familiar as it was to him, it looked new and strange and in some way, mysterious.

He went wearily up the cement steps and into the lobby, and Mr. Grillman was waiting there, still in his suit-coat and night-shirt, sitting huddled in front of the desk, looking old and very tired.

"Oh, hell!" Dodd exclaimed. "I forgot all about calling you and telling you…."

Grillman smiled wanly. "It's all right, Mr. Dodd. Mr. Brown got home a long time ago. I put him to bed and called the doctor, and the doctor said he would be fine if he stayed in bed and rested for a few days. I want to thank you again for being so kind as to help him and me. I didn't know what to do…."

Dodd leaned against the desk. He was dead-tired, and his head ached with a steady, ringing beat that made the whole room vibrate in front of his eyes.

"What are you sitting up for?" he asked. "There isn't anything else wrong, is there?"

"Mr. Pennant," Grillman said. "He's not playing his radio."

"Swell," said Dodd. "Maybe I can get some sleep."

Grillman shook his head worriedly. "I can't understand it. I know he's in. I saw him come in about a half-hour ago, and he was very drunk. He always plays his radio when he's drunk, but he's not playing it now. Do you suppose I should ask him if he's all right, Mr. Dodd?"

Dodd said: "No. Let well enough...." He stood there for a long moment, both palms pressed flat against his temples. "What did you say this bird's name was, Mr. Grillman?"

"Pennant. Mr. Pennant."

"Pennant," Dodd repeated slowly. "Well, well. I don't think I've ever seen him around here. Is he a tall guy who wears glasses and keeps his hair slicked down with grease?"

"Why, yes," said Grillman.

"Have a black mole at the corner of his mouth?"

Grillman nodded. "Yes."

"Well, well," Dodd repeated. "He always plays his radio when he comes home tight, you say?"

"Yes."

"But he's not playing it now?"

"No," said Grillman. "And I know he's there. I saw him come in, staggering. I was a little worried about him, and I listened at his apartment door, and I could hear him moving around inside, opening and shutting drawers and banging things around."

"Is that a fact?" Dodd said. "Mr. Grillman, would you like to do me a favor?"

"Why, certainly!" said Grillman. "I'd be only too glad, Mr. Dodd, after all you've done...."

"Good. Have you got your master key?"

"Why, yes."

"All right. Here's what I want you to do. In just exactly two minutes, you go to the door of his apartment and knock on it. Never mind if he tells you to go away. You say that you're worried about him and that you're going to unlock the door and come in and see if he's O.K."

"But—but—"

"Will you do that for me?"

"Well, yes. But I don't understand...."

"Never mind. I'll tell you about it later. Start your act in just two minutes."

DODD ran across the lobby and down the front steps. He turned to the right and trotted to the mouth of the alley that ran along the north side of the apartment building. There was a row of ash cans sitting against the wall, and Dodd sat down carefully on top of one of them and waited.

It was very quiet in the alley until one of the windows on the ground floor of the apartment slid up cautiously and slowly. A man began to climb out of the window. He was very awkward about it. He got one leg through and then the other and then sat on the sill for a moment. He finally jumped down into the alley.

He staggered a step or two before he caught his balance. He was holding a bottle in his right hand.

"Hi, there," said Dodd. "Remember me, Mr. Brown?"

Brown whirled around with a wheezing, agonized gasp. He stared unbelievingly at Dodd, still sitting on top of the ash can, and then turned and started to run down the alley.

"Hey!" Dodd said sharply. "Stop!"

Brown kept on running desperately. Dodd drew the police revolver out of his hip pocket and fired.

Brown's legs crumpled under him, and he fell flat on his face. Dodd stared at him in incredulous amazement. He had fired straight up in the air. The bullet couldn't possibly have come anywhere near Brown.

Dodd got off the ash can and walked slowly and cautiously toward where Brown lay, holding the revolver poised for another shot.

Brown didn't move. Dodd knelt down beside him and turned him over. Brown's eyes were wide open, bulging horribly, and his lips were pulled back in a twisted, set grimace.

"Damned if he didn't have a bad heart," Dodd muttered to himself.

The bottle Brown had been carrying hadn't broken, and Dodd picked it up and looked at it. It had an old fashioned gaudily red label that said *Milton's Magic Mixture—A Positive Cure for Drunkenness.* There was no formula printed on the label, no indication at all of what the magic mixture might be.

"Well, I'll be damned!" said Dodd blankly.

"Mr. Dodd!" Grillman shouted hysterically. He was leaning out the window through which Brown had appeared. "Mr. Pennant is—is sitting here and—he's dead! He's got a knife sticking right in him, and the blood…. Mr. Dodd, what will I do?"

"Stop yelling," Dodd said.

"Who—who's that there? Why—it's Mr. Brown! Is he hurt? What's the matter with him?"

"He had a heart attack," Dodd said absently.

"Oh!" said Grillman. "Oh, oh! This is horrible! What *will* I do, Mr. Dodd?"

"Go on back in the lobby."

Dodd got up and walked to the mouth of the alley. He was still staring at the bottle of Magic Mixture, as though he were trying to convince himself that it really existed.

He was going up the steps of the apartment building when tires squealed behind him, and Milton shouted: "Oh, Mr. Dodd! Wait!"

He came puffing across the walk.

"Mr. Dodd, I've just been down to the jail, and I find that you alone are responsible for having Brown released from custody, and I want to thank you again from the depths of my heart and apologize for the way I spoke to you earlier this morning before I understood what had happened. I thought I'd drop in here on my way home and see how poor Brown was making out. That infernal heart condition of his is an awful thing."

"It's not bothering him now," Dodd said. "He's lying back in the alley there—dead."

"Eh?" Milton said, staring. "You said—dead?"

"As a door nail. Take a look at this bottle."

Milton's plump face turned pale. "What—what—that—"

"Now just why," Dodd asked, "should a man who can't drink at all commit murder and burglary to get hold of a bottle of medicine that is supposed to cure drunkenness?"

"I—I don't know.... I'm horribly shocked, Mr. Dodd, to hear about Brown. I must go and see if I can help...."

"Oh, no," said Dodd. "Do you see what I've got in my other hand? It's a gun, and it's loaded. You march up these steps and right into the lobby. Go on."

Grillman was waiting for them inside the door, wringing his hands in helpless panic. "Mr. Dodd, what will I do? The tenants are asking questions and yelling at me, and your telephone is ringing and ringing...."

"Tell the tenants to shut up and let the telephone ring," Dodd ordered. "Milton, come over here to the desk."

MILTON seemed to have shrunk inside his top coat. His face was the color of wet clay. He walked meekly over to the desk and stood there, shivering a little.

Dodd put the bottle of Magic Mixture down on top of the desk and pointed at it. "Start explaining."

Milton took a deep breath and started, stuttering over the words in his haste to get them out. When he had finished, Dodd reached over the desk, picked up the apartment-house telephone and dialed police headquarters and asked for Hennessey.

When Hennessey answered, he said: "This is Dodd. Pull Meekins off whatever telephone he's using and put him on this line, will you, Hennessey?"

Meekins' voice said angrily: "Well, why didn't you go home like you said you would? I've been working my head off. I checked with the gas company and the telephone company and the city directory and called everybody I knew, and I couldn't find any trace of any guy by the name of Banner who looked like you said this guy did. And then Harry Shuman from the Four Deuces Club called me back just now and said he had been thinking about the matter and that there was a guy by the name of Flag that had come around there a few times and got oiled. So I thought maybe this is one of those smart guys who changes his name by using some other word that means the same thing. So I checked on all the Flags and couldn't get the right answer, and then I looked up 'banner' in the dictionary and I found—"

"That a guy named Pennant who answers to the description I gave you lives in this apartment building," Dodd finished.

"Oh, hell," Meekins said in a discouraged voice.

"Never mind," Dodd comforted. "He doesn't live here any more. Are Limes and Lillicott still there?"

"Sure."

"Call them. I want to talk to them."

THERE was a pause, and then Limes' voice said gruffly: "Well? What the hell do you want now, Dodd?"

"I want to apologize for making you let Brown loose."

"Now you listen, Dodd," Limes said. "I'm not going to take any more ribbing—"

"This is straight," Dodd said. "Brown killed that girl, but not with his car. He batted her over the head with the same wrench Meekins found in his back seat."

"What? What did you say? Lillicott! Get on that extension and listen to this!"

There was a click, and Lillicott said: "I'm listening."

Dodd went on: "Meekins and I were right, too. Brown was framed. He framed himself."

"What!" Limes yelled. "Are you crazy? Why, nobody would be so nuts—"

"Shut up and listen to me. That frame was so obvious—Brown meant it to be—that your case wouldn't have stood up in court for five minutes. Brown couldn't drink and had plenty of proof that he couldn't. There were no skid-marks on the pavement and hardly any blood where the accident was supposed to have occurred. The dents in the car fenders didn't match the places where the girl had bruises and cuts. There was no way her face could have gotten mashed like it was, and there was no way Brown could have gotten bumped on the back of the bean as he was.

"Any defense attorney would have made you two look like a pair of clowns if you had dared show up in court with that kind of case. But the fact that he was so obviously framed gave Brown an apparently clear bill of health. That's why he fixed things the way he did."

"Well, why?" Limes demanded. "I mean, why did he kill the girl in the first place?"

"I'll tell you. Brown worked for the Milton Medicine Company for thirty-odd years. He knew a guy by the name of Sellers, who is the night watchman of the old Milton warehouse on San Pedro. Sellers is a feeble old boy and has a lot of trouble sleeping in the day-time. But he was too conscientious to sneak a sleep at night unless someone was watching the place. Brown used to go down there twice a week and sit around while Sellers napped. Probably he did it at first just as a favor to Sellers, but he got to prowling around in the warehouse while Sellers slept, and he found something."

"What?" Limes asked.

"A medicine called Milton's Magic Mixture. It's a cure for alcoholism."

"For what?" Limes said.

"Alcoholism. A cure for guys who drink too much too often."

"Aw!" Limes said. "What are you trying to give me? What would Brown want with a cure for drunks?"

"If you'll shut up I'll tell you. This Magic Mixture is really fancy stuff. After you take it a while, you don't want to drink any more liquor. It absolutely cures you."

"Huh?" said Limes. "Say, I don't believe just takin' any medicine would—"

"Taking this medicine would. It's full of morphine. It cured you of the liquor habit by giving you the dope habit."

"Hey!" Limes shouted. "They can't do that! It's illegal to put dope—"

"Yes, yes. Now it is. The Milton Company put out this particular medicine fifty years ago. That was in the hey-day of patent medicines when you could shake up any old kind of concoction and start selling it. This mixture sold like wildfire, naturally. The poor guys that took it had to keep right on, not knowing what was in it of course. The government finally got curious about its success and analyzed it and issued a stop order against the Milton Company. The mixture was a bit too much of a good thing even then. So the Milton Company called it all in—all they had sold and distributed and all they had made ready to sell. There were several carloads of it. It was all stored in the warehouse."

Limes gave a strangled shout. "What! You mean—morphine—in that warehouse—carloads—"

"Yes. As soon as Brown saw it, he knew what it was and what was in it. He knew he had something. So, every time he went down there, while old Sellers slept, Brown would carry a few cases of bottles out to his car and then bring it home with him and extract the morphine from it."

"Oh, oh, oh!" Limes said in an awed voice. "You hear what he said, Lillicott? Carloads of morphine!"

DODD said: "Brown didn't get around much—he couldn't—and he didn't know where to sell the stuff. But there's a guy named Pennant or Banner or Flag—take your choice—who lived here and was quite the boy for prowling around night clubs and other spots. Brown sounded him out, and Pennant went for the idea. He said he could find a market for the morphine, and he did find one."

Limes was swearing in an undertone. "Dodd! Now don't you hold out on me! What market? Who?"

"Harry Trill."

"Oh, that fat rat! That dirty fat rat! Wait until I get my hands on him!"

"He's not feeling so well these days. You'll probably find him in some near-by hospital with a couple of chums of his by the name of Dutchy and Lug. Harry decided that he wanted more of that morphine and cheaper. It was pure stuff—in liquid form. So Harry started trying to find out where Pennant was getting it. He and his chums tried to trail Pennant, but Pennant was too smart for them. Harry had a girl working in his joint by the name of Lulu Trent. She's down in the police morgue right now."

"What? Lulu Trent! Is that her name? Lillicott, are you writing this down?"

"Yes," said Lillicott. "Keep that big mouth of yours shut so I can hear what Dodd says. Go on, Dodd."

"Lulu Trent had better luck than Harry and his boys. Better luck at trailing Pennant, I mean. Harry put her up to following Pennant, but he didn't tell her why. She located Pennant down in the warehouse district somewhere, and she's been hanging around there nights trying to spot where he went. He was going to the warehouse to help Brown with the medicine. Brown had to be careful about exerting himself, and besides they could carry twice as much of the Mixture if they used Pennant's car, too. Last night she located Pennant at the Milton warehouse. But she got too nosy, and Brown and Pennant caught her snooping around. Lulu was a smarty, she thought, and she was probably set to pull a shake-down on her own hook. Brown was panic-stricken, and he cracked her over the head with that wrench—too hard.

"Sellers was asleep all this time. He's absolutely innocent. So Brown and Pennant had a corpse on their hands. Pennant must have known Lulu from seeing her at Harry Trill's, so they understood the set-up. They framed this phony accident business to throw suspicion away from Brown—as it actually did once it became clear that he had been framed. Pennant cracked him with the wrench to make it look better, and it was Pennant who called the cops."

"Pennant!" said Limes. "Brown! I want those birds! I'm gonna put out a call—"

"Later, later," Dodd said. "Harry Trill, when he heard about the accident, sent his chums, Dutchy and Lug, down to the warehouse district to look for Pennant. They mistook me for him in the dark. We're about the same height, and both of us wear glasses. Pennant, in the meantime, had found out where Lulu Trent lived and had gone over there, trying to make sure just who it was who was backing her. Either she didn't tell him it was Harry Trill or else Pennant didn't believe her. Anyway, I came along pretty soon. The place belongs to Mama Mandalay, and just to be funny I used that old police ring that you used to use, Limes, when you were shaking Mama down at her place on Fulton."

"That's a damned lie!" Limes yelled.

"All right, all right. Pennant heard the ring and thought I was expected. He did a little window peeking and recognized me. He'd seen me around here. So he decided I was in on the business with Lulu Trent and blew a few shots at me."

"Hah!" said Limes. "*That* was the riot down on Pearl Street! Lillicott, I told you it was that damned Dodd—"

"Let me finish. Brown was pretty well scared over the murder business. The only person who could connect him in any way with the morphine or Lulu Trent was Pennant. So Brown, after alibiing himself with a doctor and what-not—though his heart was on the fritz, he wasn't as bad as he was making out at the moment—laid for Pennant when he came home and stabbed him. I happened along about then, and Brown saw me and dropped dead of a heart attack. He had been under a terrible strain, because after he killed Pennant he had to search Pennant's place to make sure there wasn't any of that Mixture lying around to connect Brown up with Pennant. That's all."

"Oh, no!" Limes shouted furiously. "Oh, no, you don't! That's three deaths, and you're not going to just walk off laughing! You've got a lot more to explain! I want to find you there when I get there, you hear? I mean it, Dodd! If you aren't right there, I'm gonna charge you with obstructing justice and concealing material evidence and being an accessory before and after the fact and—"

"Calm yourself," Dodd said. "I'll be here. Milton, the president of the Milton Medicine Company, is here with me, by the way."

"Milton!" Limes repeated, sputtering. "I want that guy! Storing dope openly in a warehouse! I'm gonna pinch him, and the dope squad is gonna pinch him, and the Bureau of Internal Revenue is gonna pinch him, and the Narcotics Bureau and the Pure Food and Drug and the F.B.I...."

"Now, now," said Dodd. "You are speaking of a client of mine." He put his hand over the mouthpiece of the telephone and looked at Milton. "You *are* a client of mine, aren't you?"

"Eh?" said Milton. "Oh, yes! Absolutely, Mr. Dodd! I—I stand ready to answer for—for this. I know I should have done something about that Mixture, but it was stored there before I was even born, Mr. Dodd! My father stored it. And—and it's been fifty years…. I never dreamed that anyone would remember it or know what it contained…."

"Sure, sure," said Dodd. "Mr. Milton is a client of mine, Limes. He's innocent of any harmful intent, and every time you pinch him I'm going to have to bail him right out again—for a slight fee, of course. Tell Meekins to start making out bail forms. It's about time we stopped fooling around and made us a little money."

COME UP AND KILL ME SOME TIME

DODD HAS A DOLEFUL HANGOVER BUT IT'S NOTHING TO THE HEADACHE THE BENIGHTED BAIL-BONDSMAN ACCUMULATES WHEN HE FINDS HIMSELF IN THE SOAK FOR 50 G'S BAIL. FOR SADIE'S KOOTCH-SHOW HAS JUST BEEN RAIDED AND A COP DRILLED IN THE PROCESS! THE KILLER MAY BE A KOOTCH-SHOW COMIC BUT HE'S NO JOKE TO DODD.

CHAPTER ONE

SADIE GETS SOCKED

DODD HAD both arms wound around his middle. He was sure that if he didn't keep a strangle-hold on his stomach it would fall out and bounce on the floor in front of him.

He came wavering down the hall toward his office, bent nearly double, wincing at each step. He was a tall man with wide shoulders and a long homely face. He wore horn-rimmed glasses patched on the bridge with a piece of white adhesive tape.

Reaching his office door, he fumbled back-handed for his keys, moaning in a minor tone to himself. He got the door unlocked finally, went headlong through the anteroom and plopped himself down in the chair behind his desk.

"Oh," he said. "Oh, oh, oh."

His head felt as big and unwieldy as a barrage balloon, and the mere thought of the taste in his mouth made him shudder. It was all the fault of a character by the name of Henry Rally. Rally was a book-maker, and the night before he had celebrated his twenty-fifth arrest and acquittal on that charge. Dodd, being Rally's bondsman, had been included in the party that followed.

Rally's tastes ran to brandy with beer for a chaser and blondes with big breasts. Dodd moaned at the memory and put his head down on the desk and abandoned himself to despair and suffering.

The telephone on the desk rang shrilly. It felt exactly as though someone had slugged him on the ear with a sledge hammer. He yelped in agony and fumbled hastily to get the phone off its cradle before it could ring again.

"Dodd," he said feebly. "Bail bonds."

"Hart speaking. Take this down."

Dodd found a pencil. "Right, Lieutenant."

"*Grass Shack* on Dorado. Two for ten nineteen and one for ten twenty. Judge Mizner in Department 12. Vice squad from Central. Rolling now."

Dodd scribbled busily. "Thanks, Lieutenant." He put the telephone back on its cradle and touched his throbbing temples gingerly with his finger tips.

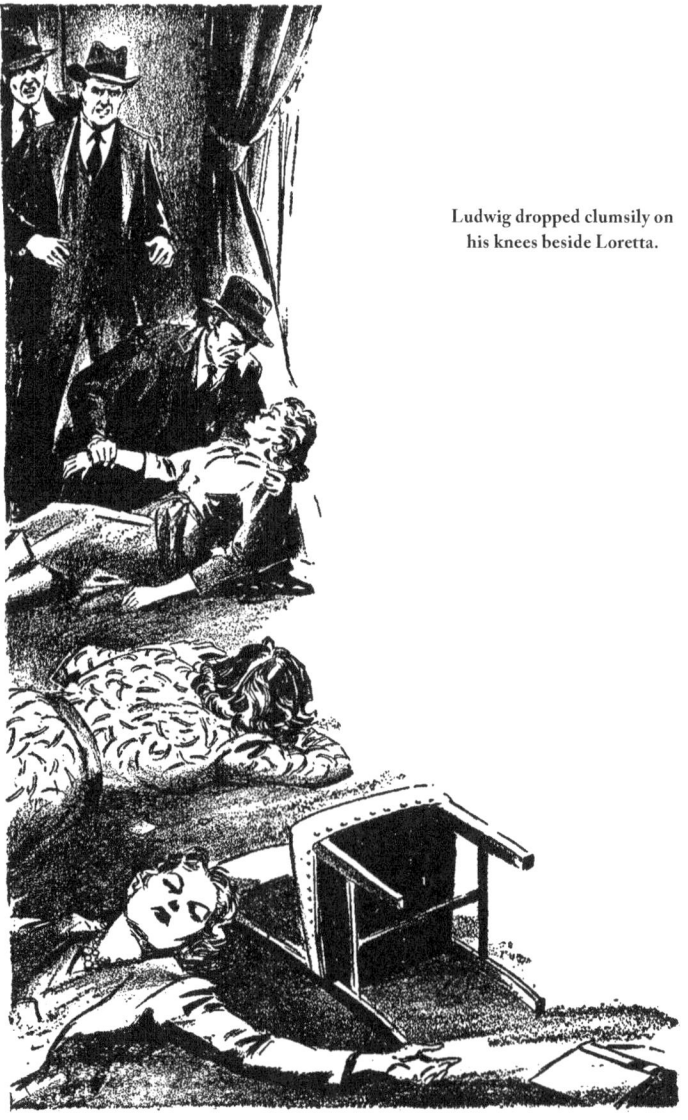

Ludwig dropped clumsily on his knees beside Loretta.

"Brandy," he muttered to himself. "Beer for a chaser. *Ugh!*"

He picked up the telephone again and dialed a number. After a moment a polite voice said into his ear: "Police department."

"Sergeant Hennessey," Dodd requested. "Booking desk."

The line clicked, and another voice said: "Sergeant Hennessey speaking."

"This is Dodd, Hennessey. Is Meekins there?"

"Naw, Dodd. He went out to get a beer. Say, what about that drawing?"

"Drawing?" Dodd repeated.

"Sure. On the lottery."

"Lottery?" Dodd said vaguely.

"You know. That there Luxembourg lottery. I got three tickets. When they gonna have the drawing?"

Dodd's bloodshot eyes narrowed behind his glasses. "Any day now," he answered. "See you later."

He depressed the breaker bar on the phone, let it up and dialed another number. He waited quite awhile, and then a voice answered shortly: "Well, what?"

"This is Dodd. Is Meekins there?"

"Yeah, he's here. Hold it."

DODD waited again, and after a moment Meekins said: "Hello, boss. How you feel?"

"Lovely. Listen, you rat. Did you sell Hennessey some of those Luxembourg lottery tickets you bummed off Pottsey Hanks the last time we bailed him out?"

"Well, not exactly. You see, I owed him some dough, and I give him three tickets, and he canceled—"

"You brainless louse!"

"Well, what's the matter with that?" Meekins demanded in an aggrieved tone. "Them tickets is genuine, and Hennessey's got as good a chance to pull the grand prize—"

"Do you know where Luxembourg is?"

"It's in Africa, ain't it?"

"No!" Dodd said explosively. "It was between France and Germany."

"Oh!" said Meekins. "I see what… Say! You don't think that guy

Hitler grabbed off the grand prize for himself, do you? Why hell, that's illegal! He can't do that!"

"Write him a letter," Dodd advised. "But in the meantime, you give Hennessey his money. You know damned well we can't afford to get him griped at us. And there's something else for you to do. Do you know anything about a place called the *Grass Shack?*"

"Sure. That's the name of Sadie Wade's new kootch show down on Dorado Road at the beach."

"I thought that was it. The vice squad is going to pull the joint, and I want you—"

"Oh, no," Meekins interrupted.

"What?" Dodd said.

"They ain't gonna pull Sadie."

"And why not?"

"Because it ain't her turn yet."

"What do you mean, stupid?"

"She ain't supposed to be knocked over any more than once a season, and they got her once already."

"Never mind that. Lieutenant Hart just called and said the vice squad was on its way out there now."

"Sadie's gonna be mad," Meekins warned.

"I don't care whether she's mad or not. You get over to Judge Mizner's court and bail her out when they bring her in. She and her barker will be booked on violation of Section 1019. One dancer will be booked on violation of Section 1020. You know what the bail will be, so get the papers fixed up and give her some snappy service."

"All right. Say listen, boss. The last time I had a hangover a guy told me—"

"Shut up!"

Dodd slammed the phone back in its cradle. He put his head down on his desk again, and the smooth varnished wood felt luxuriously cool and soothing against his cheek. After a while he began to snore in muted little flutters.

The telephone went off and slammed him in the ear. Dodd jumped a foot in the air and came down so hard he cracked his neck. He sputtered profanity, grabbing for the instrument with both hands.

"Hello! Dodd speaking."

"This is Sadie Wade, Dodd. Have you got a sawed-off little monkey with a bald knob working for you?"

"Sure," Dodd said. "That's Meekins. He's my runner."

"Did you tell him to bail me out?"

"Certainly. I hope everything—"

"Well, why don't he do it? You think I've got nothing to do with my time but sit around in this damned rat-trap of a jail?"

"What?" said Dodd. "What's this? Didn't Meekins bail you out?"

"He did not. He won't do it."

"Well, why not? I told him to. Where is he?"

"Right here. Tell him again. And make it plain this time. I want bail, and I want it right now!"

Meekins' voice said: "Listen here, boss—"

"You scum! Didn't I tell you to bail Sadie out?"

"Sure you did. But listen—"

"I don't want to listen! Put—up—that—bail!"

There was a crash and a crackling sound from the other end of the line. Meekins protested incoherently: "Here! You can't— Quit shovin'!"

Sadie Wade's harsh voice snapped in Dodd's ear. "Did you tell him?"

"Yes," said Dodd. "And when I get hold of him I'll do more than tell him. I'm sorry, Sadie. He's a dope, and I guess he probably didn't understand. I'm always ready to give you service any time of the day or night—"

"All right, Dodd. I'm in a hurry now. See you later."

DODD hung up and sighed in a sad, dreary way. He put his elbows on his desk and braced his head in the palms of his hands. In a few moments he dozed off again.

The sun, slanting through the half-closed shutters on the window, woke him. He straightened up cautiously. His head felt better, and he grinned with relief. He went to the cooler and took a leisurely drink of water.

He was filling the glass for the second time when the telephone buzzed commandingly. Dodd picked it up and said cheerfully: "William Dodd speaking."

It was Meekins. "How do you feel now?" he asked.

"All right. Say listen, I want to tell you—"

"Wait a minute," Meekins interrupted. "Go in the front room and look under the leather lounge chair in the northeast corner. The one I usually sit in."

Dodd put the telephone down and obeyed. He felt around awkwardly under the low chair and finally brought his hand out holding a flat pint bottle half-full of bourbon. Carrying it, he went back to the telephone.

"What's the idea of this?"

"It's for you," Meekins told him. "You're gonna need that pretty quick."

Dodd felt a queer chill of apprehension. He sat down carefully behind his desk.

"What, Meekins?"

"You're in soak for fifty thousand smackers."

"Fifty thousand…" Dodd said numbly. "What? *What?*"

"Yeah."

"But I haven't got fifty thousand!"

"You're telling me?" Meekins asked. "But that was the amount of Sadie Wade's bail, and you're signed up for it."

Dodd's face was gray. "Why—why— That *can't* be!"

"Yes, it can."

Dodd swallowed hard. "What—happened?"

"Sadie had a comedian named Tracy workin' for her. A little guy that wore big pants and big shoes and a clown make-up and went around slappin' the gals on the fanny between shakes. You know, anything for a laugh."

"Go on," Dodd said tensely.

"So when the boys rumbled the joint, this Tracy pulls a gun and cracks one of the detectives—Jake Holden—with a slug in the chest and scrams out the back way."

"Oh, oh!" Dodd said in a sick voice.

"Jake ain't dead—yet. But the boys are really mad. They were holding Sadie as a material witness and for aiding and abetting. That's the why of the heavy bail. We didn't do ourselves any good with the cops by puttin' it up."

Dodd exploded. "Why, you—you— What'd you do it for?"

"Ha!" said Meekins. "I tried to tell you, but you were too busy with your hangover and your snappy service. I couldn't argue while Sadie was pushin' me around. You told me to do it, and she knew you did. What was I supposed to answer to that?"

"O.K.," Dodd said slowly. "It's in my lap. I'm sorry I popped off to you."

"That's all right, boss. I know how you felt. But you bought yourself a baby. The cops are griped, and you've signed up for more bail than you can cover, and Sadie's actin' funny."

"What?" Dodd barked. "Funny how?"

"She's worth fifty thousand dollars to us, and I been walkin' around a step-and-a-half behind her. She's steamin' mad, just like I said. I tailed her down to her joint, and I'm across the street in a dog stand now. She's got the itch. I think she's gonna blow on us, boss."

"My God!" Dodd exclaimed. "If she does, and I can't cover that bail...."

"Maybe you'll like it in jail," Meekins said comfortingly.

"Stay right there!" Dodd ordered. "Wait for me! Don't let her get away from that joint of hers!"

He jumped up and started for the door. Halfway there he stopped short, turned around and went back for the whiskey. He slammed out of the office, fumbling with the metal cap on the bottle.

CHAPTER TWO

SOCKED BY SADIE

THE BAY was a great flat blue semi circle that cut into the smooth green of the hills beyond the beach. There was some wind, and the waves wore ruffled white collars of foam as they traveled up to roll themselves over in ponderous playfulness on the sand.

Automobiles shuttled back and forth in squawking lines on the speedway that was divided in the middle by a green parkway. Dodd wormed his battered coupe through the traffic lanes and parked it slantwise at the curb.

It was late Saturday afternoon now, and Dorado Road was winding up for its weekly hoopla. A ferris wheel, already lighted, traveled its endless futile way up and down again, and loudspeakers blared their hoarse invitations everywhere. The sidewalks were thronged with people with pink sunburned faces and peeling noses, and a car went by on the high lattice-work of the roller coaster with a sudden smack-bang and thin trailing whoops from its riders.

Dodd ignored it all. He elbowed his way along, hat crushed down on his head, spectacles balanced precariously on the end of his nose.

He found the *Grass Shack* without any trouble. It was a flat-roofed dingy building with colored life-size photographs of its entertainers plastered all over the front of it. The red curtains across the doorway were closed now, and the spangled ticket box was empty. The place looked battered and rundown and sorry for itself.

Dodd made a right turn and headed across the street toward a glistening white stand with an enormous red sign over it that said: COME IN AND COOL YOUR DOGS WHILE YOU EAT OURS—ONE FOOT OF SUCCULENT SAUSAGE FOR ONE DIME. Dodd dodged around a vendor who was selling candy that looked like pink puff-balls and ducked through the door of the stand.

Aside from the white-uniformed counterman, Meekins had the place all to himself. He was a nondescript little man with a tired, disillusioned air. He was sensitive about his baldness, and he never took his hat off unless the rules required it. He was sitting at the end of the long counter holding a raw pat of hamburg over his right eye. He turned and stared glumly at Dodd with the other.

"Where's Sadie?" Dodd demanded.

"Where's my whiskey?" Meekins countered.

Dodd produced the pint bottle. There was now only about an inch of liquor left in it.

"You must feel a lot better," Meekins said, eyeing it. He removed the cap and took care of the remaining whiskey in one big gulp.

"Where's Sadie?" Dodd demanded again. "Is she still over in her place?"

"No," said Meekins sourly.

"Well, where is she? What happened?"

Meekins removed the hamburg and showed the foundation for a beautiful black eye. The lid had already swollen shut.

"That happened," Meekins said, putting the hamburg back carefully. "Right after I phoned you, she came tearing out of her joint like the place was on fire. I was sitting here, so I hopped out and trailed along—but not far."

"Why not?"

"She turned into that alley down the road, and I put on a big spurt and turned in right after her. She was waitin' for me. She didn't even say hello. She just handed me this mouse."

"She hit you?" Dodd asked.

"And how! She tagged me with an overhand right and knocked me end-over-end. When I picked myself up she was gone, so I came back here. I don't feel so good." Meekins sighed and then added casually: "She had a bag with her."

"A what?"

"A traveling bag. One of them dressing cases."

Dodd said: "She's blowing on us! Come on!"

"Where?" Meekins groaned.

"Over to the *Grass Shack*. We'll see what we can uncover."

Meekins put the hamburg down on the plate in front of him and signaled to the counterman. "Put this back in the icebox. Probably I'll need it again pretty soon."

"Hurry up!" Dodd ordered.

THEY went back across the crowded street and pushed through the faded red curtains that masked the entrance of the *Grass Shack*. There was a narrow wooden door behind the curtains, and Dodd led the way through it into the shadowed dusty dimness of the big room beyond. It was full of long rows of bare wooden benches that faced a small, low stage.

A man was sitting on the edge of the stage swinging his long thin legs dejectedly. He had a hugely swollen red-veined nose and watery-weak little eyes under fiercely bushy brows. He was wearing a checked suit and a double-breasted white vest that had an enormous gold watch chain stretched across it.

"That's Smedley," Meekins told Dodd. "He's Sadie's barker and ticket man. Smedley, this is Dodd. He's my boss."

"All right," said Smedley. "Go ahead."

"Go ahead and what?" Dodd asked.

"Curse me," Smedley said lifelessly. "Insult me. Call me names."

"Why?" Dodd asked blankly.

"Why not?" Smedley inquired. "You might as well. Everybody else does. Nobody has a kind word for me. Everything that happens in the world is my fault personally. I'm to blame no matter what it is."

A woman's voice said shrilly: "You dirty old whiskey-bum!"

Smedley closed his eyes with a martyred air. "Sure. That's right. Go ahead."

The woman came down the aisle between the benches, brushing past Dodd and Meekins as though they didn't exist. She was a big woman with wide, high shoulders and a thickly-set strong-looking body. Her hair was a brassy red and swung loose in a long bob.

"Are you blind?" she demanded of Smedley. "Can't you spot a copper before he shoves his buzzer in your pan?"

"It's my fault," Smedley said. "Sure. Everything is my fault."

"You drooling rum-pot! Why didn't you signal us? You could at least have yelled when they put the arm on you. But, no! Not you!"

"Go ahead," Smedley invited drearily. "I'm to blame."

"You're damned right you are! So just because you didn't tip us off I have to get pinched and dragged through the streets in this outfit! Look at it! Just look!"

Smedley opened his eyes cautiously. She took off an old, stained slicker.

"Go ahead," Smedley said sadly. "Hit me. Knock me down."

"I'll do worse than that! Look at me!"

Smedley peered under one protective arm. She was wearing nothing but a very scanty gilt brassiere and an even scantier gilt G-string.

"What do you think of this for a street costume?" she demanded. "How do you like it for a court appearance? Maybe you think it's just the thing, but I don't!"

Expertly she hurled the slicker in Smedley's face.

"Now!" she said, doubling her fists on her wide hips and glaring at him. "I'm through! I'm through with this one-horse show and with this one-horse town and everybody in it!"

She opened a door at the side of the stage and slammed it violently shut behind her.

"Whee!" said Meekins, tugging at his collar.

Smedley sighed drearily. "That's the way it goes. Everybody kicks me around all the time."

"Who is she?" Dodd asked.

"That's Loretta. She's our star dancer. That is, she would be if she was working for us and we had a show for her to dance in. She's temperamental."

"Is that what you call it now?" Meekins inquired. "Say boss, I think I better take a look around backstage—"

"You stay here," Dodd ordered. "What's this about having no show to work in, Smedley?"

SMEDLEY gestured tragically at the empty benches. "We're closed. It'd be bad enough—just havin' Loretta walk out. She's something special. See, the yaps like big dolls, but most big dolls are fat and they sort of droop when you put 'em in a rig like that. But Loretta's solid. She don't sag."

"I noticed that," Meekins said dreamily.

"She's a great artist," said Smedley. "But now she's quit, and the cops are mad at us, and Sadie's gone wacky."

"What's the matter with Sadie?" Dodd inquired.

Smedley moved his thin shoulders. "I'd think she was gonna do the old dutch, except that she don't act to me like a person who is gonna do that."

"Kill herself?" Dodd said. "What do you mean? What did she say?"

"Nothing much," Smedley explained. "Except she was swearing a little bit more than usual. But she had a mean look in her eye, and I can't figure out what she wanted that gun for."

Dodd jumped. "Gun?"

"Yeah. The .45 Colt she kept in her dresser. It's a regular elephant gun. Got a barrel a foot long. So she comes in here and swears at me for awhile and puts that gun in her dressing case and sails out again."

"Where'd she go?" Dodd demanded tensely.

"I dunno. She said she was goin' snake huntin'."

Meekins said: "Boss, if she gets in any more trouble, she'll sure jump her bail."

Dodd chewed his under-lip. "You're telling me. Hell! I certainly did manage to hide myself right behind the eight ball! Fifty thousand dollars!" He shook his head sharply. "Listen, Smedley. What happened here, anyway?"

"I don't know much about it," Smedley said, "on account of the cops had me on a leash out front at the time. They rolled in just like it was a routine pinch. Sadie was griped because it was out of her turn to get it. She's been payin' off regular, and she ain't supposed to be pinched only once a season when she does that. So she beefed with them backstage. She wanted to call Captain Boris and squawk."

"Captain Boris?" Dodd repeated.

Meekins said: "Head of the beach precinct."

Dodd nodded. "O.K. Go ahead, Smedley."

"So Sadie says these payoffs are getting too damned complicated. Too many people got their hand out, and a person can't make an honest living with a hide show any more. But the cops wouldn't let her call, and she swung on this guy Holden, and he slapped her back, which was no more than right, and then this little bum of an Edgar Tracy popped out from behind the fire barrel where he'd been hidin' and let fly at Holden and bored him through the chest. There was hell to pay around here for awhile."

"Edgar Tracy is the comedian?" Dodd asked.

"That's what he claimed. He never made me laugh."

"Was he Sadie's boy-friend?" Dodd asked.

"He had notions in that direction, but when I showed him this he changed his mind." Smedley took a razor out of his coat pocket and snapped the long blade open and shut again. "I'm a patient man, and everybody picks on me, but there's limits to what I'll take."

"Tracy got away?" Dodd said.

"Yeah. He lammed out the back. The little rat."

"Who is he? Where'd he come from?"

"I got my own ideas about that," Smedley said darkly. "Guys like him ain't born. They crawl out from under stones. I don't know who he is—aside from his name. He ain't never worked the carny circuits or the fairs or the burleycue stands."

"What does he look like?"

"Nothin' much. Sort of fat and sort of middle-aged and sort of dopey. You can find guys who look just like him on any street corner."

"Where does Sadie live?" Dodd asked.

"At the Langley Apartments on Keener Street."

THERE was a sudden crash from backstage. Loretta screamed and then screamed again. There was another crash, and the whole small stage shook.

A man ducked out under the curtains and jumped down off the stage into the aisle. He ran three lumbering steps and then stopped, peering cautiously back over his shoulder.

Loretta batted the curtains aside and came to the edge of the stage and pointed her finger at him warningly. She was dressed in a green street costume now.

"Scram, you bum!"

The man in the aisle wore a wrinkled blue suit and a black derby with a dent in the side. He had a beefy red face and enormously thick, heavy shoulders. He spoke protestingly to Loretta in a high, whining voice: "Now, honey-bee. Don't get mad like that...."

Loretta kicked Smedley hard. "And there's one thing more I'm through with around here! I'm through brushing off cow-footed fly-cops!"

Smedley winced. "Go ahead. He's my fault, too, I suppose."

"Now, honey-bee," said the beefy man.

"Shut up!" Loretta screeched. "Scram!"

She ducked back through the curtains. The beefy man cleared his throat with a belligerent cough and peered suspiciously at Dodd and Meekins.

"Who are these two guys, Smedley?"

"Who?" Smedley asked. "Oh, them. They're just a couple of would-be customers that dropped in."

"I'm Ludwig," said the beefy man to Dodd. "First class detective. Beach precinct. You got business here?"

"No," said Dodd. "We were just leaving."

"O.K.," said Ludwig. He turned importantly to Smedley. "You see anything of that guy Dodd yet?"

"Dodd?" Smedley repeated vaguely. "Oh, you mean the bail bond guy. No. Haven't seen him."

"Well, if you do, remember to tell him what I said."

"What was that?" Smedley asked, still vague.

"You dope! Can't you remember nothing? Captain Boris wants to see this bird Dodd, and he wants to see him right now."

"What for?" Smedley inquired.

"How should I know? But Captain Boris is plenty mad, and when he's mad he raises pure hell. He'll tear this guy Dodd to pieces and put him back together again wrong-side out. If he can't find Dodd he wants a guy by the name of Meekins. This Meekins is Dodd's stooge."

Meekins muttered under his breath. Dodd jabbed him warningly in the side with his elbow and said: "Well, we'll be moving along, Mr.

Smedley. We're sure sorry your show is closed. Me and my cousin left our plowing and drove thirty miles just to see it."

"Come again, boys," Smedley said kindly. "Some other time."

CHAPTER THREE

BORIS BURNS UP

THE LANGLEY APARTMENTS were housed in a thin, anemic-looking building covered in an off-shade of pink stucco that hadn't weathered the salt-sea air very successfully. Weeds grew high and rank in front of it, lapping over the curb into which Dodd cramped the wheels of the old coupe.

Here, up on the hillside, the wind had a sharper, colder tang. To the west the clouds were a rolled pile of red-gold that masked the setting sun, and shadows stretched long and thin ahead of Dodd and Meekins as they went up the chipped cement steps.

The front door was half ajar, and they went into the narrow, dark hallway that served as a lobby. Rows of mail boxes lined the left wall, and Dodd ran his finger down the name cards until he found Sadie Wade's.

"One twelve," he said. "That'll probably be in back— What was that?"

"What was what?" Meekins asked.

"Come on!" Dodd ordered.

Odors of meals long past swirled in the dim hallway, and the carpet was scuffed and ragged under Dodd's feet. Somewhere a radio and a baby squalled in off-key unison.

One twelve was the last door at the right at the end of the hall. It was closed, soiled-looking from the smears groping palms had left on it, and there was no sound from the apartment behind it.

Dodd stopped short about ten feet away, and Meekins ran into him from behind.

"Are you drunk again?" he complained. "What—"

"Shut up. I thought I heard a shot."

"I didn't hear—"

"It was muffled. Just a thud."

Dodd stepped cautiously up to the door and reached for the knob. He turned it very carefully and slowly, holding it so the latch wouldn't click. The door wasn't locked. Carefully Dodd pushed it open an inch and then another.

From behind him Meekins said: "There ain't no light. She ain't—"

Dodd flipped his arm back and hit Meekins hard in the chest, knocking him sideways. At the same second, he pivoted himself and swung flat against the wall.

The shots weren't muffled this time. They were sharp, whip-like cracks, and three little holes like splintered, sinister periods appeared, magically in the door panel just above the knob.

From inside the apartment feet scuffled hurriedly on the floor. A screen door slammed flatly.

"The back way!" Dodd shouted. "Go around—"

Meekins was huddled against the wall, his face pasty-white. "Oh, no! Not if she feels that way about it. A black eye is bad enough. I got no desire to spend the summer pickin' lead out of my plumbing."

Dodd ran for the end of the hall, but there was no door or window there—no way to get out the back of the building. He started for the front of the hall and then stopped, realizing that whoever had shot would be blocks away before he could get around the building. He approached the bullet-scarred door with wary hesitant steps, keeping against the wall.

"Boss," said Meekins, "let's just fold our tents and steal silently away. This is gettin' kind of out of hand."

Dodd ignored him. He kicked the door suddenly, knocking it wide open. The apartment was a gloomy cave, and the sharp acrid smell of powder drifted into the hallway.

Dodd waited for a long, silent minute and then put his head cautiously around the door jamb. The furniture in the box-like living-room resembled grotesque animals crouched and waiting in the shadows, and there was something else that moved and wavered and mumbled.

"Oh!" said Meekins in a choked gasp.

THE WAVERING thing took a sodden, slumping step toward the door and then folded down gently on itself into a lumpy pile that kept on mumbling.

Dodd reached a long arm around the door, found a light switch on the wall and flicked it. Light jumped brilliantly out of the brass chandelier that hung on a chain from the low ceiling.

"It's Sadie!" Meekins whispered.

She was a tall, heavily powerful woman of better than middle age. She was still wearing her street coat, and her flat pancake hat was tipped down drunkenly over one ear. Her face was a square-jawed stubborn mask, lined deeply with wrinkles, and the rouge stood out on her hard-muscled cheeks in raw patches.

She was sitting down on the floor, leaned back against a chair. She was holding a big .45 revolver in her lap. She had it in both hands, and she was trying to lift it. Her lips were drawn back rigidly from her square, white teeth with the effort she was making. Her eyes were wide and glassy.

"Take it easy, Sadie," Dodd said. "It's Dodd."

Sadie relaxed so suddenly her head jerked forward on the thick column of her neck. "Aw! Dodd!" She panted hoarsely, taking her breath in strangled gasps. "That—fat—smiling—little devil! I'll—kill him! You hear me, Dodd? I'll—kill—him…."

Dodd was kneeling beside her. "Sure, Sadie. Who?"

"Tracy. Wait 'til—I—get—my—hands…."

Her head slumped forward. Her hands relaxed, and the big revolver slid to the floor with a soft thump.

"Is she—dead?" Meekins asked uneasily.

"No," Dodd said. "She's hit in the left side—up high here. Call an ambulance. I'll go—"

"Nowhere," a voice finished for him. A man stepped through the door from the hall. He was short and thick-set, with a round darkly saturnine face, and he carried himself with an air of lazy confidence. He was holding a revolver casually in his right hand.

Dodd nodded. "Hello, Fesitti," he said calmly.

"Ta-da-ta-da!" Meekins said in a mock trumpet call. He had recovered himself completely. Policemen didn't frighten him a bit. "The cops arrive with a fanfare—late as usual. Where were you hiding, Fesitti? In the garbage can?"

"I wasn't hiding anywhere," said Fesitti. "I was staked out in front—watching the joint. I followed you two in here. Which one of you shot Sadie?"

"Pass the cocaine, Watson," Meekins commented. "The mastermind has just made a startling deduction."

"You'll talk too much one of these days," Fesitti said coldly.

Dodd said: "If you'd gone around in back you'd have nailed the guy that did this."

"That would have taken some brains," Meekins said. "Don't expect miracles, boss."

"How'd you like to fall down and hurt yourself?" Fesitti asked.

Dodd said shortly: "Stop fooling around and call an ambulance. Sadie's bleeding a lot."

"Too bad," Fesitti said. He walked leisurely over to the telephone stand and picked up the instrument. "Police department," he said into the mouthpiece. He nodded at Dodd. "Captain Boris wants to see you—but bad."

"I'll go down pretty quick."

"No," Fesitti corrected. "You'll go now. With me." He spoke into the mouthpiece. "Fesitti. Give me Captain Boris."

"Do you want Meekins too?" Dodd asked.

"I wouldn't take him as a gift."

Dodd nodded at Meekins. "You stay here with Sadie. When the ambulance comes, you go with her to the hospital. Stay there and watch her."

"O.K.," Meekins agreed.

"I got Dodd, Captain," Fesitti said into the telephone.

CAPTAIN BORIS looked exactly like the motion picture version of a Prussian army officer. He had a round, bullet-like head covered with a close-clipped blonde stubble of hair and no neck at all. His eyes were sinister blood-shot slits almost hidden in pink rolls of fat.

He even had what would pass as a saber scar on his cheek. It wasn't. He had acquired it years ago when he had tried to stop a drunk from beating up his wife. The wife tagged him with a flat-iron.

He looked up from the tangled mass of papers on his desk when Fesitti pushed Dodd into the cubbyhole office. He waggled one blunt finger, and Fesitti went out and shut the door carefully behind him.

"Sit," said Boris, pointing. He had a grin which was like something out of a nightmare.

Dodd lowered himself gingerly into the braced, straight-backed chair in front of the desk.

"Mr. William Dodd," said Boris. "The big shot from uptown. So you think you're going to play fun in my precinct, do you?"

"Am I pinched?" Dodd inquired. "Because if I am, I want to call—"

"Shut up. Do you know that Jake Holden died?"

Dodd's face lengthened. "No."

"Yeah. An hour ago. Jake was a friend of mine. He joined up with the cops the same year I did. He never did get past a first-class detective grade because he was honest, but I liked him in spite of that."

"So did I," Dodd said.

"Shut up. So Sadie Wade hired this guy Tracy, who popped Jake off. She didn't hire him on account he was a comedian, because he wasn't any funnier than a time-bomb. He was hidin' out, and he must have been hotter than a fire-cracker or he wouldn't have shot a cop just to keep from bein' dragged in on a routine vice raid. Sadie must know what he's hidin' from, but before I can question her you get her out on bail."

"That was a mistake."

Boris nodded grimly. "I'll bet you'll think so before I get through with you. But you ain't even satisfied with bailin' her out. You're afraid I'll pick her up again, so you take a bang at her to keep her quiet. Listen, sonny, let me tell you something. This precinct is a damned good thing, and I've held it for ten years. If you think you can push in with those row-de-dow tactics of yours, you're crazier than hell. And shut up!"

"Shut up yourself!" Dodd snarled. "I didn't shoot Sadie. Tracy did. She told me so. If that lunk-headed Fesitti had been a little smarter, he'd have nabbed Tracy when he was getting away. If you don't believe me, ask Sadie."

"I can't—yet," Boris said mildly. "I just called the hospital. She's still unconscious."

"Ask her when she comes out of it, then. She knew Tracy would be hiding out at her place—or had a good idea he would. She got her gun from the *Grass Shack* and headed right for home. She bopped my man, Meekins, when he tried to tail her. She spotted Fesitti and sneaked in the back way. She and Tracy must have had an accident. He had a gun wrapped up in a towel, and he let her have it and then blasted through the door at me."

"So you say," said Boris.

"And I can prove it!"

"Probably you can," Boris admitted. "I've heard tell that you're a guy who can prove the moon's made of limburger if you set your mind to it."

"Not only that," said Dodd, "but I told you the truth a minute ago.

I bailed Sadie out by mistake, and if she runs out on me I can't cover her bail."

BORIS stared at him out of slitted eyes. "You know you're sittin' there wide open for a felony charge?"

Dodd leaned forward. "Sure, I know it! That's what I'm yelling about!"

"Oh," said Boris. He rubbed the scar on his cheek with the back of his thumb contemplatively. "This sort of puts a different slant on things. Who tipped you off to the raid on the *Grass Shack?*"

"Lieutenant Hart at headquarters. He's a friend of mine, and he knew I'd been trying to get some business from this precinct."

"You sure it was Hart?"

"Call him up and ask him."

"Ummm," said Boris. "Did you know it wasn't a routine raid?"

"Meekins said it wasn't Sadie's turn, but I thought he was just blowing off as usual."

"He was right," Boris said. He sighed lengthily. "It's gettin' so I'm losing my faith in human nature. The mayor has got to make a speech before a women's club tomorrow, and he wanted something to talk about. So he wanted a vice raid. So I said they could raid down here if they were nice about it. I told 'em to take Sadie because she's a good pal of mine, and I figured I'd make it up to her later. But I come to find out she's hiding a red-hot in her show—and without even telling me! How do you like that?"

"It's not so good," Dodd commented.

Boris nodded gloomily. "You'd think she'd at least tip me off—her being a friend and all that. She knows I'm reasonable. I wouldn't have bothered the guy as long as he behaved, if there wasn't too big a reward on him. But the main thing is, I wouldn't have run the vice squad in on her if I'd known about this Tracy."

"Have you been shaking her down heavy?"

"Sadie?" Boris asked. "Why, no. I told you she was a pal of mine. A place like hers always makes extra trouble for the cops, and I expect her to pay for it, but that's all."

"Having any trouble is your precinct?"

Boris' lips moved in a gargoyle grin. "If I found any trouble around here, I'd shoot it and mount it and hang it on the wall. Just keep that in mind, pal."

The inter-office communicator buzzed, and Boris flipped the switch. "Yeah?"

The desk sergeant's voice said: "That guy Emil Poulson is here again. Says he's got to see you right now. Very important. He says if you don't see him he's going to see Kranz and get us all fired."

"Send him in," Boris ordered. He flipped the switch and looked at Dodd. "I hate lawyers—even worse than I do bail bondsmen. Do you know this guy Poulson?"

Dodd shook his head. "No. Never heard the name."

"You're lucky. He's a pest."

CHAPTER FOUR

RESPECTABILITY REARS UP

FESITTI OPENED the door and let in a small, plump man with a neatly pointed white goatee and a round, smiling, dough-like face. He wore thick-lensed nose-glasses attached to his coat lapel with a broad black ribbon.

"Captain Boris?" he inquired.

"That's right," Boris said.

"My name is Emil Poulson, as you are very well aware. I'm an attorney representing the Agatha Drinkwater Estate."

"O.K.," Boris said wearily.

Poulson cleared his throat with the air of a professional lecturer and said: "The Agatha Drinkwater Estate consists of a trust of a great number of miscellaneous pieces of property. The beneficiary is, of course, Agatha Drinkwater, who is a widowed lady of advanced years."

"So what?" Boris asked.

Poulson continued in his precise informative way: "One of the pieces of property owned by the Estate and leased by its accredited agents—of which I am one—consists of Blocks 12, 14, 18, and 19 of the southeast quarter of the north section of Silvester's addition to White's quarter section of the suburb—"

"Hold it," Boris requested. "If this is a tax beef, you've got the wrong party."

"It is not a tax—ah—beef. As I say, the Estate owns Block 19—"

"Yeah, I know. Go on from there."

"The third lot of Block 19—is occupied by an amusement concession known as the *Grass Shack*."

Boris pulled his beefy body upright. "Is that a fact?"

"It is. Now the rental agreement, or lease, between the Agatha Drinkwater Estate and the—ah—*Grass Shack* contains certain provisions and covenants to be fulfilled on the part of the lessee."

"The who?"

"The *Grass Shack*. The owners of said concession agreed that they would operate a lawful business on the property."

"Well, they are," said Boris. "It's a hide show."

Poulson took off his glasses and tapped them on his forefinger. "But not a lawful one—not according to the legal definition of such outlined in Brass Ring vs. Greeley, 113 General Sessions 304. According to my reports, the *Grass Shack* has twice been raided already this current season by the Vice and Morality Squad of the police department."

"Oh, those were just routine raids," Boris explained.

"Routine?" Poulson repeated, raising his eyebrows.

"Sure. Those guys on the vice squad have to do something to justify their existence. If the show wasn't lawful, I wouldn't let it run in my precinct."

"The proprietor of the show—one Sadie Wade—pleaded guilty to the charges of operating an indecent show the first time she was arrested."

"Oh, sure," said Boris. "That keeps the reformers happy, gives the papers something to print, and gets Sadie some free advertising. Just a matter of business."

"Not the kind of business the Agatha Drinkwater Estate prefers to be associated with," said Poulson. "It is my intention to cancel the lease held by the *Grass Shack*."

"I wouldn't do that."

Poulson nodded his head slowly and meaningly. "Ah. I suspected you had an—ah—interest in the place. That's why you've been trying to avoid seeing me."

"Let's get this straight, chum," said Boris. "If you mean, do I own a piece of the show—I don't. If you mean is Sadie paying me protection money—sure."

"Graft," said Poulson.

"Nuts," said Boris. "What do you think I live on—my salary?"

"Graft," Poulson said solemnly. "My suspicions—as trustee—have been justified. Good day." He made a smart about-face and headed for the door.

"Wait a minute," Dodd requested. He looked at Boris. "You going to let him throw Sadie out?"

"I fail to see how he could prevent it," said Poulson, frowning at Dodd in a dignified rebuke.

Boris shrugged. "Why not?" he said to Dodd. "Sadie crossed me up—hiding that Tracy."

"You haven't talked to her. Maybe she has an explanation. Give her a chance. Besides, she owes me dough for bail bond fees."

BORIS squinted thoughtfully. "O.K., Poulson, don't cancel that lease. If you do, I'll put the joint on the black list and nobody will dare rent it."

Poulson took off his glasses and stared at Boris incredulously. "Graft," he said in a dazed voice. "And now threats."

"That's right," Boris agreed.

"Why—why, I'll have your job, sir! I'll see the mayor—the police commissioner. You haven't heard the last of this!" He went out, slamming the door.

Boris shrugged amiably. "Acts screwy," he commented. "He oughta be in with the old lady."

"Old lady?" Dodd repeated.

"Yeah. This Agatha Drinkwater. She's in the state asylum. Cuckoo as they come. She chopped her old man up with a hand-axe and was tryin' to run the pieces through a meat-grinder when they nailed her."

Dodd stared at him unbelievingly.

"Fact," Boris said. "Oh, you meet all kinds of people in the police business. The guy I'd like to meet right now, though, is that Tracy."

"What do you know about him?" inquired Dodd.

"Nothing, damn it," said Boris. "We haven't got any pictures of him except in costume, and he put enough paint on his pan so he might be Hitler under it and nobody the wiser. His description fits one out of every three guys that go by the front door. Lived in a hotel. No papers or letters in his room. Had no friends. Nobody knows where he came from or why. We couldn't even get any prints that we were sure were his. Maybe he's a phantom for all I know. I guess I better call up the hospital and see if Sadie can talk yet."

He picked up the telephone from his desk. "Get me the receiving hospital," he said into the mouthpiece.

Outside in the hallway a voice said wearily: "Aw, why don't you go drown yourself, drip?"

Dodd's head jerked up, and he looked at the closed door of the office.

Captain Boris spoke into the telephone: "This is Captain Boris. About Sadie Wade, the patient— What? *What?*... Escaped? What the hell do you mean, escaped? You just got through telling me she was unconscious.... Oh, you *think* she was faking, do you? When you make up your mind about it, let me know. And in the meantime, you find her! You hear me? You find her or I'll come down there and tear you up like confetti! And shut up!"

He slammed the telephone back on its stand. "She got away! Scrammed out of the joint! I'm gonna kill somebody! I feel it comin' on!"

Dodd got up and jerked the office door open. Meekins was leaning against the wall outside, while Fesitti glowered at him dangerously, blocking the way to the office. Meekins was holding an ice cube wrapped in a paper napkin. He was running the ice tenderly back and forth along the line of his jaw.

"You!" Dodd snapped. "I thought I told you to stay at the hospital and watch Sadie!"

"You did, and I did. Until she left."

"Come in here!" Dodd ordered.

Meekins slid past Fesitti. "All right. So this is how it was. I was sitting in the corridor not ten feet from the door of her room, talking to this cop by the name of Bromski."

"That's the guy I assigned to watch her," Captain Boris put in.

"Sure. So Bromski had to go to the john. He went to look for it. Sadie must have been watchin' through the keyhole, because right away she popped out of her room. The nurse just got through tellin' me she was unconscious, so I think maybe she is delirious or something. So I take hold of her nice and gentle and try to lead her back inside the room. She tagged me with that same overhand right. On the jaw this time. Knocked me cold. I'm telling you, I didn't hire out for a punching-bag—"

"Shut up," said Boris gloomily, holding his head. "I'm pretty sure I'm going to kill somebody now. Any minute."

"Was Sadie dressed?" Dodd asked.

"Nope," said Meekins. "She had on one of them long hospital nightgowns. Looked like a circus tent on the prowl."

"She can't get far in that outfit," Dodd said. "She'll be picked up right away."

"You don't know them guys I got working for me," Boris told him. "There ain't any of them could find his own mouth with a spoon. Why do things like this have to happen? As if I ain't got troubles enough—"

THE INTER-OFFICE communicator buzzed, and Boris snapped the switch. "What now?"

The desk sergeant's voice said: "Ludwig is here."

"So he's here. So what?"

"He's got Smedley with him. Smedley's drunker than an owl. Ludwig says he can't watch him and the *Grass Shack* both at the same time and what should he do?"

"My God," Boris said, disgusted. "Tell the gravy-brain to throw Smedley in the drunk tank and to go back to the *Grass Shack* and stay there and to keep away from that ten-ton fanny shaker of a Loretta while he's at it."

Meekins nudged Dodd. Dodd looked at him inquiringly. Meekins had discarded his ice cube and now he made motions with his fingers as though he were counting money and jerked his head in the direction of the booking-room outside.

Dodd frowned. Meekins nodded his head in a positive emphatic manner.

Dodd said slowly to Boris: "I'll go Smedley's bail on the drunk charge."

"Sure," Meekins said quickly. "Smedley's our pal, and he's a good guy. He's probably just upset about all his troubles and about Sadie."

Boris said into the communicator: "Give Smedley to Dodd and Meekins." He nodded to Dodd. "You can have him without any bail, if you want him."

"Right!" said Meekins gratefully. "Thanks, Captain."

"Want us any more?" Dodd asked.

"I don't want anything but a long vacation," Boris answered. "Get out. Go away. Don't bother me. Wait a minute. I mean that last. Get the hell out of my precinct and stay out. I've had enough of you."

Dodd and Meekins went out into the hall. Meekins was all for heading right for the booking desk, but Dodd seized him by one thin arm and jerked him up short.

"If this is another of your crack-brained ideas—"he hissed dangerously. "What do you want to be pestered with a drunk for? Haven't we got enough trouble?"

"Smedley ain't drunk," Meekins whispered.

"How do you know?"

"He can't get drunk."

"Listen, stupid," Dodd said, "anybody can get drunk."

"Nope. Not Smedley."

"And why not, may I ask?"

Meekins said: "Look. I *know* he can't. I know a guy who runs a cartoon in the papers about strange facts and odd characters and such. He told me about Smedley on account he wanted me to persuade Smedley to let the guy run a picture and some dope about him in his cartoon. Smedley's got something wrong with him. This guy give me a lot of big words on it—but the idea is that alcohol don't absorb into Smedley's blood. Liquor don't have any effect on him. It's a fact. Smedley wouldn't let the guy run his picture in the cartoon because Smedley picks up a lot of side money bettin' guys in bars he can drink a quart of whiskey down and then walk a straight line or stand on his head or whatnot. He can do it, too. A quart of whiskey don't mean any more to him than a quart of water would to you."

"Ummm," said Dodd, staring at him skeptically.

"It's true!" Meekins said. "And if he ain't drunk and is pretendin' he is, then he must have a reason for it. Come on."

Dodd followed him into the booking-room. Smedley was parked in a corner on the floor, legs and arms trailing limply rubber-like in all directions, head tilted forward on his chest. His eyes were closed, and he was muttering unintelligibly to himself.

Ludwig, the beefy detective with the dented derby, was standing at the booking desk.

"You can have him," he said. "You're sure welcome— Say! You're the two guys that was at the *Grass Shack!* Why didn't you tell me you was Dodd and Meekins?"

"We were incognito," Dodd answered absently.

Ludwig stared. "In what?"

"Disguise. We're so good at it we don't even recognize ourselves sometimes. Give a hand, Meekins."

They took hold of Smedley's limp arms.

"Upsi-daisy!" Meekins said, heaving.

SMEDLEY came up to his feet. He wavered back and forth loosely, eyes still tightly shut. Meekins and Dodd started him toward the door. He dragged his feet, but they hauled him along willy-nilly.

"You're gonna wish you hadn't," Ludwig warned. "He's out like a light. Don't go droppin' him in some gutter and leavin' him there, neither!"

"Oh, we wouldn't do that," Meekins answered. "Smedley's our pal."

"Sure," said Dodd. "We love Smedley dearly."

They half-carried Smedley down the cement steps and along the crowded sidewalk to the nearest corner, They turned on to a narrow residential street lined with slatternly little cottages. Scattered street lights made feeble blobs in the growing darkness, and halfway along the first block they came to a narrow alleyway that had high hedges on either side.

Dodd looked at Meekins over Smedley's drooping head. Meekins winked in answer and said conversationally: "Hold him up a minute, boss. I got to tie my shoe."

He let go of Smedley and crouched down. Dodd shoved Smedley hard. Smedley went headlong over Meekins and sprawled full length into the alley with a grunt of agonized surprise.

Meekins jumped on his chest, putting a knee on each of Smedley's arms.

"Get that razor!" he said breathlessly.

Dodd found it tucked neatly away in the cuff of Smedley's baggy trousers. He put it in his own pocket. Meekins got up, and the two of them stared thoughtfully down at Smedley. He was still playing his part. He lay sprawled out lifelessly limp.

"Come on, Smedley," Dodd said.

"It's a good act," Meekins added. "But we don't like it any more."

Smedley breathed in and then out again in a long, melancholy sigh. He sat up and poked at his chest experimentally, wincing.

"Why didn't you just kill me while you were at it?" he asked wearily.

"Why didn't you drop me out of a ten-story window? What did I ever do to you two?"

"Nothing," said Dodd. "But you're going to. You're going to tell us what's the idea of this little song-and-dance."

"I wanted to get in jail, you dopes," said Smedley.

"Why?"

"I got an appointment with a guy that's in there."

Dodd crouched down beside him. "Who, Smedley? Come on and tell us all about it. We're your pals. We like you."

Smedley kneaded his biceps where Meekins had landed on them. "A guy by the name of Charley Blue. He's in the drunk tank. I want to see him about something."

"What, Smedley?"

"He was sellin' Sadie protection. I want to ask him why she didn't get it."

Dodd stood up and looked at Meekins. "Do you know this Charley Blue gent?"

Meekins nodded. "A drunk. A souse. He's a tout and a shill for floating crap games. Works uptown. I think maybe he pimps a little in his spare time. Strictly no good and a cheapie."

"Would he be working for Boris?"

"Hell, no. He was just shaking Sadie down a little on his own."

"Oh, no," Dodd denied. "Not Sadie. She wouldn't fall for any fake protection gag. She'd investigate. Who is he working for, Smedley?"

"I dunno," Smedley answered gloomily. "That's what I was gonna ask him. Sadie never told me. She don't pop off much about such matters. But I know he's workin' for somebody heavy. Sadie wouldn't pay out unless he was. She's gettin' a hell of a rough shake around here, and I think it's that little punk's fault. I'm gonna slice him up like balogna. Give me my razor."

Dodd handed it back to him. "You know," he said thoughtfully, "this sort of ties in with some other stuff. I think somebody is muscling in on Captain Boris. He accused me of it at first, and he was pretty anxious to find out who tipped me off to the raid on the *Grass Shack*. Of course, he wouldn't admit he was having any trouble, but I think he is."

"Somebody is nuts, then," Meekins observed. "Captain Boris is smart and tougher than hell, and he's got this district solidly behind him because he never gouges on anybody and he keeps things in line. Somebody is going to fall right on their face with an awful jangle."

"I think Smedley's got something," Dodd said. "I think maybe we better go talk to this Charley Blue. You sure he's in the drunk tank, Smedley?"

"Sure," Smedley said sadly.

"All right," said Dodd. "Be drunk again, and we'll pack you back to the jail."

CHAPTER FIVE

THE DRUNK TANK

WHEN MEEKINS and Dodd came back into the police station dragging Smedley between them, Ludwig was gone, and the sergeant was alone behind the booking desk.

"What's the matter now?" he demanded.

"Our playmate is a little too drunk for us to handle," Dodd explained. "Can we park him in the drunk tank?"

The sergeant tossed him a ring of keys. "Sure. There's nobody in there yet but Charley Blue. Lock the door when you come out."

Dodd and Meekins steered Smedley toward the door into the cell block. "Is Charley Blue in here often?" Dodd asked the sergeant.

"Every week. It takes him about five days to wind up, and then he falls flat on his face and stays there. The first cop that happens along totes him in to sleep it off. He's been out for about eighteen hours now. It's about time he should be waking up."

Dodd said in an undertone to Meekins: "Go get a pint of whiskey. He's going to need it."

Meekins went out the front door. Dodd half-carried the limp Smedley down the cement-floored aisle to the big cell at the back.

"All right," he said. "Stand up now. Nobody's looking."

He unlocked the cell door, and Smedley followed him inside. There were half a dozen narrow iron cots with bare mattresses placed side by side with about a foot of space between them. A man lay on his back on the one under the window. His face, pitilessly revealed by the glow of the unshaded bulb in the ceiling, was red and swollen and puffy. There was a ragged stubble of blonde beard on his cheeks. His mouth was open, and he snored in a fluttering, choked way. His scanty hair stood up in sweat-sticky clumps.

"Is this our party?" Dodd asked.

"That's Charley," said Smedley. "Don't he look pretty?"

"Like a week-old corpse," Dodd agreed.

He shook Charley Blue's slack shoulder. There was no resistance in the man at all. His head rolled a little bit. He mumbled brokenly, and a thread of saliva slid down over his chin and spread on the soiled collar of his shirt.

Meekins came in the cell with a pint bottle of whiskey in his hand. Watching Charley Blue thoughtfully, Dodd took the seal off the cap of the bottle and had a drink.

"I'm the guy that bought that whiskey, you know," Meekins hinted.

Dodd handed him the bottle. Meekins drank and offered it to Smedley.

"I never drink except for business reasons," Smedley said. "You wanta bet I can't drink all that pint and then—"

"No," said Dodd. "Give me your hat. You're not going to need it in here."

Smedley handed him the hat. Dodd punched out the crease in the crown, turned the hat upside down and held it under the tap in the water basin. When it was full, he held it carefully over Charley Blue's head and tipped it.

The water splashed noisily, soaking into the mattress. Charley Blue spluttered. His head rolled violently, and he made mumbling protests.

Dodd and Meekins and Smedley sat down in a row on the nearest cot and watched him.

CHARLEY BLUE'S eyes opened. They were red, burned holes in the puffiness of his face. He moaned as the light hit them. Slowly and cautiously he groped around him until he found the edge of the cot. He took hold of it and pulled himself up, hand over hand, to a sitting position.

He was facing Dodd, Meekins and Smedley now. He stared at them uncomprehendingly. They stared back. Charley Blue began to shake. He shook all over in spasmodic shuddering lunges that made the cot legs rattle like castanets against the cement floor. His eyes rolled glassily.

"Wow!" Meekins said softly. "This guy is one step away from the horrors."

"Hold his head," Dodd ordered.

Meekins braced Charley Blue's head against his chest, tilting it back. Dodd tipped the whiskey bottle up to his chattering teeth and poured a little in his mouth. Charley Blue gulped and shuddered and gulped again in a raging fever of anxiety. He grabbed for the, bottle, and Dodd batted his hands away.

"That's enough, now. Take it easy."

Charley Blue took deep, whistling breaths. Gradually the awful shuddering stopped and some faint shadow of intelligence came in his reddened eyes.

"More," he said hoarsely.

Dodd gave him another drink, keeping a firm hold on the whiskey bottle. He pulled it away after Charley Blue had gulped down two big slugs.

"More," Charley Blue begged.

"Nope," said Dodd.

"You'd better," Meekins warned. "He'll throw a fit."

"In a minute," Dodd answered. "Listen, Charley. We want to ask you some questions."

Charley Blue tore his fascinated gaze from the whiskey and really looked at his three visitors for the first time. He evidently didn't care for what he saw. He moved back on the cot uneasily.

"Who're you guys?" he demanded.

"I'm Dodd—bail bonds. This is Meekins. He works for me. You know Smedley, don't you?"

Charley Blue nodded reluctantly. "Yeah, I guess so. How are you, Smedley?"

"I'm alive," said Smedley gloomily. "I think."

"I don't want no bail," Charley Blue told Dodd. "Give me another drink."

"Not just now. First you give some answers. Smedley says you've been shaking down Sadie Wade."

"That's a lie!" said Charley Blue.

Smedley took out his razor and opened it. He moved the blade so that it shimmered dangerously in the light.

Charley Blue gulped. "Here, now! Get away from me with that, or I'll yell—"

"Not more than once, you won't," Smedley told him.

Charley Blue pulled his feet up and crawled to the head of the cot and huddled against the wall shaking.

"What you guys doin' here?"

"Asking you questions," Dodd informed him. "You want us to get mad and go away with our whiskey?"

"No!" Charley Blue said frantically.

"Keep your voice down. Who're you working for?"

"Nobody!"

"You're running a shakedown racket on your own?"

"Sure. What's it to you?"

"Nothing," said Dodd. "But suppose I tell Captain Boris about it?"

Charley Blue sneered shakily. "Go ahead. He don't dare lay a finger on me."

DODD looked at Meekins inquiringly. Meekins said, "The guy is punch-drunk."

"You think so?" said Charley Blue. "I can close any joint at the beach, whether it's legitimate or what, and I don't care what Boris says about it. I can get anybody down here raided any time."

Smedley said softly. "Could you get Sadie raided?"

"Sure! And you better remember— Wh—what?"

Smedley was creeping up on him with the razor. "So you're the weasel that was responsible for her gettin' pulled today, huh? Just like I thought!"

"No!" Charley Blue said shrilly, losing all his bluster. "I am not! I never did! Get away from me!"

Dodd stood up. "Come on, Meekins. We're in the way here. Charley and Smedley want to be alone."

"Wait!" Charley Blue pleaded. "Wait, now! You guys will be sorry! I'm tellin' you! You deal in bail bonds, huh? All right, my brother-in-law will get your license—"

Dodd sat down again. "Now we're getting somewhere. Your brother-in-law, eh? Who's he?"

"Kranz," Charley Blue muttered sullenly.

Dodd looked at Meekins questioningly. Meekins was staring at Charley Blue in blank amazement.

"Kranz is the councilman for this district."

"You bet he is!" Charley Blue seconded emphatically. "And you better just watch your step how you treat me!"

"Kranz," Smedley muttered dangerously. "So he's the guy Sadie's been payin' off."

"I don't like this," Meekins said, worried. "We're getting in away over our heads."

"I know," Dodd agreed. He extended the whiskey bottle cordially. "Well, if you're Kranz's brother-in-law, Charley, why that makes everything look different. Yes, indeed. Have yourself a snort."

Charley Blue tipped up the bottle and drank greedily.

Dodd jerked his head. "Come on, Meekins. You, too, Smedley. You'll have to be sober again."

The three of them went out in the corridor, and Dodd locked the cell door.

"He'll put that whiskey down and pass himself out—I hope," Dodd told them. "I want him out of the picture until I can locate Sadie."

"I don't like this," Meekins repeated. "Something is screwy around here."

"Everything is," Dodd said.

"Yeah. But I mean with what Charley said. Kranz is honest."

"An honest councilman?"

"It's true," Meekins insisted. "He's got a good law practice—civil stuff. He don't chisel. If he did, I'd know about it. Something's wacky."

"He might skid a few corners for his brother-in-law."

"Not Kranz," Meekins said stubbornly. "I mean, the guy is really honest. He makes a point of it. He doesn't even handle legitimate graft."

Charley Blue's bubbling voice sounded behind them. "Don' believe, huh?" He was leaning forward with his head pressed against one of the bars on the door, peering at them owlishly cross-eyed around it. The pint bottle in his hand was half-empty. The liquor, on his empty stomach, had hit with the force of a ten-ton truck. He was slobberingly drunk again.

"Think I'm lyin', huh? All righ'. All righ'. Kranz my brother-in-law, see? Backs me up. Always. You wanna know? You wan' proof, huh?

All righ'. All righ'. You phone. You phone yourself and see. You ask he don' back me up. Number's Ashway 6626, see? Private number, see? You phone. Go ahead. Dare you phone. All righ'."

He lost his grip on the bars and went staggering back and fell headlong on his cot.

"Come on, you two," Dodd said.

HE LED the way down the corridor and out into the booking office again. The desk sergeant stared at them in amazement.

"Smedley decided he didn't like your jail," Dodd said, handing over the keys.

Captain Boris came out of the doorway of the hall that led to his office. He rolled himself to a halt, his bullet head thrust forward.

"I thought I told you two to get the hell out of this precinct and stay out," he growled.

"We're on our way," Dodd said hastily.

Emil Poulson stepped daintily through the front door. He blinked a moment through his thick-lensed spectacles, getting used to the bright lights, and then he pointed a plump, precise finger at Boris and said: "I have been in communication with Richard Kranz, the representative of this district on the city council. He informs me that you have no right whatsoever to blacklist any property belonging to the Agatha Drinkwater Estate, and that if you do so or attempt to do so he will take steps."

"What steps?" Boris asked, mildly curious.

"He did not inform me, sir. But, as I warned you, I allow neither graft nor threats to sway me in the slightest from my sworn duties as a trustee, and if I hear any more from you on either of those subjects, I shall appeal to even higher authorities than the members of the city council. I bid you goodday."

Poulson made his abrupt, military about-face and whisked out the door.

"So long," said Boris. "Now listen, Dodd. I'm getting a little tired of talking—"

Detective Ludwig lumbered in the front door and said, "Hey, Captain," in his high complaining voice.

"What?" Boris inquired in a dangerously quiet tone.

"Well, listen, I'm gettin' tired of sittin' in that *Grass Shack*. There ain't nobody around there to talk to or look at, and I think I could do better if I—"

"So you've started to think now, have you?" Boris inquired. "What are you using for a brain?" Suddenly his voice rose to an outraged bull-like bellow. "Let me tell you something! I'm the guy who thinks in this precinct! I don't want any competition from numb-wits like you! Get the hell back there to the *Grass Shack* before I kill you right here in cold blood!"

"Yes, sir," said Ludwig, heading for the door so quickly he stumbled over his own feet.

"Wait a minute!" Boris yelled. "Take Dodd and Meekins with you and escort them out of this district—clear out! And if I see you two around here again…."

"We're leaving," Dodd said. "But what about this Poulson-Kranz business?"

"Nothing about it," Boris answered. "Like Poulson said, the Agatha Drinkwater Estate owns a lot of property around town—apartments, office buildings and such. Kranz can't brush off such a heavy tax-payer. He had to give Poulson some sort of a song-and-dance to quiet him."

"Kranz doesn't interfere with you?"

"Of course not," said Boris. "He realizes I know my business. He never bothers me. What's it to you?"

"Just wondering," said Dodd. "Did you know that you had Kranz's brother-in-law in the drunk tank?"

"Sure," Boris answered. "You don't think I let every drunk in town use my jail for a hotel, do you? Kranz is a good guy, and Charley Blue is a hell of a burden to him. Always in trouble. We lock him up whenever we find him crocked, and when we get tired of that we ship him off to the funny house for a cure. Now, scram."

SMEDLEY and Meekins and Dodd marched out of the station, with Ludwig lumbering along behind them like a clumsy shepherd dog. At the corner a half-block above the station, Dodd stopped short, frowning in a dramatically worried way at Meekins.

"I just thought of something," he said.

Meekins picked up his cue instantly. "What, boss?" he asked in a gravely concerned tone.

"This guy Tracy is a killer."

"That's right," Meekins agreed. "A desperate character."

Dodd said: "Do you realize, Meekins, that he shot Sadie because he thought she could identify him?"

"It must be true."

"Certainly," Dodd told him. "And there's another poor defenseless girl who is in danger while this fiend is at large."

"Who?" Meekins asked breathlessly.

"Loretta. You remember Loretta?"

"I certainly do," Meekins said emphatically.

Ludwig jerked to attention. "Huh? What's that?"

"If I was a friend of Loretta's, I'd be pretty worried about her," Dodd stated.

"I would, too," Meekins seconded.

"Say!" Ludwig exclaimed shakily. "Do you think Tracy might—might harm Loretta, huh?"

"There's a chance," Dodd said.

"A big one," Meekins added.

"Maybe he's even found her already," Dodd said. "Maybe even now she's lying in a pool of blood…."

Meekins put his hands over his eyes. "Terrible, terrible! Don't even mention—"

"Here!" Ludwig said, alarmed. "Stop that! I—I never thought. I'm gonna call her and see if she's safe! You guys wait right here!"

"We won't move," Dodd promised.

Ludwig lumbered toward the drug store across the street.

Smedley stared at Dodd. "Say, what're you tryin' to pull off now? That rat of a Tracy didn't shoot Sadie because she could identify him. I could do that just as well as her. He shot her because she was going to toss him to the cops or beat his ears off or perhaps both. Sadie hates shooters."

"Smedley," Dodd said, "how'd you like to take a walk for yourself?"

"What?" Smedley asked blankly.

"Beat it," Meekins ordered. "Scram."

"All right," Smedley said in a martyred tone. "Use me and then discard me. That's the way I get treated. Nobody has any gratitude or any human feeling…."

He slouched away down the street, his narrow shoulders hunched over disconsolately.

"I hope he don't go too far," Meekins observed. "We're still on him for some bail. Now what?"

"I just got a hunch. Sadie needs some clothes—needs them bad and quick. She wouldn't dare go back to her own place and just anybody's clothes wouldn't half fit her. But Loretta is as big as she is, and Loretta is a pal of hers."

"Sure," Meekins said eagerly. "Let's go."

"No. Wait for Ludwig. We can tell by what Loretta tells him whether Sadie is there or not. If she is, Ludwig is the last guy Loretta would want hanging around right now."

Ludwig came back across the street, wringing his hands. "She don't answer. I rung and rung and rung. You don't think—think she might be...."

"No," said Dodd, chewing on his under-lip. "But I think I know where she went. And I think we'd better get there, too—and soon. This mess begins to make sense now, and I don't like the looks of it at all."

"You and me," said Meekins.

CHAPTER SIX

TRACING TRACY

MEEKINS WAS pleading. "Dodd," said Meekins, "why do you want to act like this? As it is now, they'll probably only put you in prison for four or five years. If you keep it up, they're gonna hang you just as sure as hell, unless somebody murders you first."

Meekins was scrounged down in the center of the coupe's seat, packed between Dodd and Ludwig's beefy hulk. Dodd ignored him. He dropped the grumbling coupe into second gear, steered it up over the rise of the hill, and parked.

"Hey," said Ludwig. "This here is Councilman Kranz's joint. What would Loretta be doin' here, hey?"

"Tell me, too," Meekins put in. "If it ain't a state secret."

Dodd said: "I'm playing a hunch. Sadie's mad. The reason she's mad is because she thinks somebody crossed her up. She's looking for that person, and I think this is the place she'd look. I'm guessing that Loretta will be with her."

"Kranz is honest," said Meekins.

"Come on," Dodd ordered shortly.

The three of them got out of the car and walked between two square cement pillars, their feet crunching on the gravel of the drive. The lawn went up ahead of them in a long, easy sweep that ended against the brightly peering squares of the windows in the house at the top.

They were halfway up the hill when brilliant light seemed to jump at them from every direction. Arc-lamps hidden in stunted ornamental shrubs and in little clumps of flowers all over the lawn blazed in their eyes. They stood frozen rigidly in surprise, like three queer bugs pinned on a bright green carpet.

"Somebody turned on the lights," said Ludwig.

"That thought occurred to me, too," Meekins agreed shakily.

Dodd was marching steadily forward.

Some of the lights were turned to reflect on the house itself, and it was like a stage setting with its walls gleaming white and the blue of a drape moving slightly in an open window.

Dodd tried the latch, and the front door swung ponderously and silently back.

"Dodd!" Meekins wailed in protest.

Dodd walked into the hallway and looked around him. He nodded toward the wall at the right of the door.

"That must be the switch that controls the arc-lights on the lawn," he said.

Under the switch there was a long, broad smear of blood that glistened brightly against the immaculate white plaster.

"Oh, oh, oh," Meekins whispered.

Dodd walked toward the graceful sweep of the stairs. He touched the ornamental banister and then looked at his finger. There was blood on it.

Dodd climbed the stairs slowly and quietly. After a moment of uneasy hesitation, Meekins and Ludwig tiptoed after him. At the top, Dodd paused, staring at a red hand-print on the white wall.

"Somebody around here got hurt, I bet," said Ludwig.

DODD was looking down the hall toward an open door with a light showing through it. He went quietly in that direction, keeping against the wall, and Meekins and Ludwig followed after him, single-file.

From behind him, Meekins said, "Oh, my God," in an awed whisper.

It was a bedroom, furnished by and for a woman, all white and gold and blue.

Loretta lay doubled up on the floor under the windows on the far side of the room, one bloodied raw fist flung out in front of her, the other arm doubled under her twisted body.

Sadie Wade lay face down just inside the doorway, breathing in low labored groans, the muscles of her square jaw rigid and protruding, her eyes closed tightly.

A third woman was in a tumbled pile in the corner of the wall behind the bed. She had crouched there, trying to hide, and someone had beaten her until her features were a formless smear. She was dead.

Ludwig shoved Dodd and Meekins aside and dropped clumsily on his knees beside Loretta. He was breathing in little sobbing gasps, and he turned her over with infinite gentleness and cradled her head against his chest.

A siren began to wail in the distance.

"That's all we need," Meekins whispered.

Dodd swallowed against the cold, hard knot in his throat. "Sadie phoned for an ambulance. Then she went down and turned on the lawn lights to guide them. She just made it back and then fainted."

He stepped over her and leaned down toward the telephone lying on the floor. The little cardboard slip on it listed its number as Ashway 6626. It had a long cord on it, and he followed it with his eyes to the point where it disappeared into one of the spaces that had been occupied by a drawer in the bureau.

"That's it," he said to himself.

The siren was closer. Dodd picked up the telephone and dialed. "Captain Boris," he said when the sergeant at the beach precinct station answered him.

"Well?" Boris said.

"This is Dodd, Captain. I'm at Kranz's house. Kranz's wife has been murdered."

Boris didn't answer, but Dodd could hear him breathing noisily.

"Loretta's in a bad way," he went on slowly. "And Sadie Wade is here, too. She's fainted from loss of blood."

"Got anything more to report?" Boris asked thickly.

"Do you dare arrest Kranz?"

"I dare arrest anybody."

"Do it, then. And pick up Smedley. And see if you can sober up Charley Blue. I'll be down in a minute."

"You're damned right you will," said Boris. "And you're gonna grow a long gray beard before you get out again!"

Dodd depressed the breaker bar on the telephone, let it up again, and dialed long distance. When the operator answered, he said: "Give me the State Insane Asylum at Carterville."

"While you're at it, reserve a room there for me, too," Meekins requested shakily.

CAPTAIN BORIS was smiling his nightmare smile, and his eyes were narrowed down to menacing slits.

"Dodd," he said. "Don't worry about going to jail or any little thing like that. Don't let it cross your mind. Have you made any payments on your life insurance lately?"

Dodd was sitting glumly in the chair in front of the desk. He was not happy. Perspiration kept gathering on his forehead and rolling down his cheeks.

Meekins was sitting in a chair in the corner, trying to be inconspicuous.

Ludwig came in the office, his feet clumping heavily. "You want I should go back to the *Grass Shack,* Captain?"

"No," Boris said in a kindlier tone. "Go out and sit by Duffy at the desk. I left orders for the hospital to call as soon as they learn anything."

"Yes, sir," Ludwig said in a dazed, dull voice.

Dodd wiped some more sweat from his forehead.

"Aren't you feeling well, Dodd?" Boris asked. "That is very surprising to me." He flipped the switch on the inter-office communicator. "Duffy, what about Charley Blue?"

The desk sergeant's voice said: "Nope. The doc says he can't be brung around. He is due for another cure or maybe a coffin."

"How about Smedley?" Boris asked.

"No word. The boys can't locate him."

Through the communicator they could hear the telephone on the sergeant's desk ring. His voice answered it.

"Police, beach precinct.... Oh, yeah.... Yeah.... Yeah."

Ludwig's voice begged hoarsely: "What about Loretta?"

The sergeant said: "And the other—the red-head?... Yeah.... Yeah.

I see. Thanks." The receiver of the telephone clunked. "Cheer up, Ludwig. Hey, Captain."

"Yes?" Boris answered.

"That was the hospital. They gave Sadie a transfusion and it looks like maybe she'll come around. Loretta's got two badly busted mitts. They figure she put her hands up over her head to prevent whoever it was from beatin' out her brains. She's got an even chance."

Boris looked at Dodd. "Two murders—Jake Holden and Mrs. Kranz. Two assaults with intent to commit murder—Sadie and Loretta. That's quite a score, Dodd."

"Here's Fesitti, Captain," said the sergeant's voice through the communicator.

"Send him in."

Fesitti ushered two men ahead of him into the office. "This guy was with Kranz," he said. "Right away he started to holler about the Constitution and stuff, so I brought him along."

Emil Poulson took his nose glasses off and waved them warningly under Boris's nose. "This is the most outrageous violation of civil rights that I have ever encountered in all my years of practice! I warn you that I shall see to it that—"

"Shut up," said Boris.

"Never mind, Mr. Poulson," Kranz said wearily. He was a tall man, very thin, stoop-shouldered, and he looked unutterably tired. "Captain Boris is an old friend. He wouldn't have sent for me unless it was important."

"I'm sorry I had to, Councilman," Boris said uneasily. "This is bad—all around. I can't tell you how I sympathize…."

KRANZ made a wearily futile gesture. "Don't, please."

"All right," said Boris, drawing a deep breath. "The dope sitting in front of the desk is named Dodd. He's in this up to his ears, and he wants to say something now. Go right ahead, Dodd. We ain't waiting any longer—for Smedley or Napoleon. Speak your piece and make it good—awful good."

Dodd said: "I know who Tracy is. Up to about five years ago he toured through the sticks playing the leading man in tent shows. His name was mostly Shane—sometimes Shelley and sometimes Sands. He worked a racket along with his acting. Those tent shows stayed a week or so in each town they touched. He'd pick up some likely widow with a little dough and get her to invest some in him for one reason or another."

"Go ahead," Boris told him.

"He was pretty successful," Dodd said. "He had the line—being an actor and all. Very romantic. But this tent show stayed too long in one town, and the widow he picked was tougher than average. He got the dough, but she insisted that he marry her or she'd call copper on him. He wasn't having any. He shot her."

"Uh!" said Boris, startled.

Dodd went on: "He must have been a good actor, at that. He sold the jury on the idea that he was nuts. Instead of hanging him, they put him in the state asylum at Carterville. He escaped a couple of months back."

"Well, well," Boris said slowly. "He must have thought the vice squad was the boys from the booby hatch comin' to take him back."

Dodd nodded. "Probably. He knew it wasn't a regular raid because of Sadie squawking. He thought the cops had been tipped off to him."

"By who?" Boris demanded.

"The fellow that got him the job—Charley Blue. Charley has spent quite a lot of his spare time in the asylum—taking cures for chronic alcoholism—and this Shane got to know him there. Charley is a great one for running off at the mouth. He boasts about his brother-in-law—Kranz, here—being a councilman. Shane came to Charley and got Charley to hide him by making Sadie Wade give Shane a job."

"How?" Boris asked.

Dodd sighed. "Now we come to the tough part. I figured out what I just said as soon as I talked to the asylum. Now I'll have to do a little guessing. Charley Blue is a dope. I don't think it ever occurred to him to use his brother-in-law, Kranz, for anything but to get him out of jams now and again. Shane gave him a new idea. Shane told him how to threaten Sadie. Charley did, and Sadie gave Shane the job. That was easy, and Charley began to think he'd been passing up a good thing here. I'll bet it was right about then that he went to see Kranz."

Kranz nodded wearily. "Yes. He wanted to act as my agent. He wanted to shake down people in my district—call it collecting campaign funds or something like that—and split what he got with me."

"What did you say?" Dodd asked.

"I threw him out of my office."

"All right," Dodd answered. "But Charley didn't quit. He went to

Mrs. Kranz—his sister. She did what he asked. She put in a private telephone—hid it in her bureau with the bell silenced to a buzz so Kranz wouldn't hear it if it rang while he was around.

"Charley went right ahead with his scheme. He shook people down in this district—protection, campaign funds, everything. Some of them wanted proof that he was fronting for Kranz. All right, says Charley. Call Ashway 6626. If the person did, Mrs. Kranz answered. She made an appointment to see the doubtful person. What more proof could he ask? After all, she was Kranz's wife."

Boris swore quietly. "And that souse used my drunk tank for an office!"

Dodd sighed again. "So that was the setup when this raid was pulled. Tracy-Shane got into a panic and shot Holden. Sadie was plenty mad at both him and Charley Blue. Tracy, having great confidence in his abilities as a woo-pitcher, hid in her apartment and thought he could talk her into keeping him under cover. No sale. Sadie was going to turn him up to the cops. He shot her.

"Then Sadie was really mad. She sent Smedley to get after Charley Blue in the drunk tank and started after Kranz herself. She figured Kranz was responsible for the jam she was in and it was up to him to get her out of it. She was pretty weak, and Loretta went along with her to help her.

"In the meantime, Tracy-Shane was in mighty warm water. He needed some protection—right now. He went to see Kranz on his own. There he found out that Kranz wasn't back of Charley Blue at all. It didn't take him long to pump the whole story out of Kranz's wife. He thought Mrs. Kranz must have some of the money Charley had been collecting. He tried to find it. He didn't. That enraged him and he beat her...."

Kranz made a little moaning noise.

"Sorry," Dodd murmured. "Loretta and Sadie walked in right afterwards, while he was still searching. Sadie, being weak, stayed downstairs. Loretta went up to look around. She ran into Tracy-Shane, and he smacked her down and got away."

"Where to?" Boris inquired.

"Right here," said Dodd. He turned around and took the small, pointed beard of Emil Poulson in his hand and jerked. The beard came away in his hand, and Emil Poulson's round, pink face looked nude and different suddenly.

"He's got a wig, too," Dodd said. "And false eyebrows and pads in his cheeks and plugs in his nose."

"Quite," said Emil Poulson, smiling pleasantly. "Good make-up job, eh? You didn't have to be so dramatically rude, Mr. Dodd. I would have admitted my identity, had you asked me."

THE ROOM seemed small and tight and hot, and the breathing of the men in it was plainly audible.

Dodd said slowly: "You learned about Agatha Drinkwater in the asylum. One of her lawyers—a guy who lives in New York—is actually named Poulson. You figured you could prowl around and raise a little money for yourself by telling the people who were leasing property she owned that you were going to cancel their leases for this and that if they didn't pay off to you. It didn't work very well, because everyone hereabouts depends on Boris to see that things like that don't happen to them."

"Oh, quite," said Emil Poulson. "Very clever of you to figure it out."

"You admit—this?" Boris said. "The murders, too?"

"Surely. Why not?"

"Why not?" Boris repeated blankly.

Poulson was patient with him. "I have been adjudged insane. Legally insane. I cannot be held responsible for any of my actions. All you can do now is send me back to the asylum. I don't mind that much, really."

"Take him out," Boris said to Fesitti.

Fesitti took Poulson's arm and led him toward the door. Poulson smiled over his shoulder at Dodd.

"You know, you're the only one who figured this out. You're solely responsible. I'll give you something to think about. If you're clever— as I am—it isn't very difficult to escape from the asylum. I will again. And I'll come and see you when I do. Remember that."

He nodded amiably and went out of the office, Fesitti fumbling along behind him.

"Oh," said Meekins in a sick voice. "Did you hear? And he means it! It don't make no difference to him, as long as he's legally goofy, if he murders everybody in the state!"

"Oh, no," said Boris. He jerked his thumb toward the inter-office communicator. "This thing was open all the time we were talking. They could hear us out at the desk—"

Ludwig's voice bellowed through the communicator: "Hey, he's tryin' to escape! Halt! Stop! I'll shoot!"

"No!" Poulson's voice screamed faintly. "I'm not! Don't—"

Shots sounded fuzzily ragged, echoing outside the walls and through the communicator at the same time.

"Ludwig is dumb," said Boris, snapping the switch on the communicator, "but he can take a hint. I'm afraid Mr. Poulson-Shane-Tracy tried to escape a little bit too soon."

THE GIN MONKEY

IT WAS THE COCK-EYED
CONCEPTION OF A CRAZY
SCULPTOR'S MAD BRAIN—
UNNATURAL, HORRIBLE,
YET STARTLINGLY
REALISTIC—AND IT
STARTED MAX CLARK
DOWN A MURDER TRAIL
THAT WAS AS WARPED
AND TWISTED AS THE
THING ITSELF. A TRAIL
THAT LED FROM ONE
MYSTERY MAZE TO
ANOTHER AND ENDED
ONLY IN A BLOOD-WELTER
OF LEAD AND LOOT.

CHAPTER ONE

CLIP JOINT

MINNIE LANDER had an office on the second floor of the Cranz Building on Call Street. It wasn't much of an office—a big desk snowed under with a couple of feet of conglomerated papers, an immense filing case, a water cooler, and a few chairs.

Minnie listed herself as a public stenographer. She did some typing for the business men in the building, but her main function was to serve as an office address for a bunch of pipsqueak chiselers of one kind and another. She also served as a business address for Max Clark, who was neither a business man nor a chiseler, but a "consulting criminologist," which might mean almost anything.

Minnie was twenty-six years old. She was small and nervous and quick-moving, and her brown hair had a way of straggling out from behind her ears. She was not what you would call beautiful if you had any regard for the truth. She wore large horn-rimmed glasses on the end of her short nose, and when she got mad she shook her fists and swore like a trooper and threw anything that happened to be handy that she could lift.

Just now she was leaning back in her chair looking thoughtfully at a paper cup she held in one hand. She tipped up the cup and drank what was in it and said: "Ah!" in a satisfied way.

Max Clark opened the office door and came in and said: "Good?"

Minnie pulled her glasses further down on her nose, squinted over them at him. "Hello, Handsome Harry," she said, waving the cup. "Have one with you on me."

Max Clark shut the door and leaned against it. "One what?"

"Gin."

"Straight?"

Minnie waved the cup again. "Sure. Am I a sissy?"

Max Clark said: "I am when it comes to drinking gin—straight."

Minnie sighed and tossed the cup in the waste basket. "Well, if you won't, you won't. A guy by the name of Holt called. He wants you to go look up a guy by the name of Salisbury, who ain't been home for three days."

Max Clark said: "All right. Thanks a lot."

He started to open the door again, and Minnie said: "This Salisbury is the bird you pulled out of the hop joint on Louie Street three months back, ain't he? The time you got two bullets in your leg?"

"Yes."

Minnie took a pencil from behind her ear and poked thoughtfully at the wad of hair at the back of her neck. She looked up sidewise at Max Clark.

"He'll probably be in the same kind of a joint now, won't he?"

Max Clark said: "Yes."

"Just sit right where you are, Fatty."

"Hmm," said Minnie, rubbing her nose doubtfully. *"Hmm."* She picked up an eraser from the desk, turned it over in her hand. "Be a little more careful this time, huh?"

Max Clark smiled at her and said: "Sure. 'Bye, Minnie."

He closed the door softly, as he always did. Minnie looked at the closed door for awhile, and then she opened the drawer of the desk and took out a small mirror and stared at her reflection.

She made a disgusted face at what she saw and put the mirror away again. She took a bottle and another paper cup from the drawer and poured herself a drink.

"Nerts," she said bitterly, and knocked off the drink in one gulp.

THE BLINDS were down, and it was dark in the room—dark and hot and strong with the smell of stale beer and sawdust. Jake was a squatting mound of white in the shadows behind the short, high bar. He was sitting on a stool, leaning backward, with his bald, round head against the cash register. He had a handmade cigarette plastered in one corner of his mouth, and his mouth was open on that side, and air wooshed loudly in and out as he breathed.

Jake jerked his head away from the cash register and opened blank, bulging eyes when Max Clark's steps, quick and hard-heeled, came tapping across the floor.

Max Clark said: "Hello, Jake," and came up to the bar and put his elbows on it and leaned over, grinning. He was tall, thin and dark. He had a knife-like hardness about him. His teeth were very white under his thin, black mustache as he grinned.

Jake stretched his fat arms up and yawned. The cigarette bobbed up and down but stayed attached to his lower lip. "Hello, Max. Hot, huh?"

Clark pushed his dark hat back, wiped his forehead with a handkerchief he got out of his coat pocket. "Some. Borzig here?"

Jake used his fat thumb to point. "In his office."

Clark put his handkerchief away. He sighed lengthily, walked along the bar, up a short flight of stairs. He pushed through thick green curtains that had glass spangles on the bottom, went along a short hall. He rapped on another door.

There was a grunt and then a sleepy mumble from the other side of the door. Borzig's voice said thickly: "Who's it?"

Clark opened the door and went into a small office. There was a couch with red-leather cushions against the wall under the two tall windows, and Borzig was lying on the couch.

Borzig was a small man with a pale, tired face. His hair was dyed blue-black, and it stuck up straight on his head in scanty bunches. His shoes were on the floor beside the couch in the middle of a circle of cigarette butts, and his coat hung over the back of the chair in front of the desk.

He rubbed his puffy eyes with the knuckles of his right hand and squinted up at Clark.

"Oh," he said. "Oh. Hello, Max. What you want?"

Clark grinned good humoredly. "I'm playing nursemaid now, Borzig. I came after that dim-witted Salisbury."

Borzig kept on rubbing his eyes. He yawned lazily.

"Salisbury," he repeated thoughtfully.

Clark nodded. "Yeah. The artist guy. Holt, his half-brother, hired me to look him up and get him back to work again."

"Oh," said Borzig.

There was a little silence, and Borzig stopped rubbing his eyes and watched a fly buzz around on the ceiling. He rubbed his chin with his left hand.

Clark said: "Well, where is he?"

Borzig blinked and said. "In a room down the hall. Wait a minute, and I'll take you to him. You pay his bill, huh?"

"Sure."

Borzig sat up with a groan and swung his stockinged feet off the couch. He bent over to put on his shoes, grunting with the effort. He stood up and reached for his coat.

He stopped with his hand extended and drew in his breath with a quick gasp.

"Max!" he said, choking a little. "Max!"

MAX CLARK looked thin and dark and dapper, showing his white teeth in a smile, leaning forward. There were glittering, excited lights deep back in his brown eyes. The .38 police revolver in his hand caught the slanting rays of sunlight from the window and glinted prettily as he moved it. He pointed the revolver at Borzig's stomach and watched him and smiled his wise, knowing smile, quirking up one corner of his mouth and shutting one eye.

Borzig coughed once, apologetically, and backed up until his knees hit the edge of the couch and he sat down suddenly. He looked up, and his eyes were very large. He made unbelieving noises to himself and tugged at his wilted collar in an aimless way.

"Why, Max," he said in a half-chiding, half-afraid tone. "Now, Max. I don't like this, Max. I don't understand this."

Max Clark said: "Just sit still." His voice was as amiable as before.

He went over to the coat. He watched Borzig as he felt through the pockets of the vest. He found a .25 automatic. He looked at the automatic, grunted to himself in an amused way, and tossed it over the back of the desk.

"It's a pretty hot day," he said lazily. "You were too anxious to put on your coat."

"Just habit," said Borzig, smiling and patting his knees with his hands. His thin face had regained a little of its faint color. He was feeling better. He smiled at Clark and nodded. "You know I wouldn't try anything with a tough guy like you, Max."

"Yeah," said Clark. He began to search through the pockets of the coat with his left hand, keeping the revolver leveled at Borzig.

Borzig opened his mouth and started to get up. Clark didn't say anything. He shifted his weight on his feet and leaned forward, hunching his broad shoulders a little.

Borzig shut his mouth and sat down on the couch again. He opened his mouth and shut it twice more and then said: "Well now, Max. This is really a hell of a note. This looks like robbery to me, Max. I don't think you got any business to go searching through my pockets."

Clark didn't say anything. He took some papers from the inside pocket of the coat and tossed them on the desk. He backed up to the desk and spread the papers out, watching Borzig out of the corners of his eyes.

He found an open envelope with some checks in it.

"Now listen here," Borzig said, protesting in a futile way. He raised his eyebrows and put out his hands pleadingly.

Clark spread the checks out on the desk and looked at them.

The checks were not made out. They were blank except for the signature. They were signed with the name, *Edward Salisbury,* in an aimlessly scrawling script.

Max Clark gathered the checks up and put them in his pocket. He looked at Borzig and nodded once, knowingly.

"Well?"

Borzig lifted his bony shoulders. He looked like a small, sullen boy, sitting there on the couch with his dyed hair sticking up in tufts.

"Now let's see Salisbury," Clark said. He put the gun back in his coat pocket and kept his right hand in the pocket.

BORZIG got up silently and marched to the door and opened it. Max Clark followed him closely down the hall. Borzig opened a door at the head of the stairs, and they went into a room that was gaudily furnished with pink lamp shades and red-plush furniture and glass beads on the low chandelier.

A blonde woman with very red lips and very red fingernails was sitting on the couch. She was smoking a cigarette and reading a magazine and chewing gum noisily, and there was a glass with a sticky rim on the floor beside her.

She sat up straight very quickly and pulled her blue dressing gown tight across her stomach.

"Why the hell don't you knock?" she asked nastily.

Then she saw Clark, smiled and wriggled a little on the couch and said: "Oh, hello," in a cloyingly sweet voice. She noticed that Clark's hand was bulging in his coat pocket, and the muscles around her mouth tightened suddenly. She looked at Borzig and raised thin, penciled eyebrows.

Borzig said sullenly: "This is Max Clark, Mae. He's a private dick. He came after Salisbury."

Max Clark looked at Mae and said gently: "Don't yell, or I'll bop you. Both of you walk into the bedroom ahead of me. Be careful."

Mae tilted her head insolently and let her lips curl up at one corner. She said: "I always did hate—"

Clark took a long silent step toward her, smiling.

Mae didn't finish the sentence. Her eyes went wide suddenly, and the color slid out of her face and left round, red islands of rouge in the middle of her cheeks.

Borzig said quickly: "Look out, Mae. He means it."

Mae got up off the couch. She swaggered a little, but she watched Clark anxiously, and she walked very quickly toward the bedroom door. Borzig sidled after her.

Salisbury was lying across the bed, sprawled out, with his head hanging over the other side. His blonde hair trailed down, lank and damp with sweat. His eyes were closed, and there was a trail of saliva from the corner of his mouth across his cheek. He was breathing in long, gurgling snorts.

Clark walked over to the bed and picked up one limply skinny arm and let it flop back again. Salisbury grumbled in a monotone without opening his eyes.

Clark jerked his head at Borzig and Mae. "Get him dressed."

Borzig and Mae worked together without saying anything to each other. Max Clark stepped back against the wall and watched them roll Salisbury around on the bed, pulling his clothes on his lankly awkward arms and legs.

When they sat him up to poke his arms through the sleeves of his wrinkled coat, Salisbury opened his eyes and looked around with an idiotically pleased expression and said: "Hello, hello."

Mae knelt down in front of him and tied his tie, jerking it tight suddenly.

Salisbury said: *"Glug,"* and felt of his Adam's apple in a surprised way.

MAX CLARK walked up to the bed and smacked Salisbury across the cheek with the knuckles of his left hand. Salisbury flopped over backwards and hit the bed so hard he bounced upright again. He goggled up at Max Clark.

"Why," he said, pleased. "It's Maxie. How are you, Maxie? Are you feeling all right, Maxie?"

Clark said: "Wake up. I want to get you out of here, and I don't want to have to carry you."

"I'm awake, Maxie," Salisbury assured him gravely. "Wide awake, Maxie. Just like the early birds in the morning. Meet my friends, Maxie. Meet Mae and meet Borzig. Very nice people in every way."

"We've met," said Clark. "Can you walk?"

"Sure," said Salisbury confidently. "Sure and sure, Maxie. Just stand aside while I demonstrate."

He stood up and his legs bent limberly under him. He made a few vague balancing motions with his long arms and then went sideways across the room, tipping more and more, until he hit the wall with a thud that made his teeth click. He blinked sheepishly at Max Clark.

"They changed the room around since I went to sleep," he explained, nodding soberly. "This wall wasn't here before."

There was a loud knock on the door into the hall.

Max Clark didn't seem to move very fast, but before the sound had stopped he was standing beside Mae, and he had his revolver out, pointing it at Borzig.

"Quiet," he said softly.

Borzig stiffened his small body into an attitude of attention, hands at his side, neck stiffly back, mouth so tightly closed that it left a white line across his face. Mae stood very still, staring up at Clark's face with wide eyes fringed with sticky black lashes.

Max Clark said: "I'd rather take him out peaceably, but I'm going to take him out. Walk into the front room ahead of me."

Borzig and Mae edged through the door.

The knock sounded again, louder, and a voice said: "Mae!"

Max Clark stepped close to Mae and let the long fingers of his left hand rest lightly on her throat. His eyes were narrow now, and glittering. His smile was very thin and hard. He said softly to Mae: "Tell him to come in and act like you mean it."

Salisbury came ambling loosely out of the bedroom and said hopefully: "Did you forget me, Maxie?"

Mae swallowed once, trying to look down at Clark's hand on her neck, and then said: "Come on in," loudly.

The door opened suddenly, and a man came in saying: "What do you think—"

He saw Max Clark and saw the revolver pointing at him and stopped talking and stood still. He was a short man, very fat, with a round, red face. He wore a white panama hat with a red-and-blue band on it, and he was smoking a cigar. He had a very big nose that was spread flat across his face. He had his coat off and was carrying it across his left arm. He wore a pink silk shirt that was wet with perspiration. He had very small, very bright blue eyes.

HE BLINKED the blue eyes at Max Clark while the silence in the room seemed to grow heavier and heavier and faint traffic noise seeped through from the street like the far-off drone of bees. He watched Max Clark steadily, without moving at all, until Borzig let out his breath in a stifled gasp and Salisbury said plaintively: "What funny people," and went and sat down by himself in a corner.

Max Clark said: "Reach behind you and close the door. Take it slow and easy."

The fat man didn't move. "Well, now," he said lazily. He watched Max Clark, and there was a calculating look in his small blue eyes.

Max Clark didn't say anything. He pulled the hammer of the revolver back with a sharply metallic click.

Mae jumped. Borzig pulled in his breath with a gurgling sound. The fat man smiled in an amused way and didn't move.

Borzig gurgled again and said quickly: "Do it, Tiny. He's a private dick Salisbury's brother sent. He'll shoot."

Tiny grinned and said: "I think maybe he would." He stepped backwards slowly, reached behind him and pulled the door shut. "Now what?"

"Drop your coat."

Tiny raised his colorless eyebrows and let the coat fall off his arm. It hit the floor with a bumping thud.

"That's my gun," Tiny said amiably.

"Put up your hands and turn around slowly."

Tiny raised thick arms and revolved himself slowly until he was once more facing Clark. "I'm going to remember you, baby," he said, nodding and winking one eye.

"Sit down in that chair."

Tiny walked sideways to the chair and plopped his bulk in it with a squeak from the springs. He took a limp handkerchief out of his pocket and mopped his face with it. He moved the cigar from one corner of his big mouth to the other and looked bored.

Clark said to Borzig: "Get his coat and bring it here. Don't get between us."

Borzig went over and picked up the coat and brought it back. Clark dipped his hand in the pocket of the coat and found a heavy automatic. He dropped the automatic into his own coat pocket.

"All right," he said easily. He relaxed and grinned his hard, tight grin at them. He looked thin and tall and dark and very sure of himself. He nodded at Tiny. "I'm taking Salisbury along with me. I don't want any trouble."

Tiny took his cigar out of his mouth, rubbed his flat nose with a forefinger. "You won't have any. We're all through with him. That's what I was going to say when I came in. Somebody stopped payment on his checks. Take him and welcome. He's a hell of a nuisance."

"You mean me?" Salisbury asked chidingly. "I'm sure you can't be referring to me."

Clark took him by one skinny shoulder and heaved him toward the door. Salisbury traveled right along until he hit the wall. He seemed surprised that the wall was there.

"More damn walls around here," he said, frowning and shaking his head in a disapproving way. He felt along the wall blindly until he came to the door. He turned the knob on the door and fell head-long into the hall.

Clark had been watching him patiently. Now he went to the door himself, switched the key to the outside. He said gently: "I wouldn't be in too much of a hurry to get out."

Tiny, Borzig, and Mae watched him silently as he closed the door very slowly.

CHAPTER TWO

STUDIO MURDER

THE ART colony is in the form of a ragged square, running from Nineteenth to Twenty-first Avenue and sprawling crookedly between Purse and Russian Streets. It is a conglomeration of narrow, roughly paved streets, discouraged-looking stores, mangy buildings, abandoned livery stables, and many very distinct smells. Most of the livery stables are used by the artists for living quarters. No one has, as yet, invented a Society for the Protection of Poor Artists—so they are left in peace. The landlords put green wallpaper over the rotting walls and hang phony cobwebs from the ceilings and that makes things all very atmospheric, and everybody is happy.

Don't feel sorry for the artists. They are not so dumb. The landlords get stuck in the end because the artists never pay any rent.

The taxi turned off the smooth asphalt of Russian Street and ground up Green in second gear, dodging around stray ash cans and hungry-looking cats, and pulled up at the entrance of an alley that went back zig-zagging between two tall wooden buildings that leaned toward each other as though they were tired.

Salisbury didn't want to get out of the taxi. He felt like talking now, and he had been doing it steadily ever since Max Clark had put him in the taxi. He wasn't saying anything particularly important. He was talking about the future of art in America and the only true reward of genius.

Max Clark got out and paid the driver and then hauled Salisbury out by his coat collar.

"Do you know what?" said Salisbury, taking all this as a matter of course and swinging back and forth like a pendulum in Max Clark's grip. "Do you know what, Maxie? I forgot to give you some very, very important news. I got a job. Think of that."

"What kind of a job?" Clark asked without interest, hauling him along the narrow sidewalk.

"Art," said Salisbury mysteriously. "Making a statue."

He commenced to laugh, and he laughed so hard he fell down in the gutter and stayed there on hands and knees, waggling his head and laughing very heartily.

Clark caught him by the coat collar and pulled him upright again. It was getting dusk now, and it was a little cooler in a damp way, and the buildings around them lost some of their ugly lines in the half-light. A few dark figures with shapeless white blotches that were faces went hurrying by on the narrow sidewalk. Nobody paid any attention to Clark and Salisbury beyond incurious side glances. Nearby, a woman who evidently thought she was a soprano, was practicing scales and missing badly on the top notes. There were several radios going full blast on different stations, and the result was a pleasant medley of jazz and symphonic music and somebody giving a talk on the value of something or other as a health food.

Salisbury's feet turned over so that he was standing on their edges, and his knees bent limply outward. His feet walked around in circles while his neck remained stationary in Clark's grip.

"You know what kind of a statue I made for my client?" he asked. "A very, very pretty statue. The statue of a yellow-and-green monkey. Did you ever see a yellow-and-green monkey, Maxie?"

Max Clark said: "No," and hauled Salisbury along the sidewalk past windows that were orange squares in the twilight.

"I did," Salisbury assured him gravely. "The last time I went on a bat I saw a yellow-and-green monkey. I had been drinking gin, and I woke up in the hospital. You remember, Maxie. You took me to the hospital. Anyway, when I woke up, there was the yellow-and-green monkey sitting right at the foot of my bed. It stayed there for three days, and we had some very interesting conversations. It's name was

Edgar or Paul, I can't remember which, and it was a very educated monkey—had graduated from Dartmouth. I call it a gin monkey, on account of the gin I drank before I saw it. Funny, huh?"

"Very funny," Max Clark agreed.

HE TURNED Salisbury into a shadowed passageway that was roughly paved with bricks and had rows of ash cans lined up like soldiers on parade against both walls. The passageway opened out into a square of hard, dusty ground with the tattered remnants of a flower bed in the center of it. At the back of the square a squat, ugly building loomed up. The dusk draped down over it and toned down the hideous blue paint that covered it.

Clark took Salisbury around to the side of the building and started him on the flight of rickety stairs that ran up steeply.

There was a movement above them on the stairs. The scrape of a foot, a soft little sniffle.

Max Clark pushed Salisbury hard against the wall and crouched a little, trying to see up into the dimness.

"Who's there?" he asked in a flat voice.

There was another movement, and a thin, bare foot in a red sandal came down on the step on the level with his eyes. There was a thin, bare leg above the sandal and a stained, blue smock above the leg.

The woman came down another step slowly. She had a face that was painfully thin even in the half-darkness. Her mouth was a red smear, her eyes blue-shadowed holes. Her voice was husky, tight.

"Did you get it?"

Salisbury raised his hand in a vaguely polite salute and said: "Hello Annie. Did I get what?"

And then she moved all at once. Something seemed to tear loose inside her, and she gave a little animal-like snarl and came down the steps in one lithe movement and slashed at Salisbury's face with her fingers hooked into claws.

Salisbury said: "My goodness," in a surprised voice and made helpless batting motions in front of his face. He got over-balanced and slid down to a sitting position against the wall. There were four red streaks on his face.

Clark caught the woman by the shoulder and felt the starved thinness of her. He held her against the stair railing.

"Now what's the idea?" he asked, trying to see her face.

Her voice came thick and choked with impotent rage. "That fool! That dirty, drunken fool! He promised to get me some heroin when he left. That was three days ago! Three days! Do you understand that? I've been hanging around here waiting for three days! Then he asks me what he was supposed to bring!" She tried to squirm out of Clark's grasp, tried to kick at Salisbury.

Clark said: "Quit it. I just pulled him out of a clip joint down on Commercial Street. They cleaned him. He hasn't got any dough, and he hasn't got any dope."

He let go of her then, and she staggered across the dusty plot of ground toward the passageway, cursing in a choked, gasping voice.

"That's Anne Carr," Salisbury explained, as though nothing unusual had happened. "She lives on the floor below me. She's a friend of mine."

"I'd never have guessed it," Clark said.

He got Salisbury on his feet again, pushed him up the narrow steps. At the top he rested Salisbury against the wooden railing, took a ring of keys out of his pocket, selected one. He unlocked the door, pushed it open. The odor of plaster-of-paris, paint, tobacco smoke, and bad gin came out to them faintly.

Salisbury said: "I think I'll just sleep out here on my front porch. It's cooler out here."

He closed his eyes and fell straight forward limply and would have pitched head-first down the stairs if Max Clark hadn't caught him. Clark shook him hard, but Salisbury's head rolled loosely, and he didn't open his eyes.

Clark dragged him inside the door. He knew where the furniture was, and he hauled Salisbury across the littered dimness of the floor and plopped him on the bed that was in the corner under the window.

Clark stepped back and felt along the wall for the light switch, and he had just touched the switch with the ends of his fingers when the first blow hit him.

The blow came out of the darkness without any warning at all. There was no sound of any movement, not even the swish of the blackjack through the air.

The weapon hit Clark on the side of the head just under the brim of his hat. It knocked his head sideways and sent little shooting streaks of fiery pain all along his face. He staggered away, trying to get his balance, trying to reach his revolver.

He never heard the other man at all, but another blow caught him on top of the head and knocked him into the wall. He felt the roughness of the wall under his hands, felt the cool dampness of the plaster pressed against his face as he slid downward slowly, and then he didn't feel anything more.

IT WAS a round head with a few ragged streaks of gray hair above the temples and a face that was reddish and weatherbeaten. It was the first thing Clark saw when he opened his eyes. The head seemed to be suspended in a thick mist just over him, and it was nodding and moving its lips at him, and he finally made out the words.

"How do you feel now, hey?"

Clark cleared his throat and spat and said: "How do you think?"

He wriggled his shoulders against the wall and sat up a little straighter. His head was aching in quick, burning jerks that seemed to travel the length of his body in gradually receding waves. He blinked a few times and made out that the round head above him had a policeman's uniform cap on it and a thick, blue-clad body attached below it.

The policeman said: "Somebody hit you, huh?"

Clark said: "That's my guess. What's yours?"

The policeman had a wet towel in his hand, and he offered it silently to Clark. Clark took it and pressed it against the burning spot on the side of his head. The blackjack had cut the skin there, and blood had dripped down over his shirt and tie. He looked down at the shirt and said slowly: "Another five dollars all shot to hell."

The policeman said: "It's a pretty nice shirt. Silk, huh? Maybe you can clean it."

CLARK got up and the jerking ache in his head redoubled in intensity. He made a face and steadied himself against the wall. He looked at the policeman and said: "How'd you get here?"

"Dame by the name of Anne Carr that lives below," said the policeman, taking off his cap and wiping the inside band with a handkerchief. "I was walking my beat over on Spaulding, and she came running up to me and says there is a hell of a racket going on up here, and so I came up to see what's what. You were sitting here against the wall, and your pal was on the bed."

Clark walked slowly across the studio and looked down at the rumpled bed under the window. Salisbury was lying there, sprawled loosely out, with his arms dragging on the floor. His face was turned sideways, and Clark could see the four livid scratches Anne Carr had left on his thin cheek. Salisbury looked limp and peaceful and relaxed, and he was smiling a little in his silly, likeable way. He might have been lying there asleep. But he wasn't asleep. He was dead. There was a small sunken groove in the back of his head, and a little blood had welled up out of the groove and matted his thin brown hair at the nape of his neck.

The policeman had followed Clark over to the bed, and now he stood with his hands behind him and his mouth screwed up judicially at one corner, staring down at Salisbury.

"The same guy that whacked you must have tooken a crack at him, too," he suggested finally. "Only hit this guy too hard. What's his name?"

Clark said slowly: "His name is Salisbury. He is—was—an artist. This is his place."

"An artist, huh?" the policeman repeated, as though that explained everything. He took a notebook out of his pocket and wrote something in it. "Who're you?"

Clark took a card from his pocket and handed it over. The policeman examined the card dubiously.

"Max Clark. Consulting Criminologist. Well, ain't that fancy, now. How come you was up here, and what was the fight about?"

Max Clark said casually: "There wasn't any fight. I'm a friend of Salisbury's. I found him wandering around on the street tight as a goose, so I brought him home. I had just got him inside the place here, when somebody hit me and laid me out."

"See who it was?" asked the policeman, pencil poised.

"No."

The policeman shrugged indifferently. "The homicide boys'll go over that with you, anyway." He snapped a rubber band around the notebook and put it away. "It sounds sort of screwy to me, but it probably happened that way, because I got a theory that all these artists are nuts, and I should hope to shout that I know plenty about them after me walkin' this beat for four years."

CLARK was still looking down at the bed, and his face looked very sullen and angry and dark with the bluish swollen lump over his temple.

The top spread of the bed had been folded over a couple of times into a rough, bulky bundle. Clark leaned over the bed and started to unwrap the spread.

"Ah—ah," said the policeman warningly. "The homicide boys are on the way, and they get persnickity if you don't leave everything just as it is."

"I'll put it back."

"All right," said the policeman. He watched curiously.

Clark folded the spread back. It was filled with crumpled plaster. A few wire forms stuck out blackly.

"Huh?" the policeman said dubiously. "What is it?"

Clark said absently: "Pieces of statue. Somebody put them in here and then hit them with something to break them up. Wanted to muffle the noise."

The policeman tipped his cap back and scratched his forehead. "Funny. I don't blame him for wantin' to bust up these statues, though. Ain't they the most God-awful things you ever saw?" He waved his arm around the room.

There were statues everywhere—on the floor, on the chairs, on the work-bench that ran along the side of the studio. Some were uncompleted, as though Salisbury had lost interest in them when he was partly through and tossed them aside. The completed ones were macabre and grotesque figures that were really distortions that reflected an insane sort of humour. The workmanship was uniformly good. Salisbury had worked with swift, sure hands. He had known just what he wanted, and he had gotten it in almost every case. The figures all had variations of the same expression. They were all absurdly senseless—impressively unimportant.

Looking at them, Clark thought that they told more about Salisbury, more about his point of view, more about his real personality, than any number of volumes could have told in words. Clark knew that Salisbury had been chuckling to himself in his gently cockeyed way when he had made the figures, and thinking about that chuckle of Salisbury's made Clark feel tight and hard and bitter, and he jerked his shoulders suddenly and swore to himself in a monotone.

The policeman had been rocking back and forth gently, squeaking his shoes, staring blankly at the ceiling. Now he looked at Clark and said inquiringly: "What?"

Clark said: "Did you take my guns?"

"One," said the policeman. "A regulation thirty-eight. How many do you carry, anyway?"

"I had two. The revolver and a Luger automatic that a guy gave me. It was in my coat pocket."

The policeman shook his head. "Not when I found you, it wasn't."

Clark walked slowly over to the window, and the policeman tagged along two steps behind him. The window was open. About three feet below was the sloping roof of a lean-to on the back of the building. The roof of the lean-to slanted down and stopped about two feet from the high board fence that ran along the alley.

Clark lit a match and leaned out the window. There were long, fresh gouges on the tar-paper roofing.

"I figure that's the way he came in and went out," the policeman said amiably, peering over his shoulder.

Clark said: "Yes."

Faint and distant in the heavy night air, a siren picked up its thin whining song.

"That'll be the boys," said the policeman, nodding in a relieved way.

CHAPTER THREE

AN EMERALD NECKLACE

THE SECRETARY was a platinum blonde, and she was wearing a black dress that emphasized her slim, rounded figure in a nice way. She opened the door and turned around and smiled at Clark and said: "Right in here, please, Mr. Clark."

Clark nodded and said: "Thanks." He was carrying his dark hat in his hand. There was a criss-cross white bandage over his temple. The white of the bandage made his face look darker and thinner and drawn in a tired way. His right eye was bloodshot. He had on a dark suit that fit him perfectly.

He stepped past the secretary into an office that had dark, richly paneled walls with a few conservative hunting prints hung here and there. There were some mahogany chairs with black-leather cushions, and in the corner next to the wall there was a big flat desk with a green blotter on it. The blotter was the only vivid spot of color in the room, and it seemed to gather in all the light and focus it on the face of the man who was leaning over it, resting his head on his hands.

Holt did not attempt to get up or move when Clark came in the room. He nodded his head slightly and said: "Hello."

He added, as though it were an afterthought: "Sit down."

He was a small, fragile man. His black hair was thin in front and shot with gray over his temples. He had a pale, weary face and eyes with dark smears under them. He wore a gray suit, and he seemed to be a toneless, negative sort of person and in some vague way, insignificant. He had a pencil in his white, well kept hands, and now he looked down at the pencil thoughtfully and turned it over and over in his fingers.

After a moment, he winced a little and said: "Terrible thing."

Clark took a cigarette case out of his pocket and selected a cigarette. It was a long brown cigarette with a pasteboard tip. He lit the cigarette and spoke in a low voice.

"Let's get this straight. I'll feel better when you know the whole story. Yesterday morning you called up and wanted me to find your half-brother. He hadn't been around his place for a couple of days, and you thought probably he had gone off on another of his periodic bats. I'd done it before, and I knew how to start to look for him. He always took a taxi when he got to feeling gay, and the boys on the stand on the corner of Russian and Green all knew him. I started there and found the boy that had taken him to a café on Center Street. I trailed him from there by his taxis. He went to about ten places. Finally he got to this place on Commercial Street. There was a taxi stand across the street, and the driver that brought him to the place had tipped off the boys on the stand to watch for him. He hadn't come out.

"A guy by the name of Borzig runs the outfit. It's not a clip joint, exactly, but Borzig is hard up, and he knew what to do with a sucker like Salisbury was when he was tight. He kept him there and persuaded him to sign a lot of blank checks. I had a little difficulty with Borzig and a couple of his pals, but I got Salisbury out all right. I took him over to his place, and I no sooner got him inside the door than I got cracked on the head."

CLARK stopped, and his thin-lipped mouth twisted wryly at one corner, and he looked down at the cigarette as though it tasted badly.

"It was my fault. Salisbury had passed out. If I had been watching it wouldn't have happened. Nobody ever got me that way before." He looked up at Holt. "I liked Salisbury. Even when he had the horrors he was goodnatured. I had to maul him around a good deal at one time and another, but he was always nice about it. Never tried to fight me." His voice grated suddenly. "And I let some mug smack him down."

Holt's small, pale face was very old, very drawn. "Don't blame yourself," he said slowly. "You couldn't help it—coming into a dark room that way. The whole thing was my fault." He twisted the pencil around and around, and his knuckles whitened. "My fault. I can't tell you how badly I feel about the matter."

Clark blew out a long thin plume of smoke and waited silently.

Holt said: "As you know I'm a vice-president of this company. The office is very nice, but the salary I get is not quite what you probably imagine it is. I say this merely by way of introduction. Several months ago I was with some friends at a former speakeasy. I met a man there. I had never seen him before. He had a necklace he wanted to sell—an emerald necklace. There were nine stones in it. Eight small stones and a large one in the form of a pendant between the two sets of four small stones. He wanted two thousand dollars for the necklace. I know something about emeralds. I knew the necklace was worth between fifteen and twenty thousand. I knew the man had probably stolen the necklace, or he wouldn't be wanting to sell it at that price. But I wanted the necklace."

Holt looked up from the pencil. "I'm to be married in two months—to Cecile Huntland. Her father is president of the Huntland Banking Corporation. I wanted to give her a present. So I bought the necklace." He hesitated a moment and then said: "The man I bought the necklace from was Ed Kiley."

Clark's eyes narrowed a little, but otherwise his thin face was expressionless. He remembered Ed Kiley. Two weeks ago Ed Kiley, top-notch jewel thief, had made the headlines for the last time. He had been found sitting beside a pile of lumber down by the river-front with his throat cut from ear to ear.

Clark said: "I know who he was."

Holt nodded. "He must have told the man that killed him that he had sold the necklace to me. A week or so ago a man called on me. He said he was Ed Kiley's partner—virtually admitted that he had murdered him. He said he and Ed Kiley had stolen the necklace together. That Ed Kiley had skipped out with it—double-crossing his friend. He knew how much I had paid Kiley for the necklace. He said that wasn't enough and demanded another two thousand."

Holt spread his hands and shrugged his thin shoulders. "I haven't two thousand dollars. My approaching marriage has been a tremendous drain on my finances. I told the man that. He called on me several times, growing more and more threatening. I didn't want to complain to the police, because the last thing I want right now is unfavorable publicity. He finally threatened to steal the necklace. I am going back to Chicago soon to meet my fiancée, and I wanted to take the necklace with me. I conceived the plan of having Edward make up a statue and conceal the necklace inside it. That way I could carry it with me without any suspicion. So that's what I did."

Clark said: "I see."

Holt went on: "Edward made up a hideous statue of a monkey and painted it yellow and green. He called it a gin monkey. It was about a foot and a half high—the image of a monkey sitting down holding its chin in its hands. It had red stones for eyes." He stopped, and his mouth twisted up at one corner, and he shivered a little, uneasily. "The thing gave me the creeps, but then most of Edward's statues did. The necklace was sealed inside that statue. The last time I called, it wasn't quite finished. I called the day afterwards, but Edward had gone off on his drunk, and I couldn't find it. He had hidden it somewhere. I think that some way this man Torrance found out that Edward had the necklace. He broke into Edward's rooms and was searching for the necklace when you and Edward got there."

Clark nodded and said: "It might have been that way."

Holt leaned over the desk, and his voice was very bitter. "Edward was my half-brother, and that necklace caused his death. I don't want the thing any more. It would haunt me." He put his small, white hand on the green blotter with the fingers spread out flat. "I'll give you that necklace if you'll find it and that man, Torrance."

Clark said: "All right. Can you describe him to me?"

"He's small—about five and a half feet. He has light hair and blue eyes and a scar that runs from the corner of his left eye to the lobe of his left ear—a straight, thin scar. He limps a little on his right foot. He talks through his nose."

Clark stood up. "I'll see what I can do."

Holt blinked at him with his tired eyes. "You'll know what to do—when you find him?"

Clark's eyes were heavy-lidded, sleepy. His smile was very thin and hard.

"Yes," he said softly. He crumpled the brown cigarette between his long fingers. "Oh yes, I'll know what to do."

IT WAS a narrow alley, very dark, crowded in close between two tall buildings. It was paved with rough brick, and the walls that lined it were brick, and far above there was a faint strip of blue-black sky with a few stars that showed very faintly through a slight mist that floated over them.

A car banged by on Commercial Street and flipped light into the alley for a second and then was gone, with only the echoes rattling noisily between the brick walls. When the echoes finally died down there was silence again until a door opened near the mouth of the alley and threw out a yellow cube of light that splashed on the rough paving and the dirty bricks of the opposite wall.

Jake came out of the door. Jake had taken off his white apron, and he now wore a wrinkled brown suit and a derby hat that sat squarely on the top of his round, bald head.

Borzig's voice said: "Good-night."

Jake yawned sleepily and said: " 'Night," and his big feet made scuffling sounds as he walked to the mouth of the alley. He was a thick shadow, standing there for a second, and then he turned down the street and disappeared.

Max Clark moved then, at last. He came out of the deep blackness at the back of the alley, and all of him that was visible was the faint round whiteness that was his face and the white V of his shirt above his coat. He moved up to the door and knocked on it softly.

Borzig's voice said: "What?"

Max Clark said: "It's Jake, boss. I forgot my wallet."

The bolt slid in its groove, and the door swung back, and Borzig said petulantly: "What did you—"

He stopped talking, then. It was a small hallway, and he was standing under the uncovered globe that was in the center of the low ceiling. He was standing there staring up at Max Clark.

He made a small sound in his throat, and he backed up a step. He smiled a little with one side of his mouth and made a hesitant gesture with his left hand. He said: "Why, hello. Hello, Max."

Max Clark stood there in the half-shadow of the open door. The yellow light coming down on top of him made him seem very tall and blocked out an immensely thick-shouldered caricature of him on the floor. Max Clark's dark hat was pulled low over his eyes, and the only part of his face that was visible was his thin-lipped mouth and his thin, hard jaw.

His lips moved a little as he said: "Anybody else here?"

Borzig said: "No. I mean—no."

"Make up your mind."

Borzig took a handkerchief out of the cuff of his left sleeve and rubbed his moist palms on it nervously. "Why, no," he said, smiling and shaking his head. "No, Max. There's nobody here. You startled me, coming in that way."

Max Clark said: "I wanted to be sure of getting in." He reached behind him and pulled the door shut. "I wanted to talk to you, Borzig. I wanted to talk to you alone."

Borzig used the handkerchief on his forehead and said nervously: "Why sure, Max. I'm always glad to talk to you."

"Did you read the papers this morning?"

Borzig nodded. "Why, yes, Max. I read that about Salisbury. That was very terrible, Max, and I wanted to see you and tell you how sorry I was that it happened to you." He nodded again in a sympathetic way. "That Salisbury, now, was a very nice fellow, and they should certainly catch the guy that done him in."

"Do you know who it was?"

BORZIG'S eyes went wider, and he backed up another step, and somehow as his eyes got larger he seemed to shrink in on himself and get smaller. He was a small, thin, nervous man with dyed hair, and his mouth twisted up at the side as though he was going to cry.

"No, Max. No, now. I don't know who it was. Of course I don't know who it was. Now, Max, I hope you aren't going to try and connect that up with what happened here yesterday."

Max Clark hadn't moved at all. He was still leaning against the door.

"The one that murdered Salisbury and cracked me came in through a window. He was waiting there in the room when we came in. An ordinary sneak thief would have ducked out when he heard us coming. We made plenty of noise. But this guy waited. And when he left he took the Luger I took away from Tiny yesterday."

Borzig's pale cheeks were sunken, and he looked much older suddenly. He had a harried, worried air, and he talked in quick, jerky tones.

"It wasn't Tiny, Max. It honestly wasn't Tiny. Tiny stayed right here after you left. He was a little sore because you took his gun, but he wouldn't knock anybody over for that, Max."

Max Clark said: "I want to see this guy, Tiny. Where can I find him? Don't lie."

Borzig spread his hands. "Well, I don't know now. He went—"

Max Clark brought his right hand out of his coat pocket, and the hand was holding his revolver. He pointed the revolver at Borzig's foot and said: "Once more. Where's Tiny?"

Borzig's voice clogged in his throat. "No! No, Max! Listen—"

Max Clark said softly: "Maybe Tiny has a friend. Maybe Tiny has a friend by the name of Torrance. A small guy that has a scar on his cheek and that limps on his right foot. Maybe Tiny has a friend like that. Has he, Borzig? Has he?"

Borzig went back a step again, and he put his hand up in front of his face with his fingers spread wide, and he opened his mouth wide with his lips loose and jerking. But the voice that spoke, then, was not the voice of Borzig.

The voice said: "Yeah. He has."

A door squeaked a little bit, and Borzig screamed. Because the door had squeaked behind him, and Borzig knew that he was between the man that had spoken and Max Clark, and he knew that there was going to be shooting. He screamed, and screamed again, shrilly, like a woman, and tried to duck, tried to shove his small, soft body against the wall and out of the line of fire. He wasn't quick enough, and the bullets that came from behind him caught him in the small of the back and picked him up and turned him half around before they slammed him in a clawing, kicking heap on the floor.

Max Clark was already moving when the door squeaked. He shoved his gun straight up in the air and hit the electric light bulb with the short barrel and felt the thudding shock of electricity against his hand and wrist. Then he crouched down, balancing himself with one hand on the floor beside him. All this happened in split seconds, while the echoes of the shots were roaring in clashing echoes between the close walls of the small hallway, and Borzig was whimpering and squirming on the floor and beating his fists against the wall.

Max Clark knew that the other man would be crouching, too. He would be crouching, peering through the crack in the door with only his head showing, and the head would be about waist high.

Max Clark aimed lower than that to be sure. He aimed very carefully, and he shot three times. He couldn't see even the faintest glimmer of light. The darkness was like a wet, thick blanket; but he knew where the door was, and he knew the other man would be there. He would wait until he knew whether or not one of his shots had hit Max Clark.

The .38 raised more smashing echoes, and with the echoes there was the sound of a scrambling fall and the ring of metal on the floor as the other man caught himself on his hands without releasing his grip on his gun.

Then there was the sound of staggering steps, and a door slammed. Max Clark got up very quickly and stepped over Borzig's small, limp body and heard the breath rattling thickly in Borzig's throat. He flattened his lean body against the wall and pushed the door wide open, but it made no difference in the darkness, except that now he could see a flat ray of yellow light coming from under a door ahead of him.

He got to that door very quickly, turned the knob, kicked it open. He was in a small, square room with wire-legged tables set around the edges. He was looking at the man who had shot at him.

CHAPTER FOUR

THE GIN MONKEY

THE MAN was small. He had a straight scar across his cheek from his eye to his ear. He was wearing a long overcoat that made him seem smaller and more shrunken than he really was.

He had been heading for the light switch on the other side of the room, but he hadn't been able to move fast enough to make it.

He was standing next to one of the wire-legged tables with his hand spread out flat on top of it and his thin shoulders hunched up. His hat was off, and his thin brown hair hung down over his white forehead. There was blood coming out of both corners of his mouth, and he was swaying back and forth gently. The heavy revolver in his thin right hand dragged his arm down toward the floor.

It was doubtful if he even saw Max Clark to realize who and what he was. It was doubtful if there was enough consciousness left in his pain-twisted mind to understand what he was doing or why. But his instinct was working, stubbornly, in his stunted, thin body, and the big revolver glinted in the light as he began to move it up slowly, leveling the barrel at Max Clark. He was swaying more now, and the barrel wobbled around in loose little circles. He opened his mouth, and blood came out in a rush over his lower lip.

Max Clark said: "Put it down, man. You're all through."

The small man didn't hear him. He was dying right there on his feet, holding on to the table, trying to keep upright long enough to shoot.

Max Clark felt suddenly sick at the thought of putting another bullet into the small, thin body before him, and he took a big chance. He threw his revolver at the small man and crouched, ready to jump backwards through the door.

He didn't have to jump. The revolver hit the small man in the chest, and he fell straight over backwards. He hit a table on the way down and landed on the floor limply, with a resounding crash. He didn't move again.

Max Clark stepped slowly around a table and leaned over him. He picked up his .38 and held it loosely in his hand, looking down at the small man.

The small man was lying on his back, arched up in the middle with his heels pressing hard against the floor. His eyes came open very slowly and they were bright and bitter and malicious through the fog that seemed to be creeping down over them, blotting out the mind behind them.

The small man stared at Max Clark and said: "Anne—Anne Carr—" while the blood rolled thickly out of the corners of his mouth and frothy red bubbles burst on his lips.

His small body relaxed then, and his head rolled loosely to one side.

There was a heavy thudding from somewhere in front. The whole building shook from it, and a voice was yelling faintly: "Open—this—door! Police! Open up!"

Max Clark went quickly across the room and clicked the light switch. He waited, in the darkness, with his head tilted, listening to the splintering sounds that came from the front of the place. He went silently through the door he had entered, feeling his way along the wall. He went through the second door and kicked his foot against the limp softness that was Borzig.

Borzig didn't move or make any noise, and Clark opened the outside door and listened. There was a resounding crash from the front and the sound of feet pounding on the floor.

Max Clark ducked out of the door, and the deep shadow of the alley seemed to come and meet him and swallow him up into darkness.

MAX CLARK walked up along the dark crookedness that was Green Street, and he was thinking as he walked of the last time he had come along this street. He was thinking of Salisbury. This was the spot where he had hauled Salisbury out of the taxi. This was the spot where Salisbury had fallen into the gutter and stayed there laughing.

At the thought of the amiable, pleasant laughter of Salisbury, Max Clark seemed to grow hard and cold inside, and there was a thick lump that burned in his throat.

He turned into the small passageway, with its row of ash cans standing there solemnly like soldiers on parade, and came out into the small open square with its tattered flower bed. The hideous blue building was a black cube looming up before him.

There were no lights upstairs where Salisbury had lived. There was no noise from there. But down below, where Anne Carr lived, there were lights in the windows.

Max Clark felt along a path that was rough and uneven underfoot, and came to two blocks of concrete, one on top of the other, that were in front of the door and served as steps.

Max Clark rapped on the door and stood waiting.

The door was a long time opening, and when it did open, Anne Carr was standing there with the light behind her, staring down at him. She wore a smock and her red sandals and no stockings. Her hair had come down over her eyes, and somehow she seemed small and sick and frightened. She held on to the edge of the door with one thin hand and stared down at Max Clark wordlessly.

Max Clark said evenly: "Hello. Remember me?"

Anne Carr moved her head, and after a long time words came thick and blurred from her throat. "Won't you—come in?"

Max Clark came a step closer, looking up so that the light fell on his thin, dark face and made it look cruel and wolfish. "I came after the gin monkey."

It didn't mean anything to Anne Carr. She didn't seem to have heard what he said.

"Won't you come in?" she said in the same deadly mechanical tone.

And suddenly Max Clark knew. He knew why Anne Carr was so afraid. He knew what was behind her, waiting for him, in that room.

He jumped forward and caught Anne Carr's thin, bare arm and jerked her out of the doorway and hurled her away from him across the courtyard. She staggered weakly, trying to keep her balance, and she gave a little helpless whimpering cry as she went to her knees in the dust.

AND THEN the man Tiny was in the doorway. Standing there solidly in his white panama hat and his wrinkled suit. And an automatic gleamed thinly in his hand, and he shot once without saying a word.

The bullet hit Max Clark when he was off balance, half-turned with the effort of hurling Anne Carr out of the line of fire. The bullet knocked Max Clark sprawling, and he felt the thick, smooth softness of the dust sliding under his body.

Tiny was standing in the doorway. He shot twice, carefully, at Anne Carr. The bullets hit her in the back just as she regained her feet, and she went slowly down to her knees again, as if she had changed her mind about getting up, and then she fell forward on her face.

Tiny turned the automatic back toward Max Clark. Max Clark got his own revolver out of his right-hand coat pocket with his left hand. He was still lying on his back on the ground, and he shot upward at Tiny.

Tiny made a breathless sound. He sagged a little, and his knees wavered like a fighter who has taken a bad body blow. But he still could move fast, and he was still thinking with his shrewd, quick mind. He stepped back and slammed the door shut in front of him.

Max Clark got up. His whole right side was numb, even his right leg. His right arm was like a dead thing attached heavily to his body.

He shot once through the door. He went up the two concrete steps, stumbling, and hit the door with his left side.

The door gave under his weight. He fell into the room head-first, rolled on the floor. He got up stubbornly, and the room was empty.

There was a lot of noise now. People were yelling and screaming nearby. But Max Clark could hear the staggering thumps that were Tiny's steps, and he followed the sounds through a dark room that was a kitchen, out another door, down another two steps.

He was in the alley that ran in back of the building, and it was pitch dark, and there were no sounds except the muffled steps of Tiny and the little moaning noise he made with each step.

Max Clark located the sound and stopped and steadied himself. He shot carefully until the hammer of the revolver clicked on empty shells and the gun ceased to jump against his hand. Then he leaned against the fence, listening.

There were scuffling sounds in the darkness ahead, and a small whimpering. Soon the scuffling stopped, and the whimpering died down into thick, breathless gasps. The gasps stopped, too, at last.

And Max Clark went forward wearily. He found the thing that had been Tiny, lying there motionless. And he found the gin monkey, grasped tightly in Tiny's hand, as he knew it would be.

He kept on going down the alley, staggering, while the noise behind him started up once more and grew in proportions until it seemed that the whole world was screaming at him.

MAX CLARK'S suit was dark, almost black, and the blood didn't show very much even under the strong light just above the littered desk. The light had a green shade, and it was just above his head. He had his hat on, and there was a dark shadow over all his face except his cheek, and the jaw muscles on that side of his face were bulging whitely.

He sat very stiffly, trying to ease the pain in his shoulder, and his right hand was clenched into a fist in his coat pocket.

He hauled the telephone toward him, took off the receiver and sat it on the desk, and dialed very clumsily with his left hand. Then he picked up the receiver and put it against his ear.

A drug clerk with a face that was almost as white and stiff as his starched jacket stood uneasily beside him. He was twisting a mixing spoon around and around in his hands nervously.

"Can't I—" he said uneasily. "Can't I—do something?"

"Go get me a drink—whiskey."

The drug clerk hesitated, then dragged his feet slowly out of the room, staring over his shoulder.

Max Clark could hear the telephone ringing at the other end. A buzz and then a click—repeated over and over. Finally there was a louder click, and a voice said: "Hello, damn you!"

Clark smiled a little, tightly, and said: "Hello, Minnie. This is Max Clark."

Minnie caught her breath with a gasp. "Max! What is it? What's the matter?"

"I want you to do a favor for me. Call Fenton Four-four-four-nine. That's Doctor Hardley's number. Give him my name and tell him to come over to your place right away. Right now. I'm on my way there. Will you do that for me, Minnie? I can't have him go to my hotel, and the doc doesn't like suspicious-looking customers rolling in at this time of the night. He's got nosy neighbors."

Minnie's voice went up several tones. "Are you hurt? Are you hurt, Max?"

Max Clark said: "Not very bad. I had an accident, and I think I broke my arm. I'll be seeing you, Minnie."

He hung up the receiver and leaned back stiffly in the chair and wiped his face with the palm of his left hand. The drug clerk came in and said: "Here's the whiskey, and the taxi is waiting outside."

He watched Max Clark drink the whiskey, wrinkling his nose like a curious rabbit. "What—what kind of an accident did you have, sir?"

Max Clark put down the empty glass and blew out his breath in a long sigh. He got up wearily and picked up the gin monkey which he had wrapped up in a stray piece of newspaper.

"I got drunk and fell out of a ten-story window."

The clerk raised his eyebrows and batted his eyes in an amazed way. "Ten stories! Did you fall all the way down?"

Max Clark was walking toward the door. "Yeah."

"Gee!" said the clerk. "Gee whiz! I should think it woulda killed you."

"It did," said Max Clark, and went out and shut the door softly.

MINNIE was sitting on the cement steps of the apartment house. She had her chin in her hands and her feet drawn up under her. She was wearing Doctor Hardley's overcoat, and it was too big for her, and the upturned collar almost hid her head. She looked very small and nervous and alone.

When the taxi came around the corner, she jumped up quickly. And when it stopped at the curb and Max Clark got out, she came running across the sidewalk with the too long sleeves of the overcoat flopping loosely in front of her.

Max Clark was holding on to the paper-wrapped gin monkey with his left hand and leaning against the taxi to steady himself. Minnie stopped in front of him and flopped the sleeves of the coat helplessly. She had been crying, and the tears were smeared wetly across her small, thin face.

"Max!" she said brokenly.

Max Clark said: "Hello, Minnie. Sorry to bother you. Get my wallet out of my inside coat pocket and pay the man."

Minnie pulled up one sleeve and reached gingerly inside Max Clark's coat. She fumbled a bill out of the wallet and poked it at the taxi driver. The taxi driver took the bill and sat there, staring at them curiously.

Minnie realized it suddenly and turned on him. "See anything green, you big baboon?" she snarled.

The taxi driver swallowed with a gulp and let out his clutch so quickly that the taxi jumped a yard.

Minnie was looking down at her hand. There was blood smeared redly across the back of it, where she had reached into Max Clark's coat. She gave a little sob.

Max Clark said: "Quit bawling, you baby. I just got shot in the arm. I plugged the hole with my handkerchief, but it leaked a little."

Minnie wiped her eyes with the coat sleeve and glared up at him, with her mouth twisting childishly at the corners. "You j-just got s-shot, huh? That's all, is it? You b-big damn fool!"

Max Clark chuckled then, and she put her thin arm around his waist and helped him up the steps of the apartment house.

THE ELEVATOR boy was very classy in a pillbox hat set jauntily on one side of his head and a gray uniform with black braid on it. He kept looking sideways, curiously, at Max Clark.

Max Clark was leaning wearily against the back of the elevator. He had his eyes half closed. Doctor Hardley had done as neat a job as was possible on his arm. It was in a cast, strapped across his chest under his shirt. The cast made his coat bulge clumsily in front and on the right side. There were deep lines around Max Clark's mouth, and his face was painfully white, as though all the color had been washed out from under his skin.

The elevator boy leaned over and hauled the door back and said snappily: "Fifth floor, sir."

Max Clark got out of the elevator and walked heavily down the long hall on a soft lemon-colored rug. He went around a turn in the corridor. He was carrying the gin monkey, now wrapped neatly in a brown paper parcel, in his left arm. He shifted the package in his arm and punched the pearl button beside the third door from the turn in the corridor.

Holt opened the door and said: "Come in."

Max Clark followed him through an entry hall, through a long, low-ceilinged living room, into a study.

Holt said: "Have a seat," and indicated a chair with a nod of his head and moved up an ash tray and poured a couple of drinks out of a decanter on the desk.

Max Clark sat the drink on the floor beside him and began to unwrap the package, holding it between his knees and tearing at the paper with his left hand. Holt sat down opposite him and spread out his legs comfortably and watched him, sipping at his drink.

SALISBURY'S gin monkey answered, superficially, to the description Holt had given. It was about eighteen inches high. It was colored yellow and green in a sort of a zig-zag pattern, and it had red stones for eyes. It was sitting on its haunches with both paws under its chin. But no description could give the same impression as the thing did itself. In spite of its weird coloring the thing was startlingly lifelike. The workmanship was beautiful, and Salisbury had managed to get an expression of sinister and sardonic humor on the face. No matter which way you turned, the red eyes seemed to follow. The statue was unnaturally realistic—horrible in some faint and indefinable way.

Max Clark brushed the brown paper off on the floor and held the monkey up in front of him, raising his eyebrows at Holt. "This it?"

Holt said, "Yes," quietly.

Clark said: "A girl by the name of Anne Carr lives below the place where Salisbury had his studio. He gave the statue to her to keep when he went off on his drunk. He told her that the necklace was in it. We met her the night I brought Salisbury home. She was on the stairs that led up to Salisbury's studio. The reason she was there was because she had heard someone in Salisbury's studio—someone smashing things. She went up to see what was going on. Maybe she thought Salisbury had come back. She saw who was in the studio. So when we came along she put on an act for us, so I wouldn't suspect she had been spying. Later, because she knew who was in the studio, she knew who had killed Salisbury, and she didn't know what to do."

Holt said in a dull voice: "Who was in the studio?"

Max Clark said: "You were."

Holt must have been expecting this the whole time. He must have known that Max Clark knew. There must have been something in Max Clark's expression, or in the way he acted, that had told him. Because he didn't move a muscle. He sat there, small and pale and heavy-lidded, watching Max Clark, while his green robe shimmered brightly and the gin monkey leered with its red eyes from its perch on the desk beside Max Clark's chair.

Max Clark went on evenly: "Anne Carr knew Salisbury had made the statue for you. She knew you were Salisbury's half-brother. She knew you had killed Salisbury. She didn't know what to do with the statue. She wanted the necklace."

HOLT didn't say anything. He sat there motionless, and after a long time he raised his drink and sipped at it thoughtfully, watching Max Clark with his heavy-lidded eyes over the rim of the glass.

Max Clark said: "Everything you told me was true. It was true because you knew I could check up and find it out anyway. You did buy a necklace from a man named Ed Kiley. You were threatened by a man named Torrance, who was Ed Kiley's partner in the steal. But when he threatened you, it gave you ideas. It gave you the idea of killing Salisbury and blaming it on Torrance. You thought up this phony stall about putting the necklace inside of a statue. You made sure that Torrance knew that you had taken the necklace to Salisbury. Torrance and a pal of his, a guy by the name of Tiny, were tailing you around, and it was easy to lead them over to Salisbury's and put the idea across. Salisbury finished the job and went off on a bat, as you knew he would. You pretended to break in his studio and smash a few statues, making some evidence against Torrance. When I brought Salisbury in, you cracked me on the head and murdered him. It was meant to look like Torrance had been searching the studio when we came in and had cracked us both to keep us quiet, but had hit Salisbury too hard. But you can see how phony the whole business looked. In the first place, Torrance wouldn't have been caught in the studio. He'd have gotten out when we came. In the second place, he wouldn't have made the mistake of hitting Salisbury too hard. And then there was my gun. I was carrying two guns. You only got one of them. Torrance would have found both of them.

"You can see that your plan was pretty lousy, even if it had worked out according to schedule; but it didn't. In the first place, Salisbury got into Borzig's layout by accident. Torrance and Tiny were hanging out there, and they recognized him. That was a bit of luck for them. They got Salisbury drunker than he was already and pumped him, meantime getting him to sign a few checks because they were broke. They found out that Salisbury had given the statue to Anne Carr. That was fine by them, and they were getting ready to grab the statue from her, when this story about Salisbury's murder broke in the newspapers. Torrance and Tiny weren't so dumb. They could read between the lines. Somebody had framed them for Salisbury's murder, and when that somebody put on the screws, they wouldn't have a prayer. Only they thought *I* was the somebody. That was natural enough. They figured I had bumped Salisbury off and knocked myself on the head just to make it look good. They started laying for me. One of them stayed at Anne Carr's place and the other at Borzig's. They were sure I'd turn up at one place or the other, because they were sure I wouldn't put the frame on them until I got the statue.

"Your plan slipped there, and it slipped in another place. You couldn't find the statue. And for some reason you didn't want to spill your little story to the police while that statue was floating around on the loose. You didn't want the police to find the statue."

Max Clark stopped and leaned over and snubbed out his cigarette, staring narrowly up at Holt. "There could be only one reason why you didn't want the police to find the statue. It took me a little while, but I figured it out. It was because you were to tight to let loose of the real necklace. The necklace inside the monkey is a fake, and you were afraid that would put the police wise that there was something phony about the case."

Max Clark reached for the statue. "Let's break it open and see if I figured it right."

Holt said, "No," in a low voice. He moved only a little bit now. He moved only enough to shove his hand forward on his knee—his right hand—and in the hand there was a small derringer. It was only a little longer than a man's middle finger, and it had twin barrels, one over the other.

MAX CLARK sat back in his chair again and grinned. It was a cat-like grin, cruel and wise and hard. He spoke contemptuously.

"You're a fool, Holt. You thought you were going to make a very successful marriage. You needed money to square some debts that would look very bad if they came out. You were being pressed hard. Salisbury had an insurance policy for twenty thousand, and you were the beneficiary. You killed him for that. For twenty thousand dollars, so you could put on a big front and marry your heiress and get yourself a soft job in her old man's company. Just for that you killed a man like Salisbury. He was a better man than you ever will be if you could multiply yourself by ten. You're a petty, greedy fool, and for twenty thousand dollars you killed a man who was a genius. And you caused the death of four other people."

Holt said quietly: "Are you through, now?"

Max Clark laughed outright. "Not quite. You're sitting there dramatizing yourself. Holt, the master criminal! I know just what you're thinking—I know just what you would think. You think that you're going to include me in your scheme. You'll say I was a partner of Tiny and Torrance, that I had a falling out with them over the loot, that I killed them and came up here to threaten you, and you killed me."

Clark leaned forward suddenly. "Listen, Holt. I wrote two letters before I came. One to a friend of mine on the *News.* Another to your would-be future wife's father. I outlined the story I told you. I told them where and how they could find proof. If I don't call at a certain place and pick up those letters within an hour, they'll be mailed. That just goes to show what a dummy you are. If you were going to shoot me, you should have done it when I accused you of the murder. Now you don't dare."

Holt's control slipped a little, then. His eyes widened, and there was something small and cringing and afraid deep inside him that showed through them, and his mouth jerked at one corner. He was a cowardly, pompous little man, defeated and broken and squirming in his ridiculous green robe.

Clark said softly and meaningly: "You don't dare shoot me now, do you, Holt?"

Holt looked down at the derringer and moved it a little so that it glistened in the light. The gin monkey, sitting on the desk, seemed to be watching them both and grinning in its cruel and sardonic way, while its red eyes sparkled. It was very quiet in the room. The life had gone out of Holt's face and left it dead. After a long time, he raised the derringer, and his forefinger whitened on the trigger, and the blunt report bounced back and forth heavily between the book-lined walls, and the powder smoke drifted thinly blue under the lamp and curled around the gin monkey's head.

There was a long silence, and then Max Clark picked up the telephone and said: "Will you send for the police? Mr. Holt has just committed suicide."